geneticist.

A car hits someone desperate to get away from me. They honk, but the woman can't escape the front bumper. Her body rolls onto the hood. As she falls to the ground, wheels roll over her, and her limp body becomes a speed bump. The driver slams on their brakes, and the front wheel crushes her skull into a meaty mess.

Well, the car honks. But the woman darts out of the way, narrowly missing the headlight. I'm disappointed she's okay. Sitting on the sidewalk red-eyed is not a reason to give someone space. I don't have a deadly disease. If I did, I'd hold her down and share it.

As I wait for Michael, I know it's now or never. I'm getting worse, and even healthy people get caught.

He pulls up beside me and puts his flashers on. I try to stand just as he pops out of the car with his hands raised, shouting, "Wait, wait!"

Pain radiates up from my hip, and I wobble. Michael catches

me before I fall and holds me tight as he walks me to the passenger seat. He insists on strapping me in like a child. I'm sickened and humiliated for the third time in my life.

On the road, a pothole is a hammer and two speed bumps are open palm slaps. Spots fill my vision by the time Michael is parking by a fire hydrant. He's driven the five blocks we were trying to walk when my hip gave out.

I wish he had said *fuck it* and taken me home. Instead, he's illegally parked.

I've always feared a cop would come by and tell me they see me, they know what I am, and they're arresting me in the interest of public safety. Illogical and paranoid thinking, but the thoughts still bounce around.

Michael grabs his wallet from the cupholder and kisses me on the cheek before rushing from the car over to the truck.

It only takes five minutes. He slides back into the driver's seat and holds up an offering of two bags of delicious smelling vegetables and beans. "Got 'em!"

Sometimes, I wonder if he thinks I'm the less intelligent one in the relationship.

We drive in silence for a while, my mouth watering and my hip pain not lessening.

His face hasn't un-scrunched yet. I'm waiting for him to say what he needs to say. He cares more than I do—about me, about us, about everything.

We get on the highway and hit traffic immediately. He starts to cry. The abruptness of it reminds me of turning on a faucet, only I know it won't be so easy to turn off.

The stop-and-go of the cars around us mirrors his words as he gets them out one by one. Through his ragged breathing, I understand that he's begging me to go see a rheumatologist, to quit Juniper Foods, to focus more on house sitting—but not ones with dogs or cats. Though teaching ESL is good for me, he thinks. I should keep that job. I don't remind him that it pays the least.

I agree to only one thing—seeing a doctor.

They tell me that my body is consuming itself—a carnivorous beast, hungry for its own collagen. That fits with what I picture as I wake up and manipulate a loose shoulder back into its socket, nearly deafening myself with the sound of crab legs being snapped.

Months of testing have led me to the tenth floor of the Janes Hospital—months of me *waiting*, months of having a hovering Michael blocking me from exploring.

I'm not prepared, I know that. I can't wait until I think I'll be able to commit the perfect crime. It truly is now or never, and I can't imagine a world with a *never*.

At the moment, all I can hope for is that Michael hearing the official diagnosis of Hypermobile Ehlers-Danlos Syndrome— hEDS—will help him breathe a little easier. He'll back off a bit, give me some space. Then, I can look at my list. I'll be able to plan and prepare.

Young Elizabeth would be so proud. *We're doing it.* She'd be disappointed that I'm jumping in before I'm truly ready, but would I ever really be?

Michael is holding my hand for support I don't need. We're sitting across from a geneticist—of all things—on hard chairs in a wide conference room with floor-to-ceiling windows.

The geneticist clears his throat a few times. Nothing about him says professional. He's a flat-faced, rumpled man with glasses like Leopold—*or was that Loeb?*—and his teeth are too long for his mouth. They probably bang together and make his jaw click when he chews.

He begins by telling us more about my genetic connective tissue disorder. Subluxations may happen in every joint, no matter how small, he tells us. So many joints already shift and rub against each other, as if a cave person is trying to start a fire with my bones. I can't imagine more. Dislocations will get worse, too. It's hard to think that more of me will slip, slide, and fall out like broken doll parts. He rattles off a laundry list of co-morbidities that can be associated with the disorder, listing doctors that may help with what I'm experiencing now and may experience in the future.

Michael is writing things down furiously. Occasionally, he interrupts with questions. "What kind of medical aids will help the most? Should we get a shower seat?" and "Where is the best place for the doctor types she'll need?"

They discuss the failure of my body around me, and their words evoke an image of me in a wheelchair. Feeble, under a blanket, I've lost weight and have aged decades. But it's only a few years from now.

My mother's voice penetrates the spiraling. *"It took me three weeks to name you. Did I ever tell you that?"* She asked me that every year on my birthday. So, of course, the answer was always rhetorical. *"I wanted to make sure I got it right. I named you after the great Elizabeths that came before you. They were strong and loving, brutal and kind. They were what they needed to be to make it in the world, just what I want you to be, and they did what they needed to do to make their mark, just like I want you to do."*

"And if you're thinking of having children—" The geneticist's voice is ghostly as it floats over me.

When I was a child, the other kids in the neighborhood often talked about their future kids, naming them after themselves or pop stars or flowers. They'd make their dolls get married so they could have said kids. I was busy imagining sets of baby teeth on the nightstand. Did baby fingers snap off easily, and if so, how easy were they to preserve? I wondered if learning those things firsthand was worth having children for.

The only part of my future that I'm really thinking about involves satisfying the part of me that watches horror movies and stabs fruit, that reads true-crime and learned to tie a noose at age nine. I've never wanted to do it to fulfill those dreams my mother had for me—she's dead now anyway—or to be famous; I'm hoping my crimes won't be discovered until long after I'm dead.

This is about me. I have finally found something I want to be. I want to be just another Elizabeth, one that blends in with everyone else. No one suspects your average woman.

The geneticist is still talking. His oversized teeth slam into each other, occasionally going over and pushing into his lips, as he says inane words that all amount to *things will probably get worse*. Finally, he says something I can't help but pay attention to. "You should start using a cane."

Michael turns to me and squeezes my hand. "See? It's time."

Nodding, I agree to appease both of them. But I doubt I'll use it for much else than to bash people's brains in.

2

crystal.

Other murderers make it look so easy; they talk about how quickly they can kill a person and move on with their day. Here I am, bumbling my first attempt.

This was an inevitability—me with a knife clutched between two steady gloved hands, heart thumping so hard my ribcage aches with every beat.

Soft snoring rises above the automatic vacuum whirring. Crystal Keaton programmed it to begin at 2:30 a.m. about seven months ago after I told her how well the sound drowns out stray horns and barks. I still remember the text I received a few weeks after I house sat for her, telling me how she'll never sleep without the vacuum again. *You saved my life*, she joked.

In the 3 a.m. blue haze, her pale lips are nearly invisible. Behind them, she has small but straight teeth, lightly stained from a lifelong tea habit. The gap between her two front teeth is thin. Her fine blonde hair looks gray, as if she's aged decades since I last saw her.

I've been standing here too long, but I want to savor the moment. In case I only get to do this once, I want to remember how the room smells faintly of sleep and rose perfume I don't remember Crystal having in her collection.

She's got a quiet tower fan in the corner of her small bedroom. I have a Polaroid photo where the sun is shining on the slatted plastic; it's one of four photos I have of items in her house. The fan moves to the right and chills the air. Crystal is bundled under the khaki sweater blanket that lives on the couch downstairs. It's covered in fur and is probably being used to keep her connected to the dog she put down only a week ago because some treatment was expensive.

Crystal's collarbone peeks out from the oversized and faded t-shirt she wears as a nightgown. Her bone presses through her skin more than the last time I saw her, as if she took that odd mash-up diet too far—or her dog's murder actually hit her as hard as she said on social media. I've only peeked in on her often enough from incognito windows via other people's computers to know that she's a very fake person.

I might stop by the kitchen to see what she is eating. I always tell myself I'll diet, but then remember I don't need to. And even if I did, I wouldn't because I don't want to.

She rolls from her right side to her back, and I know it's time. Crystal is a very talkative person and told me she wakes up when she's on her back, which is why she hates dreaming because she's never sure if she'll toss and turn.

I tense. *Now or never*, right?

Just like I've practiced over and over on gourds and melons and couch cushions, I raise taut arms and follow through to the location I've identified as her heart. Mine thumps wildly with the thrill of the action. Everything I've planned for, everything I've wanted, is happening. Before the knife reaches her, a spike of paranoia shoots through me; I should be anywhere but here, doing anything but this.

Too late.

I'm so glad it's too late. But as the knife connects with bone and reverberates back to me, my shoulders begin to ache. Have I waited too long? Has my window for this passed?

I imagined the knife would slide in between the two ribs, puncturing the muscle that keeps her alive in one swift, smooth movement. It wouldn't hurt my body. Her murder would be so easy that I'd barely be sore in the morning.

I hadn't thought to make a Plan B. What a colossal fucking mistake I've made.

Crystal wakes up screaming, reaching for her chest to inspect what I'm sure she assumed was phantom pain. She sees a person and the glint of a knife and thrashes her whole body. I may be more stunned than she is. She throws her hands out in front of her and whimpers. I freeze, and she scrambles back. I've lost the upper hand. I've lost *her*.

Her mouth gapes open in horror. "… Elizabeth?"

Oh, fuck. It's dark, and she's scared and bleeding. How does she recognize me?

A moment in her kitchen slides into my brain—a joke about never forgetting a face. Only now do I realize it was no joke. I didn't comb through our discussions thoroughly enough. Mentally, I laugh at myself. Past Me would have shrugged that off. After all, there was never a version of tonight that involved her living. Her recognition of me is—and always would have been considered—irrelevant.

Even so, I'm shaken. The cocktail of thrill and paranoia has given way to a hot flash of icy fear. I thought this might be a one-time thing because I have a body that's falling apart. What if it's a one-time thing because I'm caught?

Heart in my throat, I don't respond. Instead, I hop on the bed and crawl towards her. She's cornered, trapped against a wall.

As she shoves and kicks, I know she's matched me in strength. It's unexpected, slight as she is. That flash of fear comes back.

I had anticipated many feelings tonight, but worry that I may get caught, that Crystal may overpower me, or that everything will go horribly wrong did not make the list. They don't mention any of this in the true crime documentaries.

Crystal pushes me backward, and a pain radiates in my hip.

I slash at her. With the first slice, she screams, and I worry about the neighbors. I tug her from her cornered animal position. She thrashes, and I'm blinded with pain. I become a child handed a head of lettuce, given only the instructions to *chop it up*.

I lose count of the stabs. I thought I could be a person with an M.O., but it's hard when everything is chaos.

Her arms are limp across her chest, but she's still breathing. I push her dead appendages out of the way and feel along her ribcage, counting the ribs. Once I find the place I need, I place the knife against her cotton shirt and heave myself onto it. The weight of my exhausted body and the lack of resistance make it much easier. My shoulder makes a small, hesitant *pop*, threatening me. I wince and ignore the burn, pushing a little further.

She stills, and I flop onto the bed beside her, listening to my own heavy breathing and wait for the sirens. Minutes pass by, and I hear nothing else but the quiet vacuum banging into the legs of furniture and the tower fan.

I lay beside her for a few more minutes, waiting to feel changed. My mind is cluttered. This didn't feel like *me*. Everything seemed to go wrong. There will be so much cleanup and with very little thought, I know at least five things I could have done better. I see room for improvement, should there be a second opportunity. And I hope there is. Killing Crystal hasn't sated me. It made the need stronger. I can't be this bad. I'm usually good at whatever I try to do, despite putting the least amount of effort into it.

The clock reads 3:48 a.m. when I crawl off the bed, soaked in her blood. The earliest riser in her neighborhood leaves the house at *exactly* 6:15 a.m. every day of the week. He must have OCD.

As I stand, I feel like I've been chasing someone through the woods—running, small hops, ducking, all the micro-movements that exhaust you. Cleaning alone could take two hours. After all of my mistakes, resting beside her may have been my biggest.

I push a curl from my face. *Okay.* My first order of business is her body.

I roll her in her bloody sheets—pee mixed with the rust permeates the air—and tie the edge of the fabric in a knot. As I go to pick her up, my left shoulder follows through on its threat from earlier and slides from the socket. Tears fill my eyes. *Not now.* I push through and heave her up, mostly using my right arm. My spaghetti arm does only minor work.

Holding her like I'm about to give her the Heimlich, I walk backwards a few feet. Her weight dragging on the carpet makes my back bend and my shoulder burn. I lean her in her open closet and shut the door behind her. With socked feet, I brush the drag marks until the look blended with the rest of the carpet's pattern.

I can't do anything else until I fix myself.

I rush into the door jamb—shoulder first. I gasp as resistance gives way, and the ball goes back into its socket. Bile hovers dangerously close to my tonsils. A few breaths later, I'm able to refocus on the cleanup. I remind myself to take stock of the *little victories*, just like my mother told me to do. She'd call washing my hair on a day I was sneezing a *little victory*. Being able to erase myself from a crime scene almost qualifies as a *big victory* by that standard.

I brought some cleaning supplies in a large suitcase outside the door, but she has some of my favorite brands, so I collect a few sprays from under the bathroom sink as well. Then, I get started.

Cleaning is an arduous process, making sure I'm not found in the mess. Though I'm wearing gloves, I wipe everything down, take the sheets, empty the vacuum's hatch, grab the stick vacuum for the stairs and her room in case I left behind hairs—emptying that after, as well.

I pause to catch my breath, pain threatening to overtake me again. If housewives can lift burning cars from toddlers, if the need arises, I can do this.

I strip, tossing my bloody clothes in three layers of plastic bags. With only underwear and a shower cap on, I use an old towel to wipe down what I can of the blood spots that are already growing tacky on my skin but don't rinse off in the sink. I saw a docu-series where that was what cinched it for the murderer. I stuff the towel in with the clothes, triple knot the bags, and toss the bundle by the foot of the steps.

By the time I'm done, the house smells of lemon, rosemary, and vinegar, and I've redressed in clean, nondescript clothes. Her bed is freshly made, though blood is already soaking through the new pinstriped gray sheets.

I glance at the clock—6:01 a.m.

A quiet panic rises in me, and I traverse down the stairs one at a time. Falling would be an unneeded complication. I do my best impersonation of rushing into the kitchen to scribble a note in handwriting that resembles Crystal's. I tape it prominently to the refrigerator for her sister, who pops in every week or two. I hope she won't start smelling too badly by then. But that will depend on a lot. "Went to the store. Be back in a bit."

6:09 a.m.

With those six minutes, I decide to turn up the air conditioner. I summit the stairs in record time and toss two comforters and a quilt onto the bed to cover the blood-soaked sheets.

I deserve a medal.

After one more sweep that reminds me of my father when we would stay in hotels and he would check drawers we never opened and the closet we never even looked in, I collect my cleaning supplies and bloody, plastic bundle.

6:13 a.m.

I sneak out the back door, locking it behind me. I'm hit with the faintest scent of cut grass and car exhaust—tell-tale scents of the suburbs.

Once I'm behind the wheel, I glance in the mirror to confirm I'm presentable enough that if I'm caught on camera, no one will be able to tell I just slaughtered someone in their bedroom.

6:14 a.m.

It's good enough.

I shamble from the house and slip into my car. Holding my breath, I turn the key and the engine roars to life. I do a quick scan. No one is running out and accusing me of murder. So I pull out of her driveway, as if I'm a normal person visiting a friend, and turn right down Sycamore St. In my rearview mirror, I see the bald man in a suit step out onto his porch and stretch. The lights of his car flash on.

I turn my attention back to the road and take a left at the stop sign, becoming fully out of his sightline.

As the sun rises from behind cookie-cutter homes, I tell myself that killing Crystal went alright. My hands shake, my chest pounds, everything hurts—and will hurt more in the morning—but it could have gone worse.

Apparently, I go on auto-pilot. I'm halfway home and haven't noticed my speed or stop lights. More importantly, I wasn't watching for cops.

But no one heard Crystal scream or saw me drive away. I won't get caught.

I'll be jittery with excitement soon, I'm sure.

3

different.

I stop at a breakfast place miles away from Crystal's house and get a to-go order. The place is a greasy spoon, so they rarely pay attention to people. If they do, they should only see a woman exhausted, getting breakfast in basic jogging wear. My pink poppy-patterned cane is the only thing that sets me apart from the background. But between killing Crystal, moving her body, and cleaning her house, I'm an over-baked potato. Stick a fork in me, I'm done. Though I hate admitting I need my cane at all, I can't imagine getting out of the car without it.

By the time I arrive at my current home away from home, it's almost 9 a.m. My left shoulder may as well have been torn off by a rabid dog, then stitched back on by a vet, it hurts that badly. My right aches from bearing my weight while I waited on hash browns and a stack of pancakes.

I want to crawl into bed and sleep forever.

Pulling into the driveway is a relief. I'll shower and wash my clothes, then donate them with a bag of other clothes tomorrow.

The mansion that looms in front of me is my favorite house yet. I've house sat for over two hundred people since I started this job five years ago, but this is by far the largest home and nicest house in Janes, which is why they couldn't let it sit vacant for two weeks. They also told me to drive their car while they were gone, keep the engine warm. They pointed out the lack of a navigation system as if it was a feature of accepting the job.

"Where you go while we're gone is honestly none of our business," they said.

I can read between the lines. We stay out of yours, so you stay out of ours. An agreement I can get behind. Normally, I get to know the people that live in the house I'm staying in; I touch their belongings, rummage through unopened mail, rifle through bedside drawers and tops of closets, sniff their shampoos. With the Vickersons, I have done none of those things.

With more detergent than is necessary, I start the washing machine for the first of at least four washes; between the towel, the outfit I wore while I was committing my first murder, and the one I wore home.

As if it's what I've *really* been waiting for, I step into the enormous master shower, which could fit most people's whole bathrooms. I take a deep sigh.

The water makes the blood on me become pink acrylic paint washing away in streaks. There's nothing dark or disturbing about it as it swirls along the iridescent mermaid tile and is sucked down a drain, miles and miles from the scene of the crime.

Tight back muscles release. Warm steam flushes my face while hot water flushes my skin. The sensations are more transcendent than the murder, but I can relive the moment I stabbed Crystal for the first time without thinking of the pain. I wish this was how I felt when it was happening.

I want to ride the high of killing a person who deserved it. Crystal had a laundry list of offenses—punching a woman in the face for bumping into her at the mall, tripping a child down a flight of cement steps at a hockey game because they made her spill beer on her dress, kicking a man in the nuts because he asked her for a cigarette when she was alone and it was dark outside. She told me many stories with pride, unprompted anecdotal shares while she showed me around her home. On my way out, a stray cat wandered onto her stoop and meowed. She knelt down and slapped it. I may not like animals, but I still wanted to slap her back for the homeless creature.

I want to float out of the shower onto the couch with fleshy fruit and a glass of wine as I allow the thrill and awe of what I've done to sink in. But I can't. Work looms over me. Maybe that's why I haven't been able to enjoy it. Maybe if—*when?*—I do this again, I'll need to when I have a day off after. I might need a day to decompress and allow my body to relax before I can actually enjoy it. The memory could always be better than the act for me, as there is no pain then. This time I didn't know that might be the case, so I have to put that off until after my shift at Juniper Foods. My day will drag on for eternity.

An image floats in: the change hitting me in a few hours while I'm walking down the frozen food aisle. It will hit me that I'm different, that what I want and need has become so unusual I can't function in normal society. Like when I first bled through my pants during gym class, my cheeks will redden, and I'll rush to the bathroom to check for any visible signs—horns, slit eyes, scales, words magically etched into my skin.

Becoming different sounds enticing, if not a little scary. Imagining a glow that people might see, having them suddenly see me as a more confident or socially adept version of myself lights up my nerves. They'd attribute it to Michael or getting a diagnosis, loving my job or spending more time with my best friend Adela.

I lather vanilla rose-scented soap harder into my skin to hide the metallic scent of Crystal, smiling with imaginings.

I don't have it in me to try more than I do. What if this could make me more of a sheep and less of a wolf? With each kill, I was more of what the collective *they* wanted? I've learned how to be like them as much as I can along the way, taking notes from documentaries and films, from books with serial killers bemoaning the importance of an appearance of normalcy. If I blended more, if killing made me less *me* and more *one of the group* that could only help me get away with it, help me do this more.

The change may be like being pregnant, and some people just *know.*

Wow, Elizabeth! You look so great today. First murder, huh? We knew you could do it! Keep it up, it's fantastic for your skin!

Jesus, Elizabeth. You're so late to the game, you may as well quit while you're behind.

You've already messed up and are bound to get caught before you can perfect it.

Didn't you know that hiding a body is passé? The smell will make its way to the street in a matter of days—if the sister doesn't show up first.

Congrats! I can tell your first kill was a success. By that I mean you did it. Remember that practice makes perfect.

I scrub until the water runs clean. My skin stings from the pressure.

A small light creeps into the bathroom. My heart, on the verge of bursting at every flash or sound, thuds. The police have to announce themselves, right? I haven't been so in my head that I missed something like that.

Shouldn't I be more collected than this?

The Vickersons don't get home until Tuesday—and today is Saturday. Nobody else is supposed to be here.

"Elibet?" a deep muffled voice calls out. "It's me."

I turn off the shower and grab the long-handled scrubby brush. Only one person calls me Elibet, and she doesn't have a key. Again, I stay quiet. I wonder what my voice sounds like now that I've killed someone. I worry it isn't the same.

"Elizabeth! It's Michael! Just wanted to let you know I'm here!"

Oh. A flare of anger hits me as hard as I hit my shoulder into the door jamb hours ago, but I still unfurl clenched fists from the brush. There are half-moon nail indentions in my palms. I've not been able to totally relax my shoulders since 1992, but they calm back into their usual non-hunched position, and I stretch tight toes. My breathing returns to normal as I turn the water back on.

He has no right to come into the Vickersons' home. I give him a key to everywhere I go in case of an emergency—in case *I* have an emergency. Just because I don't want to use a cane or talk about my disabilities doesn't mean I don't acknowledge their existence. We've had this talk—*only for emergencies, only for emergencies, only for fucking emergencies.* On top of that, he has no right using Adela's nickname for me, but I do so love hearing it, so I'll let it slide.

I don't call out to him, though. I say nothing in response. I just rinse the rest of the soap out of my squeaky-clean hair and rub some conditioner in it.

4

paint.

Five or ten minutes later, I saunter out of the bathroom into the master bedroom—a room almost as large as my entire apartment. Hurrying for others has never been in my nature. Short curls are tumbling out from under the terry-cloth wrap that's precariously atop my head. The rest of me is nude and air-drying.

Michael is sitting on the Vickersons' bed. I can smell him from here. His scent brings images of slick skin and clawing and screaming and me riding his face.

Perfectly straight teeth peek from the left side of his mouth; it can't stay closed when he flashes that lopsided smile of his. "Hi," he says.

"Why'd you let yourself in?" I ask, trying to keep my voice at its usual cadence of monotone. There's a bit of edge to it, though. The frustration at him waltzing into someone else's home isn't clear enough for him to pick up on it, as is often the case. He's rarely aware of my genuine emotions. I like that about myself.

"The key you left on your kitchen counter, in case of emergency." He answers a question I didn't ask, then holds it up like a prize.

"Is this an emergency?"

His thick eyebrows creep towards each other as he says, "No, I just wanted to see you."

As is customary in our relationship, I say nothing and wait for him to hang himself.

He doesn't this time. Instead, he changes the subject. "I walked past the washing machine. The water was pink. What was that? Looks like you're washing whites and reds together. Or was that blood?" He chuckles, and his dull blue eyes attempt to sparkle.

Cheeks flushing, I say, "It was paint." I know it was a joke, but I can still feel the phantom warmth of Crystal on my back.

"Hey, I was just joking. I know you can do laundry." He smiles instead of laughs this time.

Trying to calm my irregular heartbeat, I choke out a lie. "I went to the craft store to get more candy wrappers so I can give some honey butters out to my new class, and someone smushed a paint bottle when I was walking by. My shirt was either a toss or donate situation, but I thought someone could use them for scraps, so I'm getting what I can out."

I bought more candy wrappers hours before I went to Crystal's house, so it seems fate is offering me a handout.

"That's nice of you. So many people would have just tossed them."

Michael closes the distance between us. His footsteps make no sound on the pristine cream carpet. This would be a terrible home to murder someone in. Carpet is a no-no, if not just because the smell of wet carpet reminds me of wet dog, which is almost as vile as vomit. In truth, I don't like animals. Sure, I'll sit for them, but I really don't like them. They love me, though. I guess it's not true what they say about animals being a good judge of character.

"That's why I love you, you know?" he adds, tilting his head down.

"I love you too," I say perfunctorily. Though I do, I wish we didn't say it as often as we do. Once a week would be enough for me. Maybe even only on special occasions.

"That's why I'm a lucky man." Michael kisses the three mole-like freckles on the crevice between the bridge of my nose and eyebrows and caresses the curves of my naked body. "I wish I could ravage you right now."

His hands are nice—soft and warm. "But we have work soon." I yawn.

"Oh, no! Did you not sleep well?" he asks. His face pinches with worry.

Michael is a dramatic, if not very good boyfriend, the kind that believes soup and crackers make colds go away quicker, kisses heal wounds, and bear hugs soothe fear. He's handsome, kind, and gentle, and one of the few men I've dated. I gravitate towards women—but there was something special about him.

What I think drew me to him more than anything was how little ambition he has to rise above his current station in life. I love that I don't have to feed his ego, help him through school, cheer at sporting events or poetry slams, celebrate achievements I don't care about, and give him more of my time than I want to because he's accomplishing things.

When I was casually dating, I often didn't ask about people's lives. There's something to be said about not having to be there emotionally for another person that I really enjoy—need, crave, want, *deserve*.

"No. I didn't sleep much. Spent most of my night reading short stories that I immediately forgot. They were fine, but insomnia will do that," I add, to make it clear that it's not my fault I can't remember.

"You're favoring your left arm. Did something happen?"

Sometimes he's more perceptive than I would prefer. But he

hasn't noticed that I've just murdered someone. Whether that's good or bad, he's still oblivious enough to keep around for now. "Shoulder just dislocated again. No big."

"No big? That's the fifth time this month." It's the 27th, so that's not too bad. Still, we've had the same fight on and off for the last three months, and I'm not getting any more entertaining. "Have you been using your cane when you leave the house yet? I didn't see it by the door…"

"No," I say, not adding any more. Face impassive, he has no clue what I'm feeling.

The air conditioning kicks in, and I shiver. I should put clothes on now.

He accepts that I have opted out of the cane conversation. "What made it dislocate this time?" He grabs my clothes and hands them to me, his eyes lingering on my breasts.

I didn't plan for this question, but I think back to the craft store. I nearly fell over when I tripped on a box in the middle of the baking accessory aisle, so I say, "There was a sewing machine box in the wrong place and…"

Before I finish my lie, he fills the story in for me. "And you wanted to put it back. You sweet woman. You need to stop being so good and take care of yourself."

Michael sees me in the way I'd like to be—normal, good. Another reason I'm with him. When we first met, he hoisted me up on a cushioned pedestal. I've been there ever since.

I wince as I maneuver my sore shoulder into the offensively uncomfortable, Crayola red work shirt that's a little snug on a good day. My pink pleated skirt is much easier to slide on. I wear white knee-high socks because the store gets chilly.

"Gotta grab my lunch, then we can go," I say.

I would normally sit down and enjoy breakfast, but with the pain coming back, I'm more queasy than hungry.

He follows me into the chef's kitchen that I would kill to

have, but it would garner too much publicity—the killing, not the kitchen, though it's worthy of a magazine.

Michael touches everything as I collect my lunchbox and orange juice. The Vickersons encouraged me to consume any and everything I could while they were gone.

"Okay, all set," I say, breaking the spell the appliances have over Michael. He's not had much throughout his life.

His family was lower-middle class, and he hovers just above them. People like him are used to not having much, so they settle a lot, he told me. He'll always have a roommate. He'll own the same jeans until the holes in them have become fashionable again. He'll never ask about the luxurious steak or lobster that says market price; instead, he buys the one that's a flat $12.95 and comes with a salad. But I'm his golden ticket, he says—an unthinkable prize. Despite being looked at as some winnable object, I'm flattered.

"Want to ride together?"

"Can't. I have to use their car a lot. I made a promise, and I think they have security cameras they can check to make sure I did." They may or may not—it's probable they have some that delete themselves every 24-hours in case the FBI shows up (I assume they are Mafia)—but Michael doesn't need to know this.

Michael nods.

"I'll meet you there then. I love you," he says, as we walk to the door together, fingers interlaced.

We pass through the living room, and he makes a remark about the coldness of the furniture and how the gray and black contemporary art makes him sad. I shrug, indifferent.

Thanks to this job, I've crossed something off of my bucket list. The freedom they gave me, their car and bathroom and washing machine allowed me to go for it.

As far as I'm concerned, everything the Vickersons love is *perfect.*

5

earworm.

Michael and I reach Juniper Foods around the same time. He parks far away for the *extra exercise* while I slide into the closest spot I can find.

The looming grocery store has a tan, stucco façade meant to make it homier than its natural food competitors' storefronts, which are plain cement. Instead, it looks dated and out of place in the bright, smooth shopping complex it gloms onto for life-support.

I meander towards the *whooshing* electronic double doors, knowing Michael will catch up to me as if his last name is Myers not Goode. After a few moments, a clammy palm meets my right one. Leave it to Michael to be mindful of my shoulder. It's not what hurts the most anymore. Pain is like that—ever-changing, moving around, ebbing and flowing. A pinch in my hip sears and has overshadowed even my all-over pain. Unrelated to Crystal, I *could* actually talk about it without lying. Though I hate talking about my pain, hate thinking about it or bringing it up, dwelling on something so all-consuming. If my focus is elsewhere, I can sometimes put pain on a back burner. Besides, who knows what will hurt worse or less or next? So I don't tell Michael about the pinched nerve that appeared from nowhere. I can't have him treating me like my forehead says, "FRAGILE: HANDLE WITH CARE."

The recycled air is chilly as we walk into work. We hold cupped hands in companionable silence like elementary school children.

I'm still waiting for Michael to comment on my new confidence or the obvious change in me, or for my heart to explode, or for my brain to melt and drip through my ears. But with every passing moment, I'm closer to thinking that *I've gotten away with it* despite having done so much wrong.

"Hey, guys!" Sid calls out. Their dark brown pageboy haircut moves in one piece as they turn to wave.

"H—" Before either of us can respond, they are back to weighing two large honeydew melons. I salivate, picturing running my fingers across the slightly bumpy rind as I suck the juicy peach-colored flesh within.

Michael doesn't let go of my hand as we stroll towards the break room slash sign-in room slash room where Jamie lectures us whenever one person did something wrong, but she doesn't want to single them out.

We stroll through the cereal aisle, and I let the sounds of the store wash over me. My pink and cream Oxfords occasionally squeak softly on the linoleum, while muffled beeping from the registers and self-checkout stations surrounds me. They echo in the brain on and off all day. Even when it's slow and no one is checking out or I'm not working, the quiet noises are uninteresting earworms.

A small child is whining in the—I close my eyes for a second to listen—international aisle. Chatter is picking up as the Saturday morning crowd discusses their weekend party plans.

Michael groans, and I don't have to ask why. Someone chose the squealing cart. The noise is a stuck pig fucking a bleating sheep.

"Why haven't we gotten rid of that yet?" he asks, dropping my hand to wiggle his fingers in his ears.

"Because Juniper." I shrug. If we didn't have cameras, I would steal it and leave it in Severest Marsh to rust.

A man with a sweaty, green-tinted toddler on his hip jogs towards us. "Excuse me? Do you work here?" he calls out. We meet in front of the boxed rice. "Do you work here?" he asks again.

Our shirts say *yes,* but I want to say *not yet.* I'm not on the clock, after all.

Michael tells him that we do.

The man heaves a sigh so dramatic that I'm surprised the snotting child doesn't slip from his arms and fall to the floor face first. She'd probably crush her nose, leaving orange-red blood speckles on the linoleum. That's not my favorite color, so I'm indifferent.

Noticing her drooping, he shifts her up higher on his hip. Now she's at an angle that if she fell, she may crack her soft skull. The floor would look almost white with the deep crimson pouring out on it. That's my second favorite red, but she's a child. Though I wouldn't mind seeing the inside of a skull, I'd prefer it to be someone on my list—one of the many people I've made notes about their life-ruining behaviors.

The man is asking about soap. He reeks of desperation, both figuratively and literally. Michael starts to point him in the right direction, and the child screams. I can't stand the sound, so I walk away. I may not kill children, but the thought of my hands around her throat still pops into my head.

As I head towards the back room, I see Jamie. Her bangs are especially round today and perhaps a record-breaking space away from her forehead. She nods approvingly at me, though I don't know if it's because I walked away instead of killing a kid or made it to work on time.

Once I clock in, I tell myself that the first person I interact with will set the tone for the day. I'll have to avoid all annoying people. Sadly, working at a grocery store, that's nearly impossible.

Jamie asks me to start at the register, and I instantly get a line.

The first woman that comes through my line is on the phone. She's talking loudly as she puts her items on the conveyor belt. All fruit and juice.

"Yeah, yeah… Totally. I'm getting it now so I can start the diet with you. Well, I don't want to be like that fat bitch across the street. How her husband fucks her I'll never know. Did I tell you she was pregnant again? Baby number four? I mean, I'd abort them if I were her. She's just going to feed them shit, and they'll all turn out like little piggies." The prematurely wrinkled, orange-skinned blonde is showing more than anyone wants to see. Excess skin hangs from her neck like a turkey jowl, and her heels look out of place with her worn jeans. She's truly nothing to write home about.

All of her fruit is in one bag, banging around and bruising itself. I pull out the oranges to weigh them. I hit accept on the 3.4 lbs the screen displays. As I put them in the paper bag, the oranges become her eyes, and I want to sink my thumbs into them. I itch to feel the wet smoothness of her baby blues. I want to push in her eye sockets, see if I can pop her eyeballs out like the seed of a very ripe avocado.

I hate people like her. They are just as bad as people like me.

If this were an older time, she wouldn't be sliding her credit card into a machine and hitting buttons. She'd be handing me a check with her name and address on it. Her fate would be different then. Instead of going home to be horrible, she'd be on my list. Her time to be horrible would be cut short sooner than later.

She takes the bag and leaves without me saying a word to her or vice versa.

I crack my neck, do mini lunge stretches, and a big twist in either direction for my back's sake. The woman with just three boxes of chicken stock doesn't notice.

A few customers later, I catch Jamie's attention. She swoops by the register, and I tell her that it's going to be a roaming day as soon as my line lessens. I claim back pain. She knows about my hEDS, so I can pull the card if I need to. In reality, I can't smile at another shitty person. Walking through the store, it's much easier to avoid eye contact.

6

cruciferous.

"Hey, you," Michael says. I like that he is a floater. When I'm away from the register, he can *bump into me* on the floor. It keeps me from getting too bored. It's just another reason his lack of aspirations is a positive thing for me. "I made a decision," he says with a voice that sounds almost stern.

"Did the cruciferous veggies inspire you?" I saw him putting lettuces back where they belonged when I was checking out my last few customers. He was intensely considering a head of cabbage before he put it back. Maybe that's when he had one of his *serious thinking moments*, as he calls them.

"No, you did," he says, his brows pinching together.

I'm having a hard time focusing as my stomach is cannibalizing itself in order to stave off hunger until I take a lunch break. I have been hanging out at the end of the cereal aisle, vaguely acknowledging customers when they walked by. Even if I hadn't been frustrated, I knew I had to leave the register when I could *smell* feta through the vacuum-sealed plastic.

The woman buying it was rude enough that I considered hitting her in the head with the salami log I was about to scan. I saw myself lying on the floor, shoving crumbly cheese in my face, her blood pooling slowly under me—a better alternative to the sickly child's. And even in a daydream, I didn't bother to wipe the dribbling cheese sweat off my cheek.

Right, he has something serious he wants to say. I focus, and say, "Okay... Shoot." The word makes me realize I don't like the idea of using guns. I'm still learning about myself at thirty-six.

"I—I applied to the Janes Police Academy!" Michael says. Pride beams off of him a glow that's blinding astronauts at the space station.

My mouth dries; my right eye twitches. I wait for the wink or punchline. Every second I don't respond, his face falls a little, the light fades a little. I find the death of his excitement a little arousing. I love him in my own way, though, so I'd rather just not be with him than hurt him. How upsetting for me.

"Really? When?" I walk down the aisle to look busy, to move, to find a package of Havarti I can squish. The cold of the refrigerators hurts my prematurely aging and sore-from-killing body.

"About four months ago. I was going to tell you, but I wasn't sure I really wanted it. I haven't had ambitions in a long time. I did once. I remember I wanted to be a firefighter. My dad told me it was stupid, and I'd get myself killed. He said if that's what I wanted, I should go for it. But he said it in that way that made me feel small and horrible, so I gave up on it. When someone tells you that your dreams are stupid, that *you're* stupid for wanting them over and over again, you give up. I'm twenty-four now. I need to do better."

It occurs to me that I should be offended. I'm twelve years older than him. Though I'm passively looking for a better and more stable job, I enjoy my varied days at the grocery store. Plus, there's my ESL course and house sitting. There's a certain thrill in never knowing whose house I'll be sleeping in next.

But really, it's my newfound goal that makes me feel I'm also aiming for more. His dream involves a well-lit path, while mine is an unpaved, darkened back road.

"Do you, though? Do you need to *do better?*" I ask. "What's wrong with your life? Is this about him? Your dad, I mean?"

"No, and there's nothing wrong with my life—with *our* life. I just want to live alone or maybe support y—" He cuts himself off, knowing I still enjoy my independence and don't want to quit anything or have him move in to take care of me. "Um, myself, a little better. And I—I just want to have goals again. I'm in great shape, and I know two detectives just retired, so…"

Blood running cold, I parrot, "Detectives?" Being a cop is one thing.

"Yeah, homicide. I know it takes a long time, and they'll have long since found someone before I can get there, but it just feels like a sign. People are moving up, so maybe I can get in line now. And who knows, maybe I can move up quicker because they need people! I hear our homicide rate is the highest it's been in a long time. Though, that could just be the media circus surrounding the Hockins' murder. That whole thing got out of hand," he says. "Can you imagine if I had been a part of that? Tracking down clues, interviewing people. Even just to be the cop on the scene the day of… What a dream."

I saw the photos of the Hockins' woman, her face covered in blood—The Vampire Widow. If Michael's dream is to be on a scene like that, it's his dream to be on the scene of Crystal's murder and maybe other future murders of mine.

"I honestly haven't been this excited about anything since you and I started dating." Michael fidgets with his shirt collar. "So… What do you think?"

Only moments ago he was self-assured, but I made him doubt. Sometimes I want to slow clap for myself.

"I think it sounds like a huge undertaking. Don't most people join the Academy straight out of high school?" I ask with no clue if that's true.

I know enough about DNA and crime scenes to assume I probably left some of me behind last night despite cleaning, but I know little about the inner workings of the police department. I just don't want him joining. I'll have to come up with a reason.

"No, you have to have 60 credit hours of school or some equivalent of experience." He's a pamphlet, reading himself. "Since I have a Bachelor's, I don't even have to take the academic proficiency test."

Did I know about his degree?

I say nothing.

"Will you—will you support me?" His face is vulnerable. I like vulnerable. I'm a sucker for it because I can exploit it.

Jamie's voice calls for our baker over the P.A. system. Michael looks up at the ancient speaker in the back corner of the store.

Before he looks back at me, I cringe. "Yes, of course, I'll support you," I say.

"I know you will!" He's back to himself, all self-doubt and worry gone, replaced with smiles and love. "Besides, you've been doing it all along, right?"

I chuckle, so he thinks I'm being cute rather than angry. Supporting him will make it difficult for me to kill again, which is especially sad given that the first time didn't go as hoped. If I stop now, it really was just a checklist item. I want to find what feels best and enjoy it. I'd have that memory to cling to as I become a lump of a disarticulated skeleton and sack of pain. I'll just have to be even *more* careful. Given that I have a gap in my *how-to-get-away-with-murder* education, that's going to be difficult.

Michael turns from the yogurt section of the open refrigerator and pulls me into a hug, careful to keep his hands off my skin. Even in moments of joy, he's conscious of things like my nerve damage.

Though he's become a man with desires beyond my body and having an extra shift at work, he may be worth compartmentalizing for. He could also be another part of my life I have to toss aside so I can be myself, like Justine, when she caught me pinching the soft spots behind a kid's knee under the lunch table in middle school. That girl kept quiet because she was doing much worse. Justine saw what I was doing, saw the real me. And truly seeing *me* is looking into darkness. Very few people can handle that.

pomegranate.

We walk side-by-side through Juniper Foods until I pass one of the five clocks hanging throughout the store.

"Break time." I'm a trained dog hearing a bell. *Finally.*

Sid's voice crackles above us, picking up store noises. "I need assistance at the register, please."

"Damn," Michael says. I know what he's thinking. He tries to sneak at least a few minutes with me in the break room, even if we don't have a break together. "Well, duty calls." He swivels his head, then drops a chapped-lip kiss on my cheek before rushing towards the front of the store. The first time he did this, I almost told him to bite me, put the flesh of my cheeks between his toothpaste commercial teeth, but he's so normal that I kept that as an inside thought.

Today, I'll take my fifteen alone. I revel in the idea of the reflection time I'll get.

Out of my peripheral vision, I see a short woman raising their hand in that familiar way customers do, their mouth lolling open as if they are pantomiming speech. They hurry towards me. Keeping my gaze straight ahead, I pretend I don't see them. The vibe I aim to give off is: *I'm unavailable.* Whether she wants to think I'm adding the word *sorry* to that is up to her.

Once I step into the break room, I revert to having my twelve-year-old self's posture, all hunched and gnarled like an old woman who's been knitting blankets for the past twenty years. I bar the door with my body as my neck allows all ten pounds of head mass to fall forward, hanging on my muscles that never fully relax. I even allow myself a groan and hiss with pain as I wiggle and stretch, trying to see what exactly hurts the most. It's always all over, but I need to know what work has worsened and what last night's activity damaged.

I didn't want to ruin my shower by body-checking, but I have to do it sometime. After a few minutes of inhuman sounds akin to rice cereal crackling in cold milk, popping bubble wrap, plastic bags being packed, and preparations for a fist fight, I move away from the door.

The break room is mostly beige and brown. A small counter that holds fruits, bread products, and all things coffee and tea is the color of Crystal's blood on my skin. To stand in front of it is to clash; it's three shades darker than the stiff, mandatory Juniper Foods shirt that's pinching my sore underarms.

I grab my lunch box from the food-spotted refrigerator and head to the table, already preparing myself for the pain the hard seat will cause. Before I realize I've unwrapped it, my peanut butter and banana sandwich is gone. Looking at the remaining plastic container, I'm furious. I didn't expect the stabbing to go poorly, and I didn't expect the cleanup to be exhausting or to dislocate my shoulder. So I packed the same kind of lunch I always do. There is nothing hearty about it, nothing that can stick to my ribs.

I pull open the container, loving the sound of the plastic separating. Inside, bloody baby teeth await me. *My favorite.* Pomegranate seeds were attractive to me for how I viewed them long before I tasted them.

When I was a teenager, a friend flew over her bike handlebar. She was trying to impress me. She ate the blacktop. I rushed over from my seat under the carport to see her scuffed and bloodied face. Three small teeth were on the ground in front of her. Slimy and red, the smooth white was a stark comparison to the black pockmarked underneath. I remember wanting to put them in my mouth, bite them to see if they'd break like hard candy. They looked soft, covered in the saliva.

The first time I saw the inside of a pomegranate, I knew I'd found the next best thing.

My dark burgundy seeds have de-thawed enough that when I bite into them, they give way with little resistance. The center still crunches, but the outside is soft and rubbery. As the tart, cranberry-apple taste coats my tongue, I delve into postmortem thoughts.

I close dry, tired eyes, and it comes back to me as if it's a real-time movie. This shouldn't be the moment, but I can't stop it. I smile, I laugh a little, and I realize I will kill again and again until I get it right, until it feels like *me*. I'm sure it will take a long time for the paranoia to go away, for me to be comfortable in both the act of killing and in my ability to get away with it.

Crystal's face as she said my name tells me I don't care. Her blood on my clothes tells me I'll get through it. The ticking clock of my body's failing—which I'm sure I'm making worse—tells me I should do what I can as quickly as I can.

Popping another pomegranate seed onto my tongue, I suck on it. I picture it going from red to white, like the bodies I will leave behind me. I'll snatch the color from them, and it will taste just as sweet and tart.

My breathing has quickened, as if I'm coming down from an orgasm.

Without my list in front of me, I flip through anyone I can remember in case one sticks out. It would be a thrill to choose someone right here, right now. An older woman with a wicked backhand and a rude man with wandering hands come to mind. Then I remember their teeth—gray and veneers, respectively. Another person with stories about violence that make them laugh would be a contender, but they have a snaggletooth. I land on a woman with smooth teeth and a slight gap in the middle. *I love gaps.* The one crooked one is so far back, I only know about it because her mouth gets wide when she screams.

Cora Stone—a liar, a thief, a fake.

A year ago, I house sat for Cora. She was polite when she left me her keys, telling me to treat the house like mine, enjoy whatever food I wanted, watch whatever I wanted, have an orgy for all she cared. She even left me $20 "for booze or something". The week she was gone was uneventful. I cleaned up behind myself, ate very little of her food, and Michael only slept over once. I expected her at 5 p.m. on a Friday. At 1 a.m.—only an hour after I'd gone to bed on Thursday—I woke to a door flinging open and a banshee voice screaming, "WAKE THE FUCK UP!"

I watched from the corner, my arms tucked close to me, as she threw a lamp on the floor. I'd photographed it only days before.

Its thin drum shade bounced and rolled towards the trash can. Shards of porcelain and glass flew in every direction. One piece came my way and lodged itself in my leg. I stared at the small blue and white chunk, mouth agape, waiting for an explanation.

"You did this! I won't pay you! I'll sue you for my lamps!" Cora screamed. Her eyes were bloodshot, and I was worried she'd done some sort of drug I couldn't combat.

My body flashed cold. I couldn't come up with anything intelligent to say. So I calmly said, "What?"

"Did you eat all of my food, too?" Her face reddened.

Cora rushed to her refrigerator. With fervor, she ripped open plastic containers and unscrewed caps. She opened her mouth wide and shoved anything she could in with grabby hands—wet or dry, stale or fresh. Gummy spaghetti bits hung from her lips, milk dripped down her chin, chicken stock soaked her white dress, revealing soft curves and no underwear underneath.

I went to move, to run, then she gargled. Like a baby allergic to milk, it all came back up almost instantly, on the floors, on the counters.

Her body still shaking from the ferocity of it, she turned to me, finger-pointing. "Why would you do this to me? What did I do to you?" she cried.

I didn't know what I should do. If she was mentally unwell, I knew I'd be useless. I don't deal well with unstable people. My mother's two breakdowns and the only two times I ever saw her cry prove that. I sat in the corner and watched her lose her mind, waiting for the strong woman to come back. When she was taken to the mental hospital, I didn't visit her. I told myself it was because she'd be home soon, but it was fear. One of the few things I'm afraid of is ending up in one myself. I'll be unable to hide, and someone will lock me away.

So Cora's response had me backing towards her front door.

"Did you leave shit in my bathroom?" Cora spat the words out with venom. "You fucking did, didn't you?" She ran to the bathroom.

That did it. I couldn't see what would happen next, and I didn't want to stick around to deal with anyone who might strap her down, flailing and squealing, and take her to a hospital under flashing lights.

I remember glancing down to confirm I had left no blood behind. I hadn't even thought about it; I just did it. Now, I think my brain *knew*. I was unconsciously planning, making sure there was none of me there. If I ever grew brave enough, I could do what I want without being caught.

I drove away with a thin line of blood oozing into my shoe and splatters of purple Jello clinging in my curls. Canned mushrooms, vomit, and the phantom scent of feces lingered for days. I told no one about that incident; I've told no one about a lot of incidents. I just jotted them down on a password protected spreadsheet.

I would have moved on, assumed her mentally ill, having some sort of break, and let her be just another person in my life I couldn't talk about.

But months later, on a forum for house sitters, Cora Stone was called out by name as having acted the same way to someone else. The poster wasn't sure if she was unwell, but she thought she should share. Nine other people commented that she'd done the same—one of which called the cops. In the end, they couldn't prove anything. It was a he-said-she-said situation, and she seemed perfectly sweet and normal when the police came by to visit (or so the poster said).

It wasn't just that she'd done it to eleven people, it was that she'd had a nearly identical fit—the lamp, the leftovers, the comment about shit—with all of them.

Pretending to have a breakdown so she could get away with paying me only $20 is unacceptable. Some people only do this for a living, some people can't afford rent if they don't get paid, some people can't afford to feed themselves if their jobs fall through or they get stiffed.

Since then, I've asked for half of the payment upfront.

I looked her up after I realized she wasn't who she pretended to be. Her social media portrays a more accurate side to her. She had a habit of videoing herself knocking over things for views and likes. At a coffee shop, she shoved half of the stir straws into the trash, the other half on the floor. She tossed department store perfume samples on the floor. The pile tripped an elderly man. She cackled at that, then ran. It's her most popular video. Only the first video explained her behavior. She said that some businesses are just shitty, and more people should let them know that.

Having a name gives me a promise of another kill. The timeline almost doesn't matter because Cora Stone is next on my list.

8

honey.

I've been waiting to hear about Crystal's death, about a massive hunt for the monster who killed her. I've been waiting for police officers to find me, for Crystal to make the news. But her murder, like so many others, hasn't registered with the public. The morning after I killed Crystal, lovebirds wanting to have the house to themselves chopped a family to bits. Since then, there's been a massive gang shootout that ended with sixteen dead, a robbery at two banks, and a kid at Janes Elementary accidentally shot her teacher after taking her daddy's gun from his nightstand. Crystal's murder would have been much bigger news if even one of those hadn't sprung up, I'm sure.

But it's been over a month of near-sameness—day in and day out in various locations. Memories of Crystal help push me out of bed. But it's planning Cora's murder that keeps me moving.

For three days, I house sat for the McKinleys—a nice elderly couple with matching dentures, identical short haircuts, and six cats. It was a hectic job filled with antibiotics, the odor of supposedly scentless litter, the grating sound of meowing, hissing, purring, and a lot of cleaning. One of them peed on the floor twice a day. The scrubbing has left my arm exhausted.

Five other houses followed The McKinleys. Couples and single people who had braces, missing teeth, stubby teeth, and dogs and cats. It was a Rolodex of locations that kept my mind spinning, my wallet full, and my back aching. I longed for a stable gig with a stable bed—or better yet, no job for a week or two. But this is one of my busy seasons and the only way I can pay rent during my slow ones.

I still miss the Vickersons' house. They came home with more bags than they left with. One glance around the house and at the odometer, and they tipped me $200. In near-unison, they told me they'd call me around this time next year. "Please keep your schedule open," Mrs. Vickerson said. "We can't imagine hiring anyone else now."

I said I would and left, sad that I had to go back to normal showers.

This new place is a dump in comparison, but it's still nicer than my place. House sitting for a woman named Marney No Last Name is a three-week job. She paid me upfront and in cash. I'm a week in. Despite the interesting rotating house locations, the influx of new mouths in the faces of people that are mostly boring. Only one has made it to my maybe list so far.

Marney has a ranch-style home with three rooms, a kitchen almost as nice as the Vickersons with a brand new stove, a karaoke machine in a very blank living room, and a mute parrot who hangs out on a perch by the TV or in one of six open bird cages throughout the house.

Adela is on her way over so we can sing until we pass out. I'm surprising her, too. We'll be making my *famous* old-fashioned butterscotch candies—only called *honey butters* now. The first time Adela tasted them, she said that they're better than any store bought butterscotch candy she's eaten so they deserve a different name. I've not called them butterscotch since.

More often than not, I have a stockpile of them in my house, stowing some away in my oversized bag or giving some to Adela. These last few weeks have been hell as I've been without them, my sweet tooth going unsatisfied. Empty pink cellophane wrappers mock me.

I didn't need to see them to know I was missing them. I reach for phantom candies at least twice a day, only to be disappointed in myself for not making any recently. But I've been so tired. Maintaining life has been taking a toll far greater than I expected —not to mention the mental energy it's taking to plan my next murder.

The ingredients for honey butters sit on the counter, and the living room is all set up for a night of pretending we are tweens again.

With a little time to myself, I pull out my Polaroid camera. It's time to document my stay.

I miss my original camera and its tan, clunky body. This baby blue one is cute but doesn't have the same heft. There used to be something so *big*, so *urgent* about taking a Polaroid, a *don'tfuckitup* feeling that's lost with the new, smaller version.

I wander through the house to find the perfect things.

In the master bathroom, I see the water-stained shower faucet. A memory of getting a bath from my mother, her hand circling my back as she told me stories about Elizabeths that inspired her fills my mind. I was fifteen; she died the next year. Kneeling beside the tub, I snap a close-up. The picture slides from the plastic camera's mouth, and my whole body tingles.

In the guest bedroom, I take a photograph of a deep sea blue side table stuffed in the corner of the room. The color reminds me of a saltwater pool from one of the few parties I went to in high school. Someone held my head under water, and all I saw was this unreal blue.

They must have thought I was fine and able to hold my breath for a long time. I didn't struggle or panic. I gulped in water. I wanted to see what it would feel like to drown.

I find an unused table with a gouge in one corner and a single fingerprint pressed near the front. I want to know its story. *Click.* A photo slides from the thin flap.

Though it's said to make no difference, I shake each photo as they come out.

My last picture is of the inside of the freezer. There are ice crystals forming on a package of meat, browning at the edges of the gum pink wavy globs. Despite my not eating much meat anymore, there's a nostalgic feel to the wrapped beef. I still crave the deeply satisfying chew that only a hunk of seared steak can give—well, there's still the possibility of human meat. I've not taken it off the table.

I close the door and walk out of the kitchen; I've made it cold in there now. It rained early this morning, so I crack the living room's window just a hair to let some of the warm, earthy late-Spring air flow in. I'd lose my excellent reputation if the silent parrot that sleeps most of the day escaped. Though, I worry it will die on me. I've been very unlucky lately, getting old animals with *an any day now* look in their eyes.

"So sorry I'm so late!" Adela says by way of greeting, shoving her way past me with a paper bag of groceries in her hand. The name of the store is printed in cheerful green letters: Natural Grocery. It's a betrayal that I couldn't care less about.

She's 50 minutes late. I expected 45. So to me, she *is* still late.

"No problem. Kitchen's to the left around the corner," I tell her.

"Odd-shaped house. Smells nice, though!"

Her shaggy hair has grown into a mullet shape after a pixie cut she didn't feel like maintaining. She complains about it a lot; it's not long enough to do what she wants with it. Unlike my light, sandy brown, hers is the gray she woke up with at twenty-nine. Not once did Adela think to dye it. Maybe it's because gray has been popular for a while, but it's probably because it looks good on her—better than the pale orangey-red she had before.

"OH MY GOD!" she shouts. "Are we making honey butters?"

I don't need to respond to her clearly unnecessary question, because she's a smart woman. Adela has grown accustomed to my silence. She's the talker in our relationship.

"Ooooh, good shots, Elibet!" Adela is saying as I stride into the kitchen behind her.

"Huh? Oh, the Polaroids. Thank you," I say.

Adela is the only one who knows about the photographs. My stack fills six shoeboxes now. When she first found my collection of object and furniture pictures from a recent house I took, I figured she would call me a freak—a word still used very often at the time. Instead, she asked why I chose what I did and said she thought I should put them into a collection and submit them to an art gallery. *I don't know* and *hilarious* were my responses. In all honesty, I choose what I photograph because of what speaks to me—the stories they remind me of, their imperfections or uniqueness, items out of place, or objects I find so mundane and average they become interesting again. As for submitting them anywhere, well, I worried I'd get sued for being nosey and photographing houses without permission. Now, my worry is of a different kind.

There are only four photos that connect me with Crystal, as only four photos connect me with many people and their homes. She and I have no paper trail or shared phone number, as she only had a burner at the time (never said why, and I didn't care enough to ask). I deleted the line about her on the house sitting spreadsheet the moment I decided she was *the one*.

I cherish each and every one of my Polaroids more than ever. Though I have two favorites. Her unmade bed with red clown sheets that were the stuff of nightmares has become a captured memory of me soaking in her blood beside her. The chip on the third step of her stairs is a little blurry. It's now a reminder of me sneaking up to her bedroom.

"Can we make honey butters before anything else?" Adela asks, interrupting my wandering thoughts. Her excitement is adorable and one of the reasons I keep her around. "Now that I've seen it..." She motions to the ingredients laid out on the counter—all local because I'm a good person, mostly.

"Of course," I tell her.

I turn on the new stove, enjoying the *tick, tick, tick* my electric burner doesn't provide.

Adela's eyes light up, as they do every time when we make honey butters—an occurrence that still seems to surprise her. I've been making these for eight years, and she's been helping me for six. "Yes, yes! But only at the beginning. You know how I always burn it."

She doesn't; she just hates using candy thermometers.

I unscrew a honey jar and empty it into the saucepan as she tells me about her day at the bookshop—one of her three jobs. Like me, Adela would love to have only one job, but that's not in the cards for us right now. She enjoys life as it is. And our lives come with interesting stories filled with characters straight out of movies.

Adela slowly stirs in sugar, vanilla, and salt, working her way into a steady whisk. She shares a story about a child who sneezed into a kid's book on a page with a furry patch, closed it, then put it back on the shelf. I can't help but laugh as her hands wave wildly about with frustration. "Then, a customer who wanted 'just something by that Franzen guy' to impress a girl decided to take a quick pause and ask for my number. Because I guess why not, really." She commends him for going for it. *Life's too short*, she says. Still, she doesn't date tacky people. It's not her bag.

The story continues as she goes into vivid detail about his lip-smacking and leaning and fumbling, along with her thoughts as he's doing all of this.

Adela squeals, and I see that the honey is bubbling. "Your turn!" It's clockwork—both the candy timing and her child-like noise.

I take over, and Adela smiles wide, waiting for me to tell her she did a good job. After a moment of my silence, she continues talking.

As I whisk rhythmically, getting the mixture to temperature, I scan my best friend's face, as I do often. She's beautiful. Her apple cheeks used to be chubby, and I remember wanting to nibble on them to see what it would feel like. It must be why I wanted Michael to bite my cheeks—wish fulfillment, even if I was on the wrong end. I told Adela about my wants at a sleepover, and she said that if her cheeks were still chubby when we were fourteen, I could. They weren't.

She's already got faint laugh lines, which I adore. They are well-earned. Lips that are neither remarkable nor unremarkable are dry today. As she smiles, they look like they might split. But the best part of her is her teeth. I've always loved them—more than her cheeks or her giggles or her steadfast belief that I am good and worthy of her time and energy, even when I'm not showing up for her.

They are just a shade off from eggshell and smooth aside from the bottom front two that have three ridges in the middle. There is a gap between her front two. It occurs to me that both Crystal and Cora also have a gap. *Maybe I have a type.*

Adela still has her wisdom teeth and has never had a cavity. The back three teeth of the bottom right of her mouth have begun to crowd each other over the past four years. Still, she may have one of the best mouths I've ever encountered. I may be biased because I love her.

Deciding what to say or do as she smiles and I stare at her molars, it hits me: I want their teeth. I may not know how I want to kill or what will hurt me the least, but I know what I want to remember them by—beyond the Polaroids. I wish I had Crystal's. But there is still time for Cora.

I'd like to *feel* them too. I could wear dentures to obscure *any* dental impressions I might leave. I'd latch my jaw onto their flesh and sink my covered teeth into them. Will I finally be sated fully? Then there's the DNA cleanup, not to mention—

"I told him to *fuck right off* and refused to help him. Then I said he better leave and go buy 'that Franzen guy' at some other bookstore."

Her story must have gone full rabbit trail if she's *just now* getting to her response to his asking her out, but I checked out for most of it. I doubt it was of much import. Often Adela wants to have full sit-downs when she deems something important.

I laugh a little to confirm I heard her, and she begins another story. My shoulder burns again as I pour heavy cream into the bubbling honey and it begins to thicken around the spatula.

Adela must notice the pain because she rubs circles on my back like my mother, completely unaware that the Peter Pan collar of my shirt chokes me a little every time she does. It's soothing enough that I don't stop her.

Still, my forearm calls for my teeth, and my jaw clenches in reflex. I'm not alone, though, so I can't do anything about it. I conjure some images to focus on anything else but the pain: my grip on pliers, the pliers on canines, me yanking backwards. A hammer smashes my victim's jawbone. I bite their cheeks because Adela's got thin. My teeth rip the flesh of their soft upper arms in a familiar way, only I tear the chunk fully off, take it home to taste when I'm alone.

I'm not sure what I like and what I don't. I can't do anything until my thoughts become clear, less clouded with excitement.

I take the still bubbling honey butters mixture off the stove and reach for the cookie sheet. Adela rubs her hands together, excited to see it ooze from the saucepan, but she doesn't skip a beat in her current story about a man who kept staring at her from *the stacks*, as she calls the rows of shelves of books. I'll admit it sounds better.

Adela creates a narrative where he's in love with her, but he's shy, so he won't say anything. "It's like that one book that turned into that show," she says. "You know the one."

I do, but I really think it was just a guy checking her out because she's Adela.

9

rat.

Hours of throwback songs and duets and raps we couldn't keep up with have made my throat raw. It's good I have another jar of honey.

Adela pauses her song mid-chorus to tell me she's still hungry.

"Uh-oh," I say. "I can make more honey butters?" I would love to give her some of what's left, but I need a lot for my new students, and I need to refill my purse stash.

"Don't be silly! I'll just order a pizza." She sits up and reaches for her phone. "Supreme okay?"

"No olives."

Adela scoffs. "Of course not. I'm not a monster."

"Of course."

"Two larges?" she asks.

"Better add some sort of cheese sticks or cinnamon things," I say.

We aren't high. Getting crappy delivery pizza means Adela

will want to change that. I know she has something with her; she always does.

"I think I'm still going to make more candy," I say. "I've got more honey. Then we should get a little high." I haven't gotten high in months, and I was alone the last time I did. Normally, I just take a small hit to take the edge off of my pain. Losing my senses isn't good for me.

"Oooh, got any secrets? You know you always share them when you get high." She cackles and brushes the party bit of her hair from her shoulders, frowning. "I really need a haircut."

"You do," I admit. She's right about me spilling my guts when I get inebriated; it's one of the many reasons I've been a relatively sober person most of my life. I've fucked almost as many people as the number of times I've been high or drunk.

I wander back into the kitchen to start another batch of honey butters. It occurs to me that a lot of Elizabeths from the *olden days* used poison to kill husbands or travelers to collect money.

Marney has rat poison. She told me about it, saying she couldn't handle sticky traps. She said that she hoped I wouldn't need it, but if I did, it was under the sink, and I should use a lot of it. *"Those rats really don't like to die, you know? They just push through the poison, wobbling around. Sick stuff."* I'm not sure they wobble so much as die and she imagines their death.

It's boring—poison. Unless you time everything just right, get the doses *just right*, the whole effort could flop. There's something about having a secret way to hurt someone in my purse that thrills me, nonetheless.

The first new batch is normal, fine for Adela-consumption. The next, not so much.

Under the kitchen sink, the small box of rat poison is in front of the cleaning supplies. Marney's right, it is sick stuff. It's good that I'm using some of it, honestly. The rats don't deserve this.

She should just clean up the crumbs in her cupboards—of which there are plenty.

Reading the box, I try to gauge how much to put in without looking it up. I decide to use more than is suggested for rats, but not enough that Marney would be suspicious of its absence. I've also got to keep taste in mind. Poison plus honey still equals poison if I'm not careful, I assume.

With no science behind my choice, I plug my nose so I won't inhale any of the dust that plumes as I dump a glob of powder in.

10

english.

Finally, I get a new ESL cohort today. It's been three months since I've had a class—the longest I've gone. I've missed the money, but I've missed the students more. Preparing the desks before anyone arrives is a ritual to me, like peeling fruit or biting my forearm when I can't focus or the pain gets so bad I contemplate the Emergency Room.

I place welcome packets, three honey butters, and small paper water cups on high school desks. They were donated by Janes High School when they remodeled, so some have obscene words and phrases scribbled on them still visible despite the staff's attempt to scrub them away. Most of them don't wobble anymore either, which is good news. Two cohorts ago, the noise had me constantly grinding my jaw to the point of a distracting level of pain.

Since today is the first day, the students will learn how to introduce themselves in the most basic sense. The packets will help them understand what's next, how the course operates, what they'll learn, and gives them all the contact information they need. Written in ten languages, it's a hefty stack of paper that needed an industrial stapler.

By the time I've written my name on the board, straightened the papers, and put the jugs of water on the edge of my desk, students are arriving.

A small woman with bright white hair barely crosses the threshold before she shouts, "Hi, I Licia! My son say I never good at listening, but he just boring." She nods once, then takes her seat.

Licia is going to be a *hoot.*

I never know what kinds of students I'll end up with, so it's always nice to have a Licia. She makes up for customers at Juniper Foods.

This is a free, just-for-learning course with the goal of transitioning to those college courses or tests easier, should they want to go further in their learning, so I've seen ages range from late teens to seventies. I've not had a student that walked who wasn't already able to speak decent English—grammar and sentence structure are usually the problem areas.

By the time they leave, we are talking about current movies and their children's schooling, the horrifying crimes everyone glorifies, and jobs they can finally apply for. Not one of them has mentioned moving on to college or either of the exams meant to "prove" you can speak English—which, of course, they can.

It's dark outside already, despite it being just shy of 6 p.m. thanks to angry clouds. I flip on both of the large overhead lights and sit quietly, wait for the rest of the students. As they arrive, I flash a smile at them. I used to picture each one of them dying while they put their purses down or opened a notebook, then I got to know them. On a whole, they don't suck. The adults who seek this out want to better themselves, often for their families. Occasionally, I've still used them as imaginary trials for what I want to do—what I *will* do, now—but it's never personal like it is with most people that end up on the other end of my imagination.

At exactly 6 p.m., the last student—the youngest in the class—rushes in like this is a course with mandatory attendance.

"Good afternoon." I glance around the room at expectant faces with new teeth and personalities, the adult learners who believe I can teach them something worthy of their time. Only now do I realize that my cane is hanging on the desk. I've been a little unsteady now and again, so I brought it with me. That doesn't mean I want it to be front and center. "I'm Elizabeth, your instructor."

Smiles, waves, a few *hellos*. Someone has an intense perfume that I can only hope is for first impressions and will not be a staple of the class.

"Let me start by saying everything I say to you may help your fellow classmates. The same goes for them. More than anything, I want to teach you how to be comfortable speaking in social settings—at parties or parent-teacher conferences—and when to add words that are foreign to you so that people around you are put at ease. I don't think any of you are wrong for the way you speak. I'm just here to make your lives a little easier because some people in America are honestly just the worst," I say. It's my standard spiel, the one I give to show the students that, though I'll never understand their plight, I want to make their situation better. It tends to put them in a calmer frame of mind, a *trusting* state of mind.

"Today, I'd like to get to know you a bit better. So I'm hoping we can go around the room and introduce ourselves." I add that I'll correct them along the way, but they shouldn't feel embarrassed in any way when I do that. "It's all part of the process and all in the name of learning. Feel free to ask any questions you have about my corrections as I make them. Not everything in English makes sense, but I'll give you the explanation my English teachers have given me."

That gets a good deal of laughter, and a few quieter comments that all essentially agree.

The youngest voice stands out above the rest—a European accent. She simply says, "Yes, English sucks."

The class laughs again.

"It does, doesn't it?" I joke back.

Now that the ice has been broken, the rustle of opening candy fills the room. It's hard not to tell them all to leave the wrappers on the table so I can compost them. It's why I buy cellophane, so I can watch the pink crinkly plastic slowly rot away with clementine peels and banana strings.

During the moment of distraction, I allow myself to get excited about my mall trip. It's my first *proper* step towards my second kill.

Watching my students enjoy the honey butters, it occurs to me that this would be a great way to test the candy's potencies, to practice a passive way to kill. Tonight will lead to a very active way.

I think about a room of people grasping at their throats, pantomiming choking, while I just count seconds to scan to see who goes first, watch the clock tick down, prepare to snuff out whoever lived. I'd have to find a class to teach filled with bad people. How hard would it be to teach at a prison? I won't mind going to jail for trying to kill a bunch of people just like me en masse. I would definitely live up to my namesake then.

I don't know where these urges come from or why they come on so quickly, but I keep what Adela's therapist told her about grief in mind when they do: don't judge your thoughts or feelings, acknowledge them, accept them as they are, but don't call them *good* or *bad*. No values, they just *are*.

The students eating the candy all thank me repeatedly.

"You're welcome. I enjoy making them. How about we start on the left side of the room?" I suggest, noticing that Licia is in front and not having a candy. "Just tell us your name and a little bit about yourself."

It takes three days on average before their names stick, and I expect nothing different from this group. This is Stage 1 of my memorization technique. I am writing their names down with two pieces of information about them as they speak.

Licia reintroduces herself, remarking that she's Italian. Her teeth look soft, as if they are made of modeling clay or play dough. She says she blames Americans for making her so white that ignorant people think she's Russian—to which she spits and crosses herself. "It's cold. I stay inside. My bones so cold." She speaks as loudly as she had when she walked in.

I assumed Licia is hard of hearing, so I raise my voice as I add her missing word for her. She tells me not to shout, that I'm rude, and maybe I won't be a good teacher. She will be one of my favorites.

There are snickers around the room, but they are good adults and try to keep it to themselves.

The man behind Licia glances around the room to confirm he's supposed to go next. Chike's English isn't terrible, as most of my students aren't. Still, I have to correct a bit of what he says as he tells us about his life in West Africa, his three children and seven grandchildren. He stutters once or twice, but nods and takes what I suggest in stride. At the end of class, he even thanks me. When he smiles, I get to see his straight, if not a little large teeth. There is something almost unnatural about them. I will enjoy watching Chike speak.

The next four people are ethnically ambiguous and don't really tell us about themselves in any honest way. It doesn't matter. Why would I care? They'll all be learning the same words, the same way, at the same time. For ESL purposes, their native tongue and origin country doesn't matter. They all just talked about their reasons for being in the class—a common choice of topic in the introduction.

The next woman is weathered, with soft curves and creases everywhere I can see. I want to run my tongue across her teeth. They take up the prime real estate of her dimples and soft lips when she shows them fully—like she's doing now. They are Baby Bear teeth. Her eyes twinkle, and it's as if she knows my secret, knows how much I want her mouth. She's talked about herself while I was staring at her, but all I catch is the word *Philippines* and *childhood*. Suddenly, we're on to the next person.

The woman's name is lost to me. And I'm truly unbothered.

A slight man with crooked teeth shocks me so much that I almost ask him if he knows he's in an ESL class. "Hi, I'm Wendell. I look forward to this class. I enjoy stories and food. Don't let me ramble. My wife says, 'Wendell, you talk too much.' You can bring me food. Thank you." He jokes that he's a walking stereotype, having once been a taxi driver in India. The moment he could, though, he moved to America for better *everythings,* as he put it. His name is not Wendell, but his real name is a secret, he says—something to do with seeing something he shouldn't. I can't tell if he's joking or if he just really likes the American name he chose for himself.

The youngest woman with snark wants to be an actress but can't always enunciate, so she's hoping I can point out when she mumbles the most. Her name is Anita, and she says she's been studying English since she was a child, but she can't get it all right even still. *Thus the English sucks comment.* I've got less to offer her than the other students. She needs a voice coach, not me. But voice coaches aren't free. She's biting her nails to the quick. Even from the front of the room, I can see the angry skin. Her chin is an orange rind, slightly pitted with divots that are only noticeable at certain angles and probably by touch. I'd like to punch through her thick peel, hear the slight *pop* as the juice releases. Saliva fills my mouth.

I slurp, and the next student speaks. Mel has a thick accent that sounds like an amalgamation of accents from across the globe. They tell us they came here because this course is supposedly very accepting, and they need that while they're *polishing their English*. They have a gap between their front teeth. A vision of their teeth in a jar almost overwhelms my ability to offer them guidance on their introduction. I would not kill the disabled. So Mel will always be safe.

The rest of the class goes well, and everyone seems to be receptive to comments. My students are all interesting and have great reasons for being in the class. Everyone got the time and attention they deserved, and I told them all about the future of the course.

After I wish them a good night, I expect them to rush off to their lives just as I want to do. Instead, three of them hang back to chat with each other. I'm disappointed that it's not the unnamed woman. She disappeared into the small throng of students.

Licia announces loudly that she'd love to stay, but her son is picking her up for dinner. Maybe next time, she says. She and Anita leave side-by-side talking about car sickness.

Between me thanking everyone for a great first class and most of the students leaving, someone mentioned a love for crime and using crime podcasts to better their English. I love hearing all the ways people utilize the entertainment industry to better themselves.

Mentioning love has turned into a full-blown conversation. Through missing words and misused phrases, they share in their love of discussing and listening to the horrific murders of women. They all have theories, and I want to consume them all. I can't lurk in their conversation, though. This isn't the internet, where I can be invisible while being *present*.

But when I hear Wendell admit to having a podcast himself, I allow myself to listen a little more actively. The mall *will* be there in a few minutes.

"It's not so big now, but people will listen," Wendell says.

Mel and Chike now seem so swept up in Wendell I fear I'll have to usher them out of the room so I can go to the mall before it closes.

I hear Mel suggest almost at the same time as Wendell that they should do a case together. Wendell just wrapped up his last and found a new one that's gone unnoticed—his favorite ones to do.

"Okay!" Chike says, raising his hand for a high five. He has to drop his hand a little to accommodate Mel's wheelchair height but does so quickly. They are already getting on like gangbusters.

I'm pleased. This will mean I can listen in on some darkness, get some ideas.

"I like local," Wendell says.

My hand stills on the stack of papers I was putting away. There is so much crime here, *what are the chances?*

"Her name was Crystal Keaton."

I black out. Well, if there was a god, I would have blacked out.

I hear excited agreements and plans to meet at a coffee shop tomorrow at noon. I miss which coffee shop or I might have shown up and pretended to want to join them. I could still ask to be a part of their group next week.

Wendell summarizes Crystal's murder and why he's chosen her. His primary reason: the news should have been reporting about a brutal crime like this. People should be locking their doors and keeping an eye out for a man with an anger issue.

"But they put the story in a closet. Like her." Wendell is clearly practicing for the cold opening of the podcast.

His gaze flickers my way, I think. Is this paranoia again? How many women have been murdered lately? That's what he's interested in talking about, so Crystal makes sense...

Wendell couldn't possibly suspect me. Or *holy fuck.* Is that why he's taking this course?

11

hosiery.

Driving is suffering—partly from the throbbing in my hip, partly because it's going to get worse as I navigate the garbage that is the mall.

Parking is almost as horrible as driving. Every spot I see, some asshole cuts in front of me. I crash into them and leave mangled bodies in my wake—or so I wish. It's hard to find a spot. When I finally do, it's practically a city block away. Getting a handicapped placard is something I should look into. It's a hard pill to swallow—the *idea* that I can't walk from the back of the parking garage.

Three sets of double doors slide open in intervals. They close quickly like snapping monster jaws. The offensive odor of clothing stores that spray their mannequins with cologne hourly and forced cool air ooze from the speedy automatic doors. I'm already suffocating, and I haven't even stepped inside.

I have to bring my cane. The drive over was extremely painful, so I have little choice. I don't want to add attention to myself, and I know anyone under sixty with a cane garners looks. I'm probably being paranoid, but Wendell and his friends are added to the list of people investigating Crystal's murder and there won't be another shooting at an elementary school to bury the lead of Cora's murder. Walking past an ad for jewelry that's set against a fake sunset backdrop, it occurs to me that on the off chance someone connects me to any of my murders, I should have a passport. I'm landlocked at the moment.

My first order of business is to use the mall map to find Katy's. Since there was no parking in front, I've lost track of which direction it's in. Four teens and an elderly couple are standing beside the glowing electronic diagram. As if by a magnet, three of the six people point to the YOU ARE HERE star. *Yes, yes, we are.*

The moment I move and my cane hits the floor, I'm a traffic accident. People can't seem to help themselves. It's different when you aren't being appraised for beauty or sex appeal but as an object of disability. Children look confused, maybe interested; they tug on their parents' arms and ask questions. By late twenties, judgment, eye-rolling, or disgust fills their eyes, unable to imagine themselves needing something like that, so they project. Middle-aged people look away a lot. They think of their children needing a cane and themselves being on the way, and they can't handle it. The elderly are the worst, *tsk*ing and glaring. Often, they'll call their significant others over to point and whisper because if they don't need a mobility aid yet, no young person should.

Both kinds of appraisal are objectifying. I'm used to the former. I loathe the moment when people see my cane and have feelings about its existence. It's my daily frustration, not theirs. I hope one day I can beat one of them with the pink poppy-patterned metal so severely I can toss the cane beside them and say, *"You'll need this more than me now."*

As I head towards the big white words bookmarking the left

side of the mall, I shift my thoughts from the gawkers. I'm reminded of shopping trips for school when I was younger. We didn't go every year, as my parents deemed that unnecessary. The years when I had outgrown clothes like a seed growing into a plump fruit, we shopped in one department store—Katy's—for almost everything. The only exception came with my mother's belief that every person deserved to have *one* special item of clothing that fit them perfectly and made them feel like a rockstar or a supermodel or an intellectual—whatever. Often, mine has been a skirt in the same pink and cream color palette I've been wearing since high school.

Now, I have a small section of my wardrobe that fits that description. But I haven't changed sizes in six years, so I've had time to collect pieces from thrift stores or malls or boutique shops. A few came from Michael telling me to get myself an anniversary or birthday or Christmas present. A lot of women would hate that. Those women have not received a gift from Michael.

Tonight, I just need pantyhose. I worry it will look odd, maybe suspicious. What thirty-something woman wears pantyhose anymore? This isn't the Deep South. If I had swollen eyes and a red, splotchy face, things may be different. A woman in grief wears pantyhose. So says television.

I'm only grieving about not already having the hose at home. When I saw a hand-painted mask online that distorts someone's facial features but also allows them to see, I wanted to try it right then. I've had to wait.

Roaming towards the hosiery section slowly, I flip through out-of-season jackets and not-yet-in-season bathing suits. I rub fabrics between my fingers and peek at price tags—normal shopping behavior.

The shoe section is beside the pantyhose. Nestled under the perfume that blankets Katy's is the scent of faux leather with a hint of dirty socks. It's overwhelming and why I rarely shop at department stores, why I wander into detached local stores when I shop.

I see boots that go halfway up the calf with shiny buckles that remind me of my mother's old riding boots. I always thought the heels didn't look like they could support five pounds, let alone a hundred and fifty. She feared horses—my mother—but she loved the getups.

The first time I saw a horse, I wanted to feel what they felt. The bits in their mouths looked painful, but I was told it wasn't. I wanted it between my teeth to find out for sure. What would it be like to have the pressure of someone on the small of my back demanding me to move, pivot, and jump on their command?

I loosen up as I walk into the sock section. No one cares about me. I'm a woman lost in her own thoughts, *clicking* along with her cane, buying pantyhose two shades darker than herself. It could be for a costume, it could be for a friend, it could be for storing onions.

Breathing much easier now, I consider the small section. There are two brands. Both have many types. Control top has an extra thick band at the top that would hurt my head immensely. Toeless defeats the purpose. Opaque tights would be impossible for me to see through. I stop on sheer and study the many color options.

"Elizabeth?"

Something about my name, as of late, seems to make me freeze. I spin without speaking. I don't recognize the voice.

"Oh, it's you! Hi! How are you doing?"

A face like a peach stares at me with delight.

I struggle to place her. She's—she's—she's "Shia! I almost didn't recognize you. Chalk it up to bad lighting."

"Right?" She brushes her dark hair from her eyebrows and pretends to cover her eyes as she looks into the fluorescent strips above us. "You'd think they'd try a little harder to make us look nice. We're trying to spend money here, you know?"

"Exactly."

"So, how have you been?" *Have her teeth gotten longer? Her breath worse?* It's hard to tell, but I feel gaggy. At Juniper Foods, I only ever felt a little queasy. Even then, it could be attributed to her face and its slippery skin with plump, jiggly fat forehead underneath.

"Good. The same." I struggle to maintain eye contact, to respond. I'm not prepared for this.

Where was the documentary called *What To Do When You're Caught Shopping For Your Next Crime*?

I think she's waiting for me to ask the same, but as I don't care, I don't ask.

"Getting some pantyhose, huh?" Her expression verges on sad.

My hands creep to her slim neck, and I dig into her soft olive flesh.

I blink, and my hands are fists by my side.

I knew, just *knew*, I should have gone to the further away mall. It's weird to be buying pantyhose. They don't necessarily scream murder, but they don't scream normal behavior either.

"These are more your color," she says, reaching across me and grabbing "Beachy Light Beige".

"Oh, thanks so much." Now I know I need to get "Summer Suntan" to obscure my face enough that I won't be me, but not so much that I look like I'm trying to pin my crimes on someone of a different race.

Shia stares at me for another minute or so. Katy's ambient noises fill my ears, sounding similar to Juniper Foods with fewer beeps.

Meanwhile, I'm pretending to read the pantyhose box.

"Well, it was nice seeing you. Sorry for your loss," she says.

Grief means pantyhose.

"Thanks." Better to allow Shia to create her own narrative than try to craft my own.

The one downside of this is it takes one quick search to realize the few people I care about have either been dead a very long time or are still around loving and irritating me.

When she's out of eyesight, and her oppressive pity is gone, I grab two boxes of "Summer Suntan" in a size 3X and head to the checkout. I'm ready to make my mask, to visit Cora, to see if my encore performance is any better than the first.

12

muffled.

If I were a dog, my head would be out the window. Pink tongue wagging in the wind, I'd salivate, knowing I was near something excitable.

I rolled the window down all the same, the wind whipping at my face, fluffing three-day-old curls. Tongue in, I'm still salivating because I'm blocks away from my destination.

I've got a prepared kit resembling a rock climber's: workout clothes, knee and elbow pads, gloves, rope, carabiners, a pocket knife, a harness, baby wipes, a box of bandaids, and a water bottle are all stuffed in a navy blue duffle. I'm ready to try out something new. If I get pulled over, the only oddities I have are decorated pantyhose tucked under my floorboards in a plastic bag and the small wire cutters beside them. Unless they tear the car apart, they will never know about those.

Today, I look soft. Now poofy curls fall around my face in loose, frizzy clusters. I'm wearing no makeup aside from chapstick; I can't have makeup flaking off on Cora's floor and leading back to me. My shirt is a simple white cotton t-shirt and my linen skirt is lemon yellow. If I got pulled over, it's unlikely they would question me about much of anything. It's one of the few positives left about still being considered the weaker sex. Well, that, and free drinks.

After a long, uneventful drive, I pull over just past a dying shopping center. I park in front of a house that's under construction, my license plate just out of the street lamp's amber light. Only two blocks from Cora's house, I'll be walking the rest of the way.

Cora's modest home is her grandmother's and sits at the edge of a retirement community. Most people wouldn't have bothered with a house sitter. Cora believed her grandmother needed company—well, the ghost of her grandmother. Initially, I thought it was a joke. A woman has to eat, though. I should have never taken the job, but my hours at Juniper Foods had been cut. Bills don't go on pause because a womanizing boss fancies the new girl's ass. Luckily, Jamie became the manager after a few complaints, and I got my hours back. It was too late by then. I'd already accepted the job listing.

The walk is a long two blocks. A new muscle burns with each step, serving as a reminder that every kill may be the last. My body could give out at any moment, and that would be the end.

Once I'm at Cora's back door, I take my pantyhose mask out of the sandwich bag, stuff the bag into the duffle, put the wire cutters in back left my pocket, and grab the key from my right.

Copies of keys from every house I've ever stayed at are marked and tucked under one of my photograph boxes. At first, I made copies in case I got locked out. Eventually, I would leave them under the mat, in a potted plant, or on the kitchen counter for Michael or Adela. Sometimes I've even handed the keys directly to them. And now, well, now I just need them.

Pressing the door with my palm, I slide the warm key into the lock. I turn it slowly and feel the click and release as it unlocks. Turning the knob is loud. At 4 a.m., everything is. I have little time to waste since breakfast service begins at the community center in two hours.

I push the door in and hear a muffled TV.

This is it. This is it. This is it.

When I take a step in, the floor creaks. Stilling, I wait for Cora to call out, scream, turn on the lights. It hadn't creaked there before. I would remember something like that.

I quickly tug on the pantyhose mask and feel it rip by my ear. *Damnit.* It already has eye holes, so I'm not squinting through smushed, flattened eyelashes. It's as if I'm determined for her to know it's me, for this mask to be nothing but a creepy Halloween costume.

I stand a little taller and go further into the house. The trash can she keeps by the back door is overflowing, and rotting food permeates smoky air. My gag reflex kicks in, and I swallow hard. She wasn't a smoker when I house sat, but everything else is the same. She hadn't taken the garbage out when I came over, either. That is unusual, but not unheard of. Some people assume they can leave chores for *me* to do. I've never understood people who wait until the trash spills onto the floor to take it out.

I don't bother looking around much as I move towards her small bedroom.

Even in the dark, the shapes of her hand-me-down living room appear the same as before. I assume there are a few new stains on the stubby wooden table that every home in America has had at one point. Countless houses I've been in with that table, countless stains and burns and chips. Each has seen at least one story similar to the one in a friend's basement when I was fifteen or sixteen. The burns on the table are nothing compared to the burns on me and a neighbor girl. I have a Polaroid of them —the table's burn marks and ours.

The open floor plan leaves her messy kitchen open to constant scrutiny, but I have a feeling no one comes to visit.

Cora's bedroom door is ajar, and her sleeping form is alight with infomercials. Her ghostly skin flashes with the array of colors. I realize the volume is much louder than I first thought. For a retirement community house, the walls are extremely thick.

I step into her room. She rearranged it.

Her double bed, box TV, and single child's sized side table give off a rent-a-hotel room vibe that saddens me. Though the accordion closet doors are closed now, I remember the closet is large enough for my wingspan's worth of clothes at most and doesn't have a shelf above the low-hanging rack. When I stayed here, half of the closet was empty, the other half of her clothes had tags on them. An overexposed photo of those tags lives in my Polaroid box at home. I wondered if she was one of those people that wears clothes once, then returns them before they get gross. She seemed the type.

She's bought a new lamp, I notice. It's nearly identical to the other—white with blue flowers on it, a thin drum shade. The cord is absurdly long. Most people would have wrapped it up, tied it with something to hide behind a couch or table. Cora's dangles unplugged. A yellow tag hangs off of it: $12.99.

In my mind, the next hour goes smoothly. I would snip the lamp cord and make a noose from it. I'd tie it to the fan in her room without her waking up. Quickly, while she was still asleep somehow, I'd hoist her with powerful arms and core strength to the noose and let her drop. The bed, of course, would be else-where, so she couldn't touch it with her feet. Her neck would snap, the fan would definitely not break, then I'd leave.

Wouldn't that be the dream?

13

cora.

Cora's chest rises and falls, slow and even. Every fourth breath, she snorts air in through her long nose. I count. *One, two, three, snort.*

One, two, three, step. One, two, three, step. One, two, three, step. I breathe in time with her, letting out shallow breaths with her small snores. It's familiar, and I relax a little. I've done this before—even if it was only once. I've already learned so much, so I'm bound to be better at it now.

One, two, three, step. I'm at the lamp beside her. *One, two, three, move.* I grab the lamp from her side table. *One, two, three, pull.* I try to unplug the cord from the wall. It sticks. *One, two, three, pull.* It loosens and slides from the wall.

A laugh track blares. Cora kicks at the covers and whimpers. I can no longer match her rhythm. My heart thuds.

I pull my shirt sleeve up a bit and sink my teeth into my fore-arm. A calm washes over me. The pain is refocusing. To keep spittle from dripping, I lick the mark and slide the fabric down to cover the saliva.

My confidence grows again.

Though I would love to hang someone and see if my dad's spasmodic recounting of this type of murder was correct, I never truly intended on lifting Cora anywhere. It was always going to be me dragging her from the bed by her neck with a lamp cord. Whether I'd wander around the house or just tug and tug, I wanted to leave it up to the vibe.

I wait until I can match her breathing again. It feels like it takes a lifetime.

One, two, three, snort. I back out of the room. Cora still hasn't stirred.

Clear of her door, I pull the wire cutters from my back pocket and snip the cord from the lamp. I place it beside the TV, shove the cutters back in my pocket, and test the cord. Its cheap coating doesn't bend as smoothly as expected, but I can still wind it around my palms enough. After two wraps, I worry it will leave marks through the rubber gloves. I'll never be able to hold on long enough. The cord will hurt my hands. I need my leather gloves, or this could get ugly quickly.

To get to my bag, I creep through the living room to avoid the squeaky spot on the floor. I thought I'd become accustomed to the taste of garbage that permeates her house, but her room blocks it more than I realized.

Avoiding the corner of the living room table, I trip over something and fall to the floor. Palms and knees keep me from face planting.

I hear Cora's voice. "Hello?"

Fear hits me hard, and the smell of it suffocates the room's stench. As quickly as possible, I stuff the... unsettling old porn magazine collection back in its box and tilt it upright again.

There's a small shift from her end of the house. I have to do something. Time could run out before she gets back to sleep. I still need time to clean up and leave before 6 a.m., when some early risers get ready for breakfast and socializing.

I'm not strong enough to rush her, not fast enough either. My knee is throbbing, and my palms already feel bruised.

Quickly, I crouch-walk into the kitchen and slink behind the island. *Pop.* Something in my right knee snaps like a rubber band. The pain catches my breath, and I clench tense hands into fists. *I will keep quiet.*

The house rattles with her aggressive stomping. I rotate to the living room side as she checks the kitchen. Without thinking, I wrap the cord around my hands again. Pushing the pain aside is easier now; the consequences of getting caught are huge.

Cora's bare feet make a *splootch* sound on the linoleum. The sound stops, and the kitchen light flicks on. I hear the suction of the refrigerator. Apparently, she's given up the idea of someone being in her house.

This is it.

This is my shot.

I take it.

Ignoring the pain in my knee and hands, I jump from behind the island and whip the garrotte around her neck. My knee pops again with the motion, but this time, it's less painful. Cora's so surprised she tries to look at me.

Stepping to the left and taking her neck with me, she loses her balance. Cora tries to grab the corner of the cabinet, but her fingers can't gain purchase. Together, we fall to the ground with a thud. Angry fireworks fill my vision, but I laser in on the top of Cora's head to keep myself grounded, focused.

She's scrambling, panicked, trying to scream despite the cord pinching into her neck.

Her voice grows thinner as I wrap the cord around her throat again and again. Then, I put my right foot on her shoulder and pull the lamp cord tight. The hard plastic bites into my palm.

More pain blossoms, and I wince through the whirl of nausea that brings with it.

Tossing her head back, Cora seems desperate to look at me. Her eyes are mostly white now. If I'm anything but a blur, she sees a disjointed face painted over a real one on tan pantyhose. Thick sharpied eyebrows obscure my light ones and exaggerated eye makeup creates a new eye shape. An odd and crooked line, large, smeared lips, and drawn cheekbones further obscure my identity. I'm not myself, and yet, I'm more myself than I have been in years.

As she struggles, I *burn*.

Unpacking doll noises echo in the trashy, stale air. Plastic containers pop, styrofoam squeaks, cardboard tears, and a mean kid crushes a toy. The noises are my angry body giving way, loosening, stretching, subluxing.

Cora's arms wobble, her right fist swinging just above the ground uselessly.

My grip relaxes—no choice of my own—and my legs weaken a little. I'm not strong enough to make this my M.O. I try not to let my thoughts wander down the rabbit trail of not being strong enough to kill at all.

She uses her opportunity wisely and scrambles back. Cora flails her elbow backward. Bone connects bone, and my already sore knee jerks back from the impact. I roll to the left to get away from her weak assault. Everything can damage me right now.

The small moment gives her enough time to keep pushing herself back. This time, her elbow hits my eye. I don't know how this got so messy so quickly, how I let her get this close to me, or why fear gives strength. It doesn't matter.

I rally, because it's me or her, and there's no way in hell I'm going to let it be her.

I scramble further away from her so I can use my feet on her shoulders as leverage again. She hasn't gotten the cord from her neck yet, so I hold tight and straighten my legs. Everything in me screams. I'm shredding myself like cheese.

Cora's body spasms. She tries to scream and reaches for her neck, but I don't relent.

I stay that way, shaking with exhaustion, pain, and frustration for a long time. It seems to take hours for her body to slacken. Even then, I remain clutching the cord and pulling tight.

Without a doubt, I will not have the strength to take her teeth. I try not to let the disappointment overshadow what I'm doing.

As another commercial break comes back on, I release her. I crawl to her side to see what I've done. The cord has cut into Cora's throat some, and a thin line of blood threatens to drip onto the floor. I wrap the cord around her neck and try to sit her up.

On my first attempt, I get her halfway up, then she falls back to the kitchen floor. I wince for her, as if she's alive. Arms like jello are having the hardest time with her torso. Two attempts later, and Cora is upright and propped against the faux wooden cabinet.

I grab a kitchen towel and wrap it around the cord necklace. When I try to pick Cora up, I can't. She's too heavy. It takes five tries, self-talk about women and cars and mothers and children, and a mental reminder that I don't want to go to prison to lift her torso up a few inches from the ground.

I drop her right back down when I try to drag her. I stand and stretch. An achy back offers a chorus of cracks and pops.

Is this worth it?

I go into her bedroom. I don't want to put her in the closet. It may look like an M.O. Stepping over a pile of clothes, dirty dishes, and two unopened packages of spicy nuts, I kneel to look under her bed. It's too messy, with no room for Cora.

At first, I plan to pull everything out from under the bed to make room, then kick her all the way across the house. I glance at the clock. I haven't begun erasing myself from her house yet, and who knows how long that will take. Leaving her in the kitchen is the best option, despite it taking only half a second to find her corpse. The smell will take a while to be noticeable, at least.

I close her refrigerator, turn off her TV, and glance around for anything odd. I'm wearing gloves, my hair is under a mask, I put the box back where it belongs, and the murder weapon is hers.

This feels good.

Now I have two blocks to walk back to my car. Sure, it's on a flat sidewalk, but my hips are subluxed, my knee is swelling, and my swinging arms are dislocated. There is nothing easy about the walk.

My vision is blurry, spotted, and streaked with dots and lines. I'm trying to ignore the pain, push forward because I don't want to go to prison.

With each step towards the car, I grow closer to crying from the pain. My heart has shifted two of my ribs with its intense pounding, and the pops coming from me are inhuman.

Crystal's murder was messy and painful.

Cora's? The pain is undeniably worse, but it went *much* better this time. She didn't see me, nor did she scream. *Little victories.*

14

mugging.

Any woman with a bruised eye automatically looks like she's in an abusive relationship in the eyes of the public, and I can't seem to cover Cora's handiwork. Everything I've tried made it worse and scream that *Michael is hitting me, but I won't tell.* Years ago, I worked at a women's shelter in the shop that sold clothes to the battered women and children trying to put the pieces of their lives back together. I heard the lengths some go to escape fear, and I don't want anyone to assume that's my situation. Life would become a shitshow of pity, scrutiny, and Michael's pain. And I don't want the scrutiny.

Given that it's hiding or not, I let the shiner shine.

I've cooked up a decent cover story. Admittedly, it's not the *best*. Michael loves me, so he won't want to let it go, but nothing else seems realistic. If only I could stay away from everyone for a few weeks. I can barely feel the echo of Cora's elbow anymore.

The rest of my body has been drawn and quartered from holding her spasming body, while resistance training on the floor with a lamp cord and Cora's neck overshadows everything. Michael can't know that part; he'll have to think I'm hurting from the attack I've concocted.

I have a little time before I have to face the world. For a little while longer, I can have a bruised eye in peace, relive Cora's death in peace. Despite the pain I'm in, I would love to sit with it, enjoy the fact that I probably did it right this time. Go over every detail one more time.

I'm in the perfect position to do it. I'm house sitting for a man named John whose Kentucky accent is thicker than Cora's tongue is right now. He said he needed someone to take care of his senile dog, who doesn't bark. He didn't mention his abnormal house, which would probably need watching without the dog.

His home is a pale green that goes well with the rest of the carton of Easter egg houses, all pastel and shaped exactly the same as the one beside them. The inside has a Kermit meets rummage sale energy. With its overwhelming and complicated design, it's as if he's angling to be featured on an unusual homes show.

I wonder if this is a neighborhood theme. The pale pink house is silky, uncooked meat. The blue is filled with translucent spilled sports drink. The yellow is all linen and 1950s lemon motifs. And the purple house is fluffy and psychedelic.

Polaroid time. It's going to be a tough call to take only four. There is a lot of sameness with the distinct feeling that each tchotchke and piece of furniture has an attached long-winded story about its meaning.

I choose an emerald green couch first. Its fabric looks hellish to sit on, yet it's the focal point in the living room. The photo might not turn out with the floor and wall so similar, but it's for my eyes only.

Roaming through the house, I cannot take it all in. My fingers brush a face mug with cigars, and I enjoy the cool, smooth porcelain. John has so many trinkets, decorations, and general junk, but none of it speaks to me.

As I notice a bubble in the striped green wallpaper, the doorbell *jingles*. The sound is straight out of a children's animated series about fairies, love, and acceptance.

The main reason I'm here—Sir Pugsly—doesn't make an appearance. I quickly peek in on him and see that he's still curled up in his floof of a bed by a mostly empty food bowl. His chubby chest rises and falls, and slobber drips onto a permanently dark, crusty spot.

My socks sink into the plush forest beneath me with every step I take towards the front door. Not my house, so I don't ask who it is.

I look through the fisheye peephole. *What is Michael doing here?* Can I never have a moment alone? Cora's murder deserves some reflection.

Before I unlock the deadbolt, I put my camera on the multigreen table entryway table.

"What the hell was that doorbell sound? Like a pixie peeing or something," Michael says as I open the door.

"Right?" I try to relax. He's brought the big tub covered with cartoon popcorn. Without looking, I know it contains two microwave popcorn bags, three bags of M&Ms, and two cloth napkins.

"Surprise movie n—What the fuck happened to your eye?"

I flinch. He doesn't curse often, and it's even rarer to be in my direction. I'll have to curb his aggression or he may press more than I want.

He leans and goes to touch it, pulling back quickly, as if my skin will burn him. "Does it hurt? Of course it hurts. Are you okay? Of course you aren't. Tell me everything."

Taking a practiced shaky breath, I begin. "It was… It's nothing." I pause for effect as his eyebrow arches. His mouth makes an *oh* shape, and I hold my hand up. "No, you're right. You deserve the truth." Fear and sadness lace my voice. My 7th grade drama teacher would be so proud. "Someone... He... No, it could have been a..."

Michael puts his hand on mine.

I pull him into the house and close my eyes. My goal is to spin my lie all in one jagged sentence, spew it out and take only measured half-breaths.

"I was jumped. It was a man—I'm almost sure. He came from around the corner as I was taking a walk after I picked up dinner yesterday. He had a knife and told me to give him my purse. I didn't hesitate. Michael, I didn't. I just handed him what I had. But he got mad when he saw that I just had a bag from Juniper... Said he didn't want my groceries. I guess he—" I break off and tilt my head down.

It's a monologue out of any Law and Order episode, just your generic mugging and woman having a mildly hard time telling someone about it. Should this have actually happened to me, I would be mad, not sad. In fact, it may be the first man I'd try to kill.

"Take your time," Michael says, squeezing the hand he hasn't let go of softly. He's such a good man.

We really won't work out in the end.

I crack my neck to relieve building pressure and lead him further into John's green nightmare. When we get to the living room, I don't sit on the itchy furniture. I continue my speech. "He never looked inside the bag. He cursed, then punched me in the face. I dropped like he hit me harder than he thought. At first, I thought it was going to get worse, but there was a sound nearby, and he took off back down the alley he must have been hiding in," I say. "He even tossed my bag back at me. He was kind of small... Maybe he was just a kid."

I think back to the decades' worth of Law and Order I've watched—from Original Recipe to Criminal Intent. It's possible I recycled one of their stories. My mother had them on in the background as she ironed and putzed around the house. She would occasionally tell me the reasons the criminals were caught, and how if they'd only done x better, they wouldn't have been.

"You didn't—" He pauses. He can't blame the victim, can't blame the woman he loves. "Did you call the police? Do you want me to help you through the process?"

I shake my head, the bloodied notch on Cora's neck coming to mind. "No. I looked around. There were no cameras, plus he had a mask. I mean, if it was a he. It could have been a she with a deep voice, I guess. He didn't take anything, and I just want to put it all behind me. Besides, what if he was just a kid?"

"Someone tried to mug you! You can't just—"

A scenario: Michael gets outraged, stands to pace, eyes growing hard and resolute in making a choice for me. My mind comes up with two responses.

The first is calming him and reminding him I'm an adult. I said I was fine. The second involves me going into the kitchen, grabbing a knife, and stabbing Michael in the neck. Though I would enjoy seeing the many shades of green turn into many shades of brown as arterial blood pumps, I would miss Michael. He really is a good person. I'd miss his love, his teeth, the sex, and the way he takes care of things for me when I don't want to.

Opting not to kill my boyfriend, I touch his shoulder gently. "I can, and I'm going to. I don't want to deal with the police when I have nothing to tell them. I don't even know the color of the person's eyes. Worst yet, I can't remember which block I was on, just that I walked past a clothing store. Not much to go on. Let's just drop it. It doesn't hurt much, and I haven't thought about it much today—until now," I add, with an edge to my voice. "I was going to tell you when I saw you next."

"That wasn't supposed to be until *tomorrow*," Michael whines and pouts. "I'm your *partner*." He always uses that word when he wants me to be more communicative, more open and forthright —just *more*.

"Yes. Yes, you are. And I'm grateful for that. So, are you going to make me any of that?" I point to the bucket clenched in his hand so tightly, I'm surprised it hasn't cracked. "Or are we going to belabor something I've already made my mind up about?" I ask.

He nods curtly, in a way that makes one understand the definition of *curt*. "You'll be eating all the M&Ms tonight," he says, kissing me on the cheek—opposite side of my bruised eye, of course.

"No complaints or arguments here. What are we watching?" I ask.

"The third in that rom-com trilogy came out last night. How's that?" Michael suggests. I may love to watch true crime shows that accidentally tell me what to do if someone hears a scream, but there's something else I love to watch. And Michael knows that part of my soul. He knows a lot of fragments of me. It's all about which ones I allow him to see.

"Perfect. I wonder if Mary will end up with Brian or Sydney." I connect with him in the best way I can. For a moment, I realize that I'd love for him to be by my side during my next murder. He could do the heavy lifting I'm so accustomed to him doing, while I could do the planning and finish the last few moments. *A partner for real.*

Standing, Michael heads towards the kitchen. "Sydney," he says, pulling me out of my murder-couple fantasy. "It's always the hometown best friend."

15

fusses.

I weigh avocados for a crusty, balding man as he gawks at me. His eyes somehow don't water with the lack of blinking. He doesn't turn away as I scan three avocados, a loaf of bread, yogurt, plastic wrap, yellow rubber gloves, and two packages of adult diapers. I input two expired coupons he hands me without a word, and he continues to stare. His purchases tell me he's got someone chained in a basement, and he needs to clean away their presence soon. That, and he wants Avocado Toast for breakfast. His misshapen, dry lips stay in a firm line as he swipes his card. Keeping his gaze laser-focused on me, he accidentally cancels the credit card purchase twice.

I tell him how much money he saved and hand him the receipt. He tries to brush the back of my hand when I do, then winks at me as he grabs his bag. I envision his innards splayed out in a tableau along the conveyer belt. Still attached to him, I turn it on, and viscera gets caught on the sticky surface. The small space where the belt disappears into the counter to rotate underneath tugs, trying to suck his innards down, but they are too thick; they bang uselessly into the ledge. He watches in abject horror and cries, then dies of blood loss as the woman in line behind him tells him he ought to be ashamed of himself, making a mess like that. Doesn't he know he's not at home?

The woman I imagined chastising him is incredibly chatty. She starts with commentary about the man's creep level but hurries on to the changing weather and the latest episode of some show I don't watch *but totally should because there's no way I wouldn't love it.*

Junk food and processed nonsense *packaged* like health food is all Camy—she tells me her name—is buying. She's got three teen boys and a girl toddler who is both a mistake and a miracle. Her teeth resemble bits of cave drippings in shape and staining only by the gums. Camy's stories transition from one topic to the other without prompt or encouragement, while I barely make a dent in her groceries. Devastation isn't a strong enough word to describe how I feel about the size of her basket.

At some point, she moves to local news. Paying attention then, I hope she'll tell me if I'm missing something, if my face is plastered everywhere and I'm watching the wrong news station, reading the wrong articles. She lists off the *most heinous* crimes that have recently happened in Janes, and none of them are my doing.

I scan her frozen dino chicken nuggets.

"Okay, I've tried not to ask…" I see the end of Camy's basket. The final six items are soda, milk, orange juice, bleach, matches, and detergent. "But what happened there?" She points to her own eye.

None of my co-workers have done this, though they all gave some *oof, that looks like it hurts* comment.

"It was a you-had-to-be-there kind of thing," I say.

Given that she's probably only interested for gossip's sake, she drops it.

For the last leg of her grocery basket, I focus on the rhythmic beeping of my cash register. Camy saves $191.12 thanks to some crazed coupon blog, a bunch of glitches I didn't care to argue about, expired coupons I accepted, her membership card, and sales I would swear she hacked our computer to make. I've never seen savings above $60.

I turn my light off, happy to see that Camy scared everyone away.

Jamie sees me step away from the register and calls me over. "Hey there, everything okay?"

"I thought I could sneak to the bathroom," I say, not adding that *standing this long is wearing on my hips.*

She blows a frustrated raspberry. "Just hurry."

Jamie fusses with her blown-out bangs. She does this a lot—fusses with herself. Rarely can she go over fifteen minutes without tugging, pulling, shifting, moving, or checking something on or around her person. Before she's out of eyesight, I see her vigorously brushing some invisible crumbs off her chest. I don't think Jamie has been told how tacky it looks.

In the Employees Only bathroom, I curl up in the fetal position on a closed toilet lid and pull my phone out. Being egg-shaped causes a loud pop as a vertebra shifts into its rightful place. I'm watching a video on how to make faux crystals with blood when I hear Sid's voice. They are mumbling to themselves.

"Should I bother telling anyone? No, we're doing this."

A faint phone trilling fills the space their voice is no longer taking. They are calling someone.

Sid's breathing gets so loud it would fog up a small bathroom mirror as much as a hot shower. They are pumping themselves up; it's me before Crystal or Cora. As I think of their names together, I realize I'm developing a pattern I most definitely have to break. I chose them for different enough reasons, but that might get lost if they all have *C* names.

"I've thought about—No, you don't get to talk. You get to

listen. I've thought about it, and I can't do this. You ch—NO! I SAID SHUT UP! You cheated." Sid's voice is steady. I peek through the sliver in the doorway and see them shaking. "You cheated, and I'm done. I deserve better. You aren't the woman I fell in love with. I'll come get my things in an hour. Don't touch anything. Don't be there. Don't call me again. I'll leave the key when I'm done."

Sid hangs up the phone and turns to my stall. "I'm leaving early so I can change and go to Bertie's house." Their girlfriend has always just been *her*. I'm not sure I recall her having a name before now. It no longer matters, though, so I immediately erase it from my mind—like all of my customers and their names. "Can you set Isaac up on the register?"

Not really my job, I want to say. I flush the unused toilet and step out. I'm a little speechless, which is uncommon for me. "Yeah," I say, for lack of something better.

I don' know Isaac. He's new and works less than I do. Unless his shifts switch to mine, I'll probably not get to know him.

He'll be like Stock Guy—a person I see but don't talk to, a person I know only one thing about. Stock Guy is younger than me. We share occasional grunts or a *how's your day* with the promise of no response.

Isaac is obviously older than me and reminds me of an ill-proportioned, tubby Lurch, which is confounding, but there it is. I feel that's enough information. That, and if Isaac can take Sid's place for the rest of their shift.

16

irritate.

Isaac is the worst, it turns out. I'm sad I have to know his name.

I suppose his lackadaisical work ethic or zombie shuffle that scuffs the floor could have started my dislike of him, but his purposeful "forgetting" of my name was the icing on the cake. Power plays don't sit well with me.

According to him, he's only twenty-nine—though he looks like he's five years older than me—and lives with his mom. He doesn't have a car or a significant other. He's not interested in going to college *or anything like that*, and he doesn't really go anywhere but the mall to test out new lip and nail colors because he won't buy anything sight unseen, and has no intention of changing any of that. *Fine.* I don't care about his life, so he can ramble at me all he wants.

But calling me Ellie, Eliza, Ellen, Lisa, and Beth just because he hopes it will irritate me, *that* I care about. My mother named me Elizabeth for a reason. Only Adela is allowed to shorten my name.

The problem with putting him on my list isn't that we work together or knowing I'd have to circumvent a mother in the middle of the night. I'm not even worried about him overpowering me—a real possibility, in his case.

It's his teeth.

Seeing them in a pile on a plate like juicy pomegranate seeds —half-broken from my feeble attempt to yank them out—might make them better. His having braces would also put him in the running. But his mouth as it is now—beige, crowded with two snaggleteeth that shift his lip when he smiles, a bottom row with teeth at angles I barely remember from high school Geometry— he's the epitome of *not my type*.

Still, I have some testing to do. Maybe I could save my list for when I've figured myself and my methods out. One day, I'll know what I want my murders to look like, how I want them to go. I won't dislocate because I'll have it all figured out. I'll even leave a mark that brings me satisfaction. Until then, it's all experimentation.

One thing I'm doing right is picking people that aren't extremely wealthy with few family members to rally for them—or ones that are only mildly invested. I scanned the news before I left the bathroom. Both of them have been mentioned in an article as part of the crime wave, but not by name or with any details. It's clear they aren't at the top of the priority list.

A white man is killed in the suburbs, and it makes national news. Two women—one white and one biracial—are brutally murdered, and they don't even make page 6. The Janes Chronicle is usually better than that, but I'm glad they aren't able to keep up at the moment. No one seems to care enough to make a splash. Except Wendell.

Isaac says, "Thanks for setting me up, Lizzie."

I grit my teeth.

His register is ready to go. He flips the switch, and the number 6 above his station illuminates. Two shoppers with filled carts rush towards the empty line like starving people would rush a buffet. "How'd you get that shiner, Elsa?"

"It's Elizabeth," I snap, letting Isaac see a glimpse into the side of me that strangled a woman. "Trust me when I say you'd better start remembering that."

Isaac bristles. For a moment, I see his eyes bulging as I tie a plastic bag over his head. He screams and gasps, sucking in the fogging clear plastic instead of air. "Thanks, Elizabeth," he says. "Sorr—"

"Don't." I hold my hand up before Isaac gives me some half-assed perfunctory apology. I know all about those. "You've got customers."

The shoppers nearly crash into each other as they try to earn the number one spot in the queue. A person in a white tee and blue jean overalls with a buzzed head wins by a hair over the woman wearing an emerald green dress with a messy bun on top of her melon-shaped head. I'm impressed.

He opens and closes his mouth like a Hungry Hippo then reaches for a tomato on the conveyor belt. His long fingers wrap around it, and he squeezes too hard. The woman on the phone unloading her basket glares at him but says nothing.

17

brazen.

I'm a shaken soda can. In the past week, Isaac's social skills have declined. And he's lost all ability to do the bare minimum.

At register 3, I go into autopilot. The final hours of my shift are a blur of Isaac's unhappy customers. *Can I see the manager? It's never been that way before. But the sign said... Are you sure about that? You* are *new. This is ludicrous! I'm never shopping here again!*

Just as I turn the register light off, Isaac announces that he's going on break and two new employees join the fray. It's disorganized and unusual, but that seems to be what Isaac brings to the table—frustration and chaos.

Neither of us says *bye*, despite working side-by-side for hours.

I try to put Isaac out of my mind as I collect my duds. I'm ready to shed him like dead skin, so the moment I walk into the sunshine, I can be free to enjoy the day. He's even taking away the buzz of Cora. But I can't seem to shake him. I haven't been so bothered in years.

My body hurts more than ever, which can't help my mood. Even so, he shouldn't be getting to me this much.

I flip through the many ways I pictured killing people and see Isaac shaking violently, his hair standing on end. Electricity pulses around him like he's in a slapstick movie.

As I've stuck a fork in an electrical socket and my hair didn't even get frizzy, I think it would take a mad scientist-level of electricity to make such a spectacle. What happens, I wonder, when an exposed wire lays in a puddle of water and zaps an unsuspecting victim? Isaac may be a good person to experiment on. His mouth, his rudeness, his male power plays, his inability to ask for help, it's all more than I want to deal with on a regular basis.

I work at Juniper Foods three days a week, which is already three days too many. If I don't have a house or pet sitting job, then I sometimes add in a fourth or a double. I've even added a fifth day. Those weeks, I am non-functioning anytime I'm not scanning or speaking to a shopper. Jamie tries to keep me stocking lightweight items like bread and marshmallows or swaps me with someone at self-checkout.

I want to settle into the rhythm of the store—the scanning, the ease of wandering the store when I need to stretch, and the extended breaks when I'm nearly falling apart. Isaac has proved today that his presence complicates my routine.

Being impulsive isn't my favorite thing, but if I want to keep living my life, I feel I have no other choice. My sanity depends on this. *Doesn't it?*

I'm on my way out *and* have a few minutes before I need to be on the road. It's another *now or never* situation. And I will always pick *now*. My only hurdle is making his electrocution look like an accident.

Finding a place to expose a wire and set up a puddle is simple. Getting Isaac to go there will be just as easy. Knowing what I'm doing is anything but. Honestly, it's a crapshoot.

Every Juniper Foods has a mister that sprays the vegetables in the refrigerated case on the hour. The whole unit probably breaks every other month, though there's no real reason for it. Today, it will be because I cut and fray the wire.

Why would a shopper grabbing an eggplant for veggie lasagna or a bag of premade salad to make their in-laws respect them think that an employee was tampering with wiring? I can't think of a reason. I assume they'll think I'm tying my shoes or—if anything—trying to fix the wire if they see what's in my hand.

I grab nail scissors from my bag and the half-empty water bottle from my lunch.

When I get to the refrigerator, I kneel. An ex-girlfriend of mine showed me how to expose wires and twist them together. Why she did that is a reason lost to television show relationship drama and my memorization of the honey butters recipe.

The process is quick and easy, unlike everything else I've been doing lately. If it works, I may switch to something this simple. My body is proving itself unable to handle what I want already. I stave off my disappointment until I have a place to deal with it.

The scissors cut through the already-worn wire coating. Then, I strip it. If anyone from Juniper Foods watches the footage back, I'll say I saw the wire and tried to fix it. *Alas, I know now that I shouldn't have touched it.*

Admittedly, the water will be tricky. I need to spill water right beside a wire I'm sure is live. Well, I suppose at least one part of my plan *has* to be complicated or everyone would do it. The largest flaw in my plan is that he won't come, that someone else will arrive. It will work, but the wrong someone will die. Killing someone unintentionally is something I don't entertain often. I'm too careful to kill the wrong person. At least, I have been.

Now I'm being rash and brazen. There's a thrill in being so spontaneous, getting away with something right in front of every-one. It also comes with more potential complications and is prob-

ELLE MITCHELL

ably the quickest way to get me caught. But I'm fried today, and this is how I'm coping.

A shopper gets near the exposed wire; she's going to walk right by. I use this as my chance. I uncap the water bottle and stand up. We bump into each other, and my water spills on the floor. If the sad excuse for a security camera sees, it shouldn't be clear as to whose bottle it is.

"Oh, I'm so sorry!" we both say at the same time. *Keeping up appearances.*

"I'll take care of this. Did it get on you?" I ask her.

"Who knows? It's just water. You sure you don't want me to help?" The woman's kind brown eyes don't break eye contact as the lines forming on her forehead match the straight line that is her mouth.

"No, no." I tug at my work shirt. "Just part of the job. Thank you, though. Sorry again. And have a good day!" I add.

I rush back to the break room. Isaac is sitting at the table, unwrapping his sandwich. I didn't realize I was cutting it so close.

"I know you're on your break—" I start. "But could you go clean up this water spill by the vegetable fridge? It's small, so it shouldn't take long, but there's a long line at both registers. I've got an appointment, and I'm already running late, or I'd do it." Thunder claps in my chest.

"Sure thing," he says.

"Thanks," I say, sounding disingenuous even to myself.

With that, I leave the break room. I'm disappointed I can't see the bones glow blue through his body because that will *definitely* happen. It's a shame I won't be able to have access to Isaac's body either. If everything goes as planned, I could sate another desire—cannibalism. Mild curiosity is all it is. But if the meat is already cooked and ready, I'd only have to clean it. *Right?* I picture carving into Isaac, and my stomach turns.

I should eat someone better, someone I wouldn't mind

looking at while I prepared their thigh meat. I know I'll try it one day, as I'd like to try everything.

Well, maybe not everything.

Necrophilia is completely off the table, if only because I prefer my lover to do a lot of the heavy lifting.

Walking towards my car brings the buzzing back. *Three*—my kill count is about to be *three*.

The moment I put the key into the ignition, the stereo starts the romance novel I had playing on my drive to work. I jolt with the sound. I want nothing to drown out the spinning thoughts of success and failure in my head. They need to be wrangled into submission.

I hit pause and drive around the corner to watch for the ambulance. I find myself bouncing in my seat with all the anticipation of someone naked and blindfolded, waiting for a caress, a lick, a smack.

Ten minutes later, and nothing.

Twenty minutes.

Thirty fucking minutes.

Well, I failed. My gut sinks to the floor as I imagine police surrounding my house. When I get home, they will be waiting for me. I'll enlighten minds, then go to prison.

I shouldn't have deviated. This goes to show I should do my research, practice on inanimate objects, do the homework before I try on live people.

I guess now it's just a matter of consequences.

18

mouths.

I write my favorite three tongue twisters on the board, grinding my teeth as the dry erase marker squeaks. Unpacking my bag next, I pull out a copy of the poetry book we're reading from, as well as the print-outs of the poems I've chosen, a take-home assignment, water cups, and Rice Krispie treats. Looking at the shiny blue-wrapped rectangles, I'm sad. I hate how crappy they are, but I had no energy to make them myself. Killing Cora took a lot out of me. Even though my pain has lessened and my bruises have healed, moving still takes twice as much effort as before.

As I move through the aisles, putting the collection of stuff on the students' desks, I try not to think about Isaac or the water puddle or my failure.

An ancient clock above the door tells me I have enough time to eat a quick snack before any student should be here—that includes the earliest ones. The grapes are a little sweaty, but they give way between my molars in the satisfying *pop* I want. A little juice trickles onto the back of my tongue. My eyes roll back in my head, and I try not to slurp.

The air conditioning kicks on and makes the small part of my thighs that are visible shiver. My simple white slip dress and thigh-high pastel yellow socks are not enough today. Outside, it's warm for early May. Inside, it's September. I pull on a pale pink knit off-the-shoulder sweater and hop up on the edge of the desk. With the sweater on, the dress looks more like lingerie.

"Hello, Ms. Dauphine." A familiar voice cuts through any thoughts of me sneaking to the car for my black jeans, but I haven't known them all enough to connect them.

Wendell is showing his entire mouth's worth of angled teeth at me, his eyes crinkling. I'm pleased to see him too.

"Hello, Wendell." I'm shocked I remember his name. He makes an impact.

A cluster of students come in, chatting in various accents—a pleasant cacophony.

Licia arrives next, announcing herself and talking about her son's driving. The rest of the students follow in an ants-on-a-log style line. Imagery of the child's snack leads me to celery, which for the longest time I thought was cruciferous.

A flash of anger at Michael being a cop sneaks in and interrupts me being polite to my students. *Fucking cruciferous vegetables.* I blame them for Michael's decision. The whole produce department is at fault, truly. Rows and rows of brightly colored fruits and vegetables waiting for another kid just like me to stab them, practicing to be who they're meant to be.

If only he'd been stocking bread, he might have thought about working at a mattress company. In the spice aisle, he would have thought saving maidens from burning buildings was his calling. *But no.*

I breathe *in* my ESL course, breathe *out* my frustrations at my boyfriend and worry about Isaac. I mentally add not to think about Cora or Crystal.

"Welcome back, everyone!" I say, pushing my chipper voice to a comical level. To the average ear, I'm told it just sounds happy. I try not to show my disappointment as I note the missing unnamed, perfect teeth woman. I don't know why I'm drawn to her. "The first thing we'll be doing is reading tongue twisters. It's to wake your tongue up to our—as Mel put it last week—*sucky* language." I chuckle to show the class I'm being funny.

The room doesn't smell bad, so no perfume today. I'm relieved.

One after the other chooses from the tongue twisters and reads them aloud. I watch their mouths, taking in the shapes and sizes of their teeth, the way their lips change with the words they say. I'm still present enough to correct them if need be.

The students clap after their fellow learner finishes.

We give the entire class another round of applause when everyone finishes.

"Great job!" I say with enthusiasm. I tell them we'll be doing a popcorn reading of five poems in a row. We start at one corner of the room, and I have the first student read two lines. The student behind them reads two lines next, and so on. I explain this to them, asking them if I'm being clear. They say I am.

"Good. At the end of each poem, we'll discuss any word you didn't understand and discuss the poem's meaning or meanings, as well as what emotions were being portrayed. It's important to remember that art—whether written or visual is subjective—so you might pick up on different things." I explain the word subjective a little for those who haven't been exposed or had it elaborated. Finally, I tell them we'll start with a short poem to see how it goes. I've switched the lesson plan up if it doesn't resonate with the class.

The first poem is called *Breath of Bread*. It's a piece about a woman working through grief in the kitchen from a poetry collection I chose last year. Thus far, I've used it for the last three classes. It's not flowery, but the author still uses complex words and common turns of phrase that are both interesting and relevant.

Expectant faces of adult learners stare at me from old desks as I kick us off.

"The lace curtain moves in the open window's breeze. Her name is on the wind," I read.

I glance at the left front corner of the room and hesitate.

The woman provides her name. "Bernice."

"Right, sorry," I say, faking a wince. "Still learning."

She nods solemnly, then picks up the third line, and we're off. Two lines, then *pop*.

19

solved.

After class, Wendell lingers to tell Mel and Chike about the most recent rom-com his wife made him watch. He talks about the meet-cute, saying that it was, in fact, a good one. But if only the couple had said "*I love you*" earlier, the whole movie could have ended in fifteen minutes.

Mel keeps shifting their shoulders, clearly having something to say.

The moment Wendell pauses, they turn to me and blurt out that they may have solved a murder. Mel's accent is heavy with their excitement. That doesn't take the sting away—the shock, the horror, the fear, the backed-in-the-corner feeling.

"Oh?" My voice is small.

Chike takes over, but Mel seems unperturbed. Could be that it was his finding that led them here. He tells me they interviewed Crystal Keaton's sister.

Fuck.

Through stilted English, stutters, and mispronunciations, I

gather that she stopped by to grab an early breakfast with Crystal, but she didn't answer. She knocked and knocked, but no answer. Her car could have been in the garage. But it didn't sit right with her. So her sister let herself in. The smell wasn't horrible, but it was bad enough she thought there must be a dead animal lost in the walls. She ran through the bottom of the house and saw the note. But it was weird that Crystal didn't explain it.

That didn't occur to me, that's why.

Mel takes over the story now, unable to let Chike have all the storytelling glory. They roll their chair forward and backward every now and again, and I wonder if it's from too much crime-solving energy or to stave off discomfort. Some things you just don't ask. At least, some things *I* don't ask. The general population loves to ask me about my cane and my stretching. And Michael wonders why I don't like having it.

Mel tells me in rushed, short sentences that Crystal's sister went into the garage and saw her sister's car was still there. That's when she ran upstairs. Mel says they'll spare me the gory details because they would turn almost anyone's stomach. But it ended with the police showing up. There were no leads until they were informed about Crystal's falling out with a long-time friend from high school about three years ago. It seems it got ugly. There were words, one public near-fight, and a full-on threat Crystal told her sister about.

Until Mel, Chike, and Wendell came to talk to her about the case, she hadn't remembered it. She was thinking about newer problems. Crystal has moved since then. But the more Crystal's sister talked, told the story of this ex-friend, the more she was convinced. While the podcast was still recording, Crystal's sister called the police to tell them what she knew. They are investigating the ex-friend pretty much exclusively, as they have no other lead. This is more than just a *little* victory.

Wendell beams as Mel finishes the story. "We did it!"

"Thank you," Mel says.

I'm hard up for breath, but I ask, "Thank me?"

"We are together because your class."

"You did this yourselves. You found each other," I say. What I mean is, *You're the best crime-solving podcasters ever. I'm so glad meddling randoms solving murders is a thing now.*

They swivel their heads at each other and nod with approval, then turn to leave in near-unison.

I gather my things, my body tense in parts and looser than it has been in others as it susses how to feel. Wendell's voice penetrates my thoughts about what I'm going to do next.

When I look up, he is stepping back for Mel. Through his sharp smile, he tells me they've already found their new case.

A terrified heart bashes the inside of my ribcage as I wait for the shoe to drop.

20

scenarios.

I'm sitting in the car watching heavy rain pellets beat down on the windshield. My mood should be light, knowing the police are looking into someone for Crystal's murder. But for every relieved breath, there are three held ones. Until I see Isaac again, I'll be in a weird stasis. I hate that he's still bothering me. Wendell never did say whose case he was looking into next, which means I'll have angry question marks swirling in my head until I know. And though I wasn't worried before, now the fact that there is no one to interview for Cora aside from her neighbors is concerning.

I think I'm good at this, but really, I'm still an amateur. I'll probably have to stop long before I can say I've moved beyond novice.

After I tell paranoia to take a backseat, I turn the car on. Steady rhythmic wipers *swish* at the rain, only for it to come back. My view goes from blurry to less blurry. With the need to drive slower than usual, roaming around town may clear my cluttered mind.

Downtown is filled with lights and colors and people rushing from building to car to building in attempts to escape the rain; it seems like a good place to meander. Though it's a thirty-minute drive out of the way, I've got nothing to do tonight. Michael has to work the in-between late shift, so he's just waking up.

The traffic is terrible the moment I'm close to the first restaurant that can claim itself part of the "downtown area". Fat raindrops have eased to sharp sprinkles that bounce more than roll. Seeing has become much easier, therefore so has people watching.

Someone pulls out in front of another someone, and there is a lot of honking. While I wait for the cluster to unfuck, I get myself two honey butters from my purse. I untwist one and pop it into my mouth. Creamy honey coats my tongue. I tuck the pink cellophane wrapper back where it came from so I can compost it.

I hit every light after that on my trek to nowhere. The length of holding my foot steady on the break makes my low back ache, my knee sore.

At each, I watch men in suits and large umbrellas walk briskly along the sidewalks and women in nice dresses jump over puddles in heels that would shatter my ankle. Thursday is a date night for some, it seems.

Near a closed bookstore, a woman in jeans and a t-shirt strolls without an umbrella. She's completely lost in her own world. Not a single person notices her.

What would it be like to kill someone like her? No planning, no knowing her. Just snatch her off the street from a dark alley and kill her. Or follow her home, break in? There would be no connection. The closest thing would be a street camera showing I was in the area. I'm just one of many. Able-bodied men with ex-wives or lost jobs, women with muscular arms and an axe to grind against their neighbors. It would be hard to look at an ESL teacher with a cane and say she stalked a woman to murder her.

I play out scenarios in my head of all that could go wrong.

A person home in the bathroom, and I miss them. Someone pops by to visit while I'm in the act. She has weapons in her purse. She's in the FBI. Her eight brothers and sisters, parents and grandparents, friends and lovers care for her so deeply they'll never give up hunting her murderer down.

And what of timing? I don't know her neighbors or the street lamps in her area.

How do people get away with random murders? I'm exhausted just thinking about all the ways it could go wrong. And that's just the list I come up with before the light changes.

Now that I'm driving with the flow of traffic again, I know it's not for me. Planning is key. I need time to be able to rest, the ability to pivot if the person I choose is wrong. I already made a mistake and chose someone with a sister who loved her more than I expected, and that was *with* ample planning time.

I'm too tired, sore, and in too much pain to risk more than I need to.

After Cora, I know I already have a lot to reconsider. Hunting instead of choosing from my curated list may sound thrilling, but it would get me caught—or worse, injured beyond the point of being able to bounce back.

Slowly, I drive my way against the stream of salmon waiting to be cooked and make it onto the highway.

What I need is a long, hot bath with Epsom salts, a cup of tea, some Percocet, and a few good pulls from that joint Adela left in my purse.

21

emojis.

This weekend, I'm house sitting for a single room. Their living room isn't special, though it has a large TV and a nice couch. No one would break into a house for their relatively nice kitchen either. The bedroom is decorated from an article on how to get a designer room for less.

It's a gamer's paradise I'm here for. There is a hand-drawn sign on the door leading to the room. "NO FOOD. NO DRINK. NO SEX. NO FIGHTS".

I can see Mrs. Hudson throwing a controller against the wall and it breaking—the third time in one month. Then, she and Mr. Hudson jump each other for loud, violent makeup sex that knocks a screen over. *No more makeup sex in the game room*, one of them probably said. The other added, *While we're at it, let's add food. You always get crumbs in the keyboard.* That may have brought on another fight where one of them knocked an open soda onto a computer tower.

With harsh contrasting colors, glowing electronics, chairs

from space stations, and an overcrowded bookshelf filled with toys in packages and dusty boxes, Adela would love this room. I see her now: feet planted on the ground, ready to move from one screen to the next. She'd be in all the queues—battlegrounds, fishing tourneys, and working her virtual assistant job. Somehow, she'd still make it to the bookstore on time. I don't quite understand the allure of fake fishing or fighting as a wolf, but I'm still in awe of her ability to multi-task, compartmentalize, and get everything done without ever looking tired.

Meanwhile, making it to work in the morning after killing someone is a trek uphill in the snow for ten miles.

It's one of the reasons we're still friends—my awe. It's why if Adela finds out my secret, I will probably just run away, change my identity, but *not* kill her.

As I'm setting my toothbrush out on the single sink, Michael calls to ask if he can come over. I tell him I'm only here for two nights, but he can pop by. His text has a bunch of emojis in response. He does this sometimes, sends me cryptic coded messages I'm supposed to crack. The result isn't a long-lost treasure, so why would I bother? Besides, if I don't answer quickly enough for his liking, he explains himself.

Today's emojis are a woman and man holding hands, a popcorn bucket, the clapper thing people use to yell *cut*, a smiley face with a sweat bead, a kiss, a yellow male policeman, and a thumbs up. I groan. I don't want to watch a cop drama again. He's been on a kick of finding shows that have cops going through training. Wouldn't he rather watch the spy show that just came out? The entire cast is fuckable, and I won't have to hear about his wanting to be a detective again.

Despite my feelings, I don't respond. This one may be clearer than most, but I don't want to set the precedent of answering an emoji text.

The moment I sit the phone down, I pull out my camera. Its small body feels heavy in my hands. I'm too weak to do much of anything at the moment. That's the nature of hEDS for me: I never know when I just won't be able to *do*.

I make myself a small cup of water. Before it's half full, it feels like a gallon of milk. I sigh and go wait for Michael on the L-shaped couch.

22

academy.

My legs are draped over Michael, and my tailbone aches. The forty-minute wait for him proved the plush-looking couch to be extremely uncomfortable. My mother would have said that it was a piece of furniture meant to assure that your guests didn't over-stay their welcome—a just-for-appearance couch. Our kitchen table was similar to this, with brutally hard seats and spindly backs. It's where she took people she didn't like much. I enjoyed watching them squirm and excuse themselves, trying not to stretch or wince on their way out. Guests she liked—friends and family—she took to our living room, where the couch and loveseat cushions swaddled you like a baby. Adela and I spent a lot of time in there. Everyone else, I took to the kitchen, as well. And only *I* got a cushion.

"I have something to share with you," Michael says, shifting me so he can pull a folded paper from his back pocket. I try not to gasp from pain, as so much of the past month and a half catch-up to me. "I got into the Police Academy! It starts in three weeks!" he blurts out.

My head spins, and it isn't from the pain.

I thought it was a fanciful idea, a little boy's dream of wanting to be a firefighter. I've been busy trying to figure myself out, having an early mid-life crisis, if you will. Getting a cane can do that to a person—or at least me, *this* person. Now I have to deal with the fact that my boyfriend wants to be a police officer and that he's actually doing something about it.

When did he get initiative?

I stutter as I try to think of something to say, give a response that will sate him and seem authentic. He takes that as a good sign. People will often take what they want or need out of a situation—be that physically, emotionally, or mentally. Michael wants me to be happy for him, so in his mind, I am.

"I know! I was hoping. I mean, I'll be honest... I wasn't sure they'd take me. It's been a few years since I got my degree, and I haven't been pursuing anything in law enforcement, but it looks like that's okay! It's going to be such an amazing experience. Of course, I'll miss working with you. More importantly, I'll miss seeing you all the time. But it's not forever, and I can come back on some weekends." *Has he forgotten I work Saturdays?*

Michael fidgets so much that I lift my legs off of him and move to the edge of the couch where I can lean against a cushion. Once I resettle, my pelvis shifts and cracks loudly as it corrects itself. This time I do gasp, but it's with relief. Michael knows my sounds, so he just nods. Still, I note his furrowed brow. He'll be watching me more now.

"What do you mean, you'll miss seeing me?" I ask.

"Didn't I say? It's not here, it's in Salem. So I'm going to go live in their dorms for the 16-week academy. The patrol with the Field Training Officer and the Advanced Academy is back here in Janes, though." He is breathless. Michael's eyes sparkle.

With him in Salem for months, I wonder what being alone will be like. A third kill has been on my mind, of course.

Michael's still talking as my thoughts trickle in. Two kills in less than two months apart has felt risky enough. A third may look like a pattern. Will they guess how I choose them? *Paranoia again.*

Michael flashes me his goofy smile, his photo-worthy teeth.

If I'm ever a suspect, I wonder if that's how the police would figure it out. They may or may not note Michael's great teeth. But when they inevitably question Adela, they'll see the gap, and it might be easier to connect the dots. By then, they would have cataloged all similarities between the victims. *No.* I'm being silly. I killed the two women in vastly different ways.

How could the police connect me to them at this point? Nearly a year after brief exchanges doesn't exactly move you to the number one person of interest.

Risk, reward, risk, reward. The scale between the two sways. Opportunities like this don't come around often. I knew what I was going to do the moment he said the word *Salem.* Sometimes you have to talk yourself into things.

"I've talked a lot. How are you feeling?" Michael asks. "Are you okay with this?" He bounces on the balls of his socked feet. The carpet indents with each push. Jiggling legs make me glad that I'm no longer laying across him.

Thanks to the other night, my joints are looser than drunk, broken-hearted, single people. They've slipped and shifted more since killing Crystal than they ever have before. I fear I've sped up the stretching of precious connective tissue I've been able to baby most of my life, being a non-participator as I have been.

"I am. I'm happy that you're happy." My perfunctory answer pleases him. All of my perfunctory answers have.

Often I'm able to be myself, even let some dark comments sneak out—though he takes them as jokes. I recognize when it's time to be different or say things contrary to how I feel. Nothing like laugh tracks and Oscar-winning films to guide me through complicated exchanges.

I stand to stretch.

"Thank you. I am happy. I really am. I haven't been this happy since you said *yes* to going to dinner with me. I'm putting in a one-week notice at Juniper tomorrow." He pauses. There's something in the pause that says, *You could do that too.* I may be wrong. No matter, I ignore it. "I wanted it to be two weeks, but I think I need some time to myself before I jump into school."

"Nice that you're giving them the heads up." I turn and head to the kitchen. "Just making popcorn. I can't have it staring at me anymore, all unpopped and flat." My impatience is nothing new, nothing out of the ordinary.

"You're too cute. Oh! Speaking of Juniper… Did you hear about Isaac?" Michael's voice is a loud whisper, like he's conspiring with me or telling a campfire ghost story.

I gulp. A flash of Michael wearing a wire, the police waiting outside the front door. "No. What about him?"

My face is heating up, and I'm glad to be out of his eyesight. I glance in a mirror framed by a rainbow above the sink. Nothing about me shows my true feelings. Inside, I'm flushed and panting for Michael to spit the story out. Outside, I'm just Elizabeth. My blue-gray eyes aren't bulging or mostly white with the panic of a trapped animal. Lips as average as this apartment aren't curled into a snarl. No beads of sweat form on the tiny spot where they stick out and make a vague lip shape. Steam isn't coming from my ears or long nose. How I'm externally keeping it together is a mystery. It's not conscious.

"Apparently, he went to go clean up a water spill and found a frayed wire behind the veggie fridge. The water had spread *just* far enough to touch the wire. It was lucky he saw it because he almost stepped in it. Well, it was a small wire, so it's possible nothing would have even happened, but still. Crazy. Here's the funniest part... Are you ready?" Michael's voice raises over the beeping of me hitting the popcorn button.

I know I have no choice but to go back into the room for the rest of the story. He's waiting for me.

"Ready for what?" I ask, peeking my head around the wall of the kitchen.

"He claims that *you* tried to electrocute him. Said he wanted to play the tapes back and everything."

My mind jerks me back to the moment I showed him a glimpse of the real me. It shouldn't have been anything. Lots of people act that way. Adela and Michael have seen slivers, but they thought it was just a bad day. No one at work has seen anything but chipper, tired, hungover, or, at worst, neutral Elizabeth. I wanted to keep it that way. He crawled under my skin at the right moment, and I've exposed myself and put myself in the spotlight. *What have I done?*

"Ooooh boy!" he continues. He has no idea how many thoughts are exploding in my head as he speaks. "I thought Jamie was going to fire him right then and there. He was ranting and raving about how he accidentally called you Liz and you went off on him in front of customers. Said they left because they were uncomfortable." Michael laughs here, knowing that I aim *not* to make people uncomfortable.

He doesn't know that it's meant to keep attention off of me. He only knows that I'm a sweet person who tries to make people happy. He sees me as a funny woman who teaches adults skills, takes care of animals, plants, houses, and never ignores a customer. He sees what I want him to see; they all do.

For his benefit, I drop my mouth open. "Wait... What?!" I say, knowing there's more.

"He said you asked him to go clean up the puddle where the live wire was halfway sticking up. But when he called Jamie to come look at it, the wire was at the edge. She asked him if he'd touched anything, worried about him—or maybe just about liability. He said *no*. Then fifteen minutes later, he's changing his story. Isaac is definitely a big fish kind of person. I wouldn't be surprised if tomorrow you held his face to the wire. If he steps out of line for just *one* second, he's gone. Jamie is not interested in liars."

The popcorn is slowing, so when I respond, I do it from the kitchen. I'm a little louder than I would be if I were beside him when I say, "Wow. Honestly… Wow. I'm a little flabbergasted. Who knew that was a word people got to use for real?" I force a chuckle. "Hold on, popcorn's almost ready."

Five seconds in between pops. I wait… Two seconds in between pops. Ready.

Rummaging through the Hudsons' cabinets, I find a green translucent salad bowl that belongs at John's St. Patrick's Day house. I empty the popcorn out into the bowl, then rush into the living room.

Michael's already torn open the M&Ms and has it waiting for me. His consideration knows no bounds. As soon as I set the popcorn down between us on the hard cushions, he dumps in the candy. He shakes the M&Ms into the popcorn and hands me a cloth napkin.

"You know, it's funny he said all of that. It's like he took half-truths and twisted them," I say. "He *did* call me Lizzie—and Lisa and Beth. But he's the one who was making customers uncomfortable, though no one left. They just went home unhappy and probably thinking they should avoid him next time or that Juniper is going downhill. And I did ask him to clean up the spill. In fact, I'm the one that made the mess. But that's because I bumped into a woman. Obviously, I didn't see a wire, which is admittedly weird. I tied my shoes by that area not long before I bumped into the woman because I thought I saw a shoplifter, so I was trying to be sneaky. I didn't see any wire then. I didn't end up seeing the shoplifter either." I've gotten quick at lying. "To be honest, he didn't like that I told him to call me by my name. I basically told him I'd make sure he never got to work the register again if he kept pulling that macho nonsense with me. So yeah, of course, he wanted to get back at me. I'm not saying he did it himself, but the puddle wasn't that big... And don't you think I would have seen a wire?"

Michael is attentive, popping candy-coated chocolate-smeared popcorn into his mouth one-by-one without stopping. I worry he won't believe me. I worry I've pushed my luck.

But then he nods. "Fuck that guy! I think we should tell Jamie! He wants to watch the tapes. Maybe we should!" he says.

I've covered my bases. Well, I'm almost sure I have. Either way, if I don't agree, I look guilty. "Yeah, I think we should. It's funny at first—him going on about me. Then I think about it..." I add a frown as I trail off, giving the appearance of hurt.

"You know what, *no*. We won't give him what he wants. He's probably going to try and make up excuses. I just want him fired. If I can't be there to keep an eye on him, I want him gone." Michael stops eating and squeezes my hand. "I love you, you know? I just want you safe."

"I love you too." I kiss him on the cheek. "You take such good care of me," I say. Then I say the thing that will solidify him pushing Isaac out, keep us from watching the tape, and make sure he believes only me. "You're going to be a great cop."

23

latch.

"That was pretty good, right?" Michael asks.

I haven't been paying attention. At some point, my legs ended up across his again. Lost in the rhythmic feel of his hands caressing sore upper thighs, the plot faded away by the thirty-minute mark. *Of all the days to wear leggings.*

I don't answer him. I turn his face towards mine. If this was my house, he'd strip me right here. But it's not, and this is a shitty couch.

I stand and point towards to the homeowner's bedroom. I stroke his palm with my middle finger as we walk to bring him up to speed, knowing this is one of the quickest ways to get Michael aroused. Beside the bed, I always leave two towels because one never knows what will happen—even though I almost always use my own sheets.

Today, Michael will happen.

Putting down a towel is unsexy and frequently kills the

mood. He has to work to bring it back, tease and touch and lick. There is no such issue tonight.

Michael is a great lover—giving, flexible in every sense of the word, and adventurous.

He unbuttons his pants and drops them to the floor. My leggings are more complicated. He kisses a path down my tingly legs as he rolls the stretchy gray fabric down and tugs it off over my feet. On television, they skip this part. Getting naked is simple, quick, sexy. She's always in a dress, or her pants are magically on the floor. Reality is not as smooth.

I hop up onto the overly tall bed and position myself to be on the towel. *So mechanical.*

Michael runs his hands along my body as he slides to the foot of the bed and spreads my thighs. He paints swirls with his tongue on my clit until I'm wriggly.

After the hour-long teasing he didn't know he was doing during the movie, it doesn't take long. I can't orgasm with just penetration, but a few good licks will always get the job done. I'm a lucky woman in this regard, according to Adela.

My thighs shake and clamp around his head. Moans turn to screams. He doesn't stop, and I ride the roller coaster until I feel Cora's name begin to slip out. I don't analyze my thoughts during sex. Instead, I worry at the inside of my cheek and pat his head, our sign for *enough.* I've never told him why sometimes I tell him *enough* is *enough.* In truth, it's usually because I've had mine, and I want him to get his so I can get on with my day. Sometimes, too much hurts my nerves, turns pleasure into pain—not the kind that causes pleasure again. I don't want to have that conversation, though.

He hops off the bed, leaving a cold spot that almost aches with his absence. He rifles through his back pocket to grab his wallet and a condom he keeps there. I loathe the dumb rubber things. The sight of him sliding it on is repulsive, the feel can be numbing, and they remind me of teenagers hoping to *get lucky.*

So I look up and notice an imperfection in the far left corner of the ceiling. Before my arousal dies down or I create a story about the dent, Michael is in me. *Good. Just how I like it.*

He moves with the soft ticking of the wall clock, and my climax builds again. I close my eyes and a flicker of people roll through my mind.

Michael; I groan.

The leading couple in my favorite romantic comedy; my eyes roll back in my head.

Michael's breath quickens and mixes with the slick and squishy sounds of sex. They drown out the clock's counting of seconds.

The face of an ex-boyfriend who taught me what I didn't like in bed and an ex-girlfriend who proved what I liked depended more on my partner's talent; I tell Michael I want it harder.

Encouraged, Michael's speed increases.

A mash-up of Crystal and Cora; I cry out.

Michael groans into my hair, smashing hard against my breasts. It's rude and uncomfortable. As I do when this happens, I ignore it. He's what I need in a boyfriend in so many other ways—moldable, forgiving, blind to my darkness. Not being great at the physical act of sex isn't a huge deal. I get my orgasms first and always, anyhow.

Our heads are facing the opposite direction as we gasp for air. My hip throbs, and a tension grips my lower back. *Anytime now.*

My teeth latch onto the soft flesh of my upper arm without conscious thought. I bite hard, and pain mixes with the pleasure. He pounds into me and repeats *Elibet* into my collarbone.

The name brings her face to me, washing everything else away. Adela is all I see as I explode with one last orgasm.

I rip my fingernails down Michael's back as pleasure turns to pain. His skin giving way brings trickles of blood like red strands of hair. I smile despite my hurting. With a final grunt, Michael spasms, stiffens, and collapses onto me—a sated, beached whale.

I'm glad we're done. I was close to having to push him off of me, finish himself off in the bathroom like we're an unhappy married movie couple. Most times, when it hurts, I rearrange our bodies until I'm comfortable. When he's so close, I don't bother. If I have to stop us, he sulks for days. The guilt is as palpable as Pigpen's dirt cloud, surrounding him and following him everywhere. I don't need that.

All I can think is, now that we're done, he can roll over. We don't need to stay connected like mating love bugs in hot Louisiana summers, but I *do* love him in my own way, and he loves this part.

I remind him I need to pee to escape more pain and his softening penis.

Michael sleeps over. Tongue lolling from his open mouth, drool drips onto a pillowcase I bring to every house just for him. It's stained with dark splotches that even a 1950s housewife couldn't get out with all of her tricks of the trade and banned chemicals. He doesn't care.

Michael's snoring makes it easy for me to get out of bed to stretch, get medication I'm still not accustomed to taking from my unpacked bag, and wander to the kitchen for a glass of water without worrying about him waking up. I'm back at Cora's house. If need be, I'll only move with the loud notes.

While illuminated by the light of the refrigerator, I decide to throw him a going away party. He's leaving Juniper Foods—a place he's worked since he was a teenager—and that means something to him. For me, it will just be a day I don't have to force myself to smile at people or stand for hours. But he cares more; he's sentimental about it being the place we met. So I'll do what looks best to stay in the good girlfriend column.

I mentally craft a message to fellow employees that I'll send out in the morning.

As I close the refrigerator door, I see the deep imprint my teeth made on my arm. I haven't left one like that in a while.

My camera sits on the counter and begs me to take a photo, something I haven't done in a while either. I cannot ignore the desire, so I use the refrigerator light and capture tonight's bite, enjoying the sound as the image slides out.

I take the water to the bedroom and ruminate over my teeth's journey. Sometimes, I think it's good to go back, remember how far you've come.

The first time I bit myself was to calm frayed insides, to keep me from punching a girl who pulled my curls. She called me a name that I wouldn't be phased by now, and I walked around the corner of the building and bit my forearm to relieve the pressure. The girl followed me, so I punched her anyhow. I had to hide the teeth marks—my secret shame. I might have either way, because I realized I had irregular, jagged little teeth—a baby cookiecutter shark after a physical altercation with a rock.

I went home and asked for braces.

When barbed wire and little white bands covered my teeth, my bite marks changed. They got violent; the light indentions went from lasting a few hours or a day to a day to five. Occasionally, I'd accidentally tear my flesh with the edges of the braces. When that happened, I'd imagine chunks of flesh dangling there for all the world to see. I became a cannibal warrior.

My teeth straightened. I took photos of the progress—one a month for three years. I still remember the thrill of taking that first Polaroid, the thrill that each gave me—bite, photo, hide Polaroid, rinse and repeat. They are under the collection of furniture Polaroids, along with three blown-out closeups of other people's mouths—the boy I lost my virginity to, the first woman I slept with, and Adela's.

I sneak back under the covers, letting thoughts of teeth and the past melt away. I find Michael's dream-clenched hand and squeeze once.

I trap my bitten arm between weak legs and stroke my inner thigh. It sends shivers down my spine. Though it's arousing, I'm too spent to do anything about it.

I fall asleep on the side that hurts the least, rubbing my teeth's indention. I think I'm smiling.

24

photographer.

It's Thursday, and on Thursdays, we watch movies. On Thursdays, I also abscond one of the few microwaves from the building and sneak it into my room to pop a bag of extra buttery popcorn for each person and five unbuttered in case there are people opposed. I also bring movie candy in case there are insane people in my class who don't like popcorn—or worse yet, an unfortunate soul who is allergic to corn. I bring enough in case everyone wants both, though. I learned the hard way what happens if it's *either/or*.

It smells like a movie theater without all the screaming children and the irritating *pshh* the soda machine makes.

So, my desk is covered in unopened but warm microwave popcorn bags and candy bags. The students' desks have their usual cup for water and a small travel pack of tissues, because there may be tears today.

During a long day off yesterday, I began thinking of a few new ways I want to murder someone. Most seemed too exhausting, which was disappointing. I decided I'd need to watch some of the best horror movies again for inspiration. I may not have the energy to saw someone in half, but surely I don't have to come home a broken doll. If I knew how to use the dark web, I'd be on forums asking about comfortable ways to kill people.

How can I stay in the supine position and murder someone?

It may be time I design a rolling, freestanding, foldable, lightweight pulley system. One doesn't have to be an engineer for that, surely?

Before I could remind myself that I promised myself a day of actual rest, I had the spreadsheet of all of my clients pulled up and was scrolling through my notes.

It occurred to me as I read the "Other Info" column—made so I wouldn't forget little details beyond their addresses and how much they paid me—that I have a lot of reasons to kill people.

The first note I see says, "He paid in crisp dollar bills, insisted on making me count them in front of him, trying to caress my face as I did it."

He doesn't fit the bill because past-me remarked he had three chipped teeth. He must have caught me staring because I wrote, "He told me it was an accident that happened when he was in college, twenty-some-odd years ago. Dental healthcare is sad."

I kept hunting, started moving people to different sheets— Possibles, Nopes, Never Work For Again, Work For Again, Fave Clients.

There were two women on the Possible list worth investigating. But it's frustrating how many of my Fave Clients have great teeth.

I hear new voices. Licia and Wendell arrive together, already catching up.

Wendell still hasn't told me who the podcast is *investigating* next. I want to ask, but they seem keen on keeping it a secret. I'm trying to remind myself to be less paranoid. Even if it is Cora, how could they connect me?

"The smell!" Licia shouts and claps her hands. "Popcorn?"

"Yep," I say. I'm trying to sound the usual level of chipper, but it's not in me. I've got no house sitting jobs for the next week, which means groceries and rent will be tight again. Not to mention I'm still grappling with the fact that Michael is going to the Police Academy. And I still haven't chosen my next victim. "Grab a bag and some candy before you sit down," I say. "Buttered is on the right, unbuttered on the left."

Wendell points to the projector and asks if we're watching a movie. When I say *yes*, he and Licia begin hypothesizing about what kind. As they grab buttered popcorn and a bag of candy, Licia says she hopes there will be a good-looking man in it.

As the next wave of students come in, only minutes before we start, I hear the conversation has switched to sharing recipes. That's been a staple for my class. I encouraged a recipe exchange in my welcome packet. It suggested bringing a recipe to class each time or just verbally telling other students about a dish. Completely informal, it seems to bring people together in a way movies, reading, or studying have never been able to. The students found they used similar spices or techniques, even though they live on different continents and speak different languages. I really am an excellent teacher. Now, if only I could get this good at killing, I wouldn't need such a long recovery time.

The woman has come back today. I know her name now, as I looked at my class roster last week. Jemma. I will not kill Jemma for her teeth. I see no benefit in killing a person bettering themselves, if only to fit into societal norms. *Been there.*

When everyone settles, I welcome them all back. I find myself staring, as I knew I would, at Jemma's teeth, wondering what shade of white paint they'd be called and if she'll smile again when I get close enough for me to find out.

Taking a sip of water is necessary before I announce our first film, *The Notebook*. Then, I give a synopsis.

"Every Thursday, from now on, we'll be watching a movie. Though reading and comprehension are extremely important, movies and TV often reflect the average usage of words and phrases. They also become part of our everyday cultural references. While *The Notebook* is not a new film, the repetition of words within it is considered helpful for people learning English as a second language. So, what I want is for you to *actively* watch it." I explain active watching and listening for those who aren't familiar with the phrase, then add, "And at the end, we'll discuss words and phrases that tripped you up, any questions that came to mind—including about the film itself. Let's make this class fun. To make sure everyone is comfortable, there are a few scenes of a sexual nature, mild profanity, mild—" VCC's guidelines dictate I must mention everything down to smoking cigarettes. There are at least three smokers in the room, and half of the room has children, but I say them nonetheless. I end with my canned and recycled phrase, "If any of that sounds problematic or triggering, you can either skip this class or put watching another film to a vote, and I can give you the alternative film." I nod. "Does anyone have questions before we get started?"

No one does. So I hit play.

I kick my legs up on the desk. Today, I'm wearing soft, high-waisted jeans and an oversized white cowl-neck sweater with lots of folds and excess material. While the class enjoys and learns, sitting up straight and taking the occasional note, I'm continuing my hunt, staying as comfy and cozy as one can in a plastic molded chair. My nicer chair was missing when I got here; my price for the microwave, I suppose.

First, I pull up the two women that seemed the most likely to be my next victims. I start deep-diving into the first one. She's slim, with nice teeth and a closet full of blood vials.

At the part in *The Notebook* when Noah is just about to hang from the Ferris Wheel, Licia comes up to my desk. I see her in time to lock my phone.

She asks in her usual loud voice to go to the bathroom. I smile and answer her loudly back, addressing the entire class along with her. "No one needs to ask to go to the bathroom or to leave at all. You're all adults. It's to the left, down the hall on the right."

Once the door is closed behind her, I dive back in. I see that the woman is married now, which shouldn't have taken this long to figure out. Some people like to appear available, though.

I move to the second woman named Olivia Penn. Scrolling through her photography website, I'm trying to gauge how big of a name she is. The site is nice but doesn't feel special. It could easily be a drag-and-drop template, and the photos could be from her sister's wedding.

She has good teeth, though not great. *No gap.* But the dark-room in her walk-in closet doesn't match with the life she claims to lead. She proclaims to focus on weddings, engagements, all things baby, and sometimes food. Yet, the photographs hanging from clothespins are of people masturbating alone and couples performing any number of sexual acts to and with each other. She took the pictures through slits in the blinds or exposed corners of curtains. A single photo, hidden behind two men fucking against a refrigerator, was of a nude boy who hadn't gone through puberty. He was close to her, and there were no blinds in the way.

Olivia was sick. And I love the idea of taking her out, despite her teeth not being just right. Some things matter more.

For the longest time, I wasn't sure what could be done about her.

What if I called the cops and there was just the one picture? She wouldn't go to jail, but she might move. What if no one else had been alone in her house for a while? She'd know it was me who called. Then again, maybe I always wanted to save her for myself. She's flitted into my mind now and again. I've had many daydreams of my hands around her throat like the men's hands around their cocks.

"Olivia Penn?" A voice echoes through the classroom, through VCC, through all of Janes.

Flushing, I stutter, "Wh—what?" The chair I've been leaning back on slams to the floor with a loud thud. Shockwaves ripple from my hips to my neck, and I clench my fists and hold my breath. I cannot gasp here, now.

"My nephew a photographer." Kira, a student who has said very little until now, is standing over my shoulder. "I get you a good deal—maybe free. He owes me for not telling about—" She keeps talking, I think. I'm stunned that I didn't notice her walking up. Though, through the haze of pain and shock, I still want to know what secrets she's keeping.

"Oh, it's not for me," I say, trying to compose myself. I tug down my rumpled sweater. "It's a friend of mine, an acquaintance, really."

Kira looks at me and nods. "Not worth a favor. Yes." She goes and sits down then. Back from the bathroom, maybe. Or she could have gotten up just to see what I was doing.

Either way, I have crossed Olivia off my list.

I couldn't be more disappointed.

25

cake.

It's been a week since Michael told me he was accepted into the Police Academy, and I'm still not doing the best job at pretending to be thrilled.

Today, though, I should look like the good and loving girlfriend I normally am.

Today, he gets a going away party at Juniper Foods.

Today, his friends and co-workers will pat him on the back and tell him what I can't muster up the energy to say.

Today, I will curb my needs and wants for a person I love.

He hasn't caught on to our surprise—*my* surprise. I haven't bothered coming up with a clever lie. This morning, I woke up early, got dressed quicker than I ever have or ever will, and announced I'm heading out before him with no fanfare and no explanation.

Michael huffs but says nothing. We're at my house, so leaving before him is beyond abnormal. Even here, he's only allowed to use the key in an emergency or if he's told me he's coming. I told him it scared me, that if we weren't living together, someone letting themselves in and *being* there would feel invasive. Really, I just like my space.

Clearly, he's irritated at me for not waiting for him. Just like he's irritated that we aren't living together.

Though it financially straps me, being without a house sitting job is nice. I'm able to be in my bed for a few days. Given my job, I've set up my home like a retreat. Every room feels special, each nook and cranny filled with curated items—as many as possible bought from small shops, second-hand stores, or hand-made. In my bedroom, the elaborate setup of an overhead fan, two small fans with iridescent streamers, and one large standing fan all blowing at odd angles anytime it's mildly warm allows for me to snuggle under any number of my five to ten layers of sheets, blankets, and comforters. An ex-girlfriend of mine once called me a *burrower*.

While Michael is stomping around my empty apartment, slamming my antique green refrigerator closed with a glass milk bottle in hand, I'm putting up the cheesy rainbow streamers he thinks are fun. He's finishing a bowl of his beloved sugary cereal with his perfect 2:1 milk ratio. At the same time, I'm setting up my phone's speakers and the Michael Going Away Playlist. And while he's leaving the perfectly good half-full milk gallon on the counter, I'm making sure everyone signed his going away card.

During his drive over, I run around the store and confirm everyone's timed attendance so the floor would never be empty, and no customer would be wanting. This pleases Jamie.

And now, as Michael steps through the automatic door, I breeze to the front of Juniper Foods to meet him.

I link arms with him, and say, "Follow me."

His furrowed brow softens a bit, and he smooths his rumpled work shirt. "What's going on?" Michael's steps are lighter even though he's walking slower to match my pace.

It's a good thing I've planned something. Because if I hadn't, I think he'd be disappointed. The closer we get to the break room, the more he buzzes. "Wait," he says, pulling up short. "Is this about Isaac? I don't know if I can handle—"

"No. I haven't seen Isaac since the day I *apparently* tried to kill him," I say, scoffing.

We laugh together for very different reasons.

He resumes walking. "Do you know what happened to him? I haven't seen him this past week. I've asked around, but..." The word *but* hangs in the air.

I want to tell him that I killed him, that Isaac's body is in my modest backyard fertilizing my summer squash. *Didn't you see his hand sticking up from the garden? I'm no good with body hiding.* But I'd be lying. "I think Jamie fired him a day or so after because of something he said to a customer. Don't know, but no one talks about it. It's like he didn't exist. Like Skinny Tie Brian."

Michael nods solemnly and somehow doesn't laugh.

Skinny Tie Brian was a young man who wore a skinny tie over his work shirt. Jamie allowed it, but I still don't know why. Though it was possibly the worst offense in the world to my eyes, my problem wasn't the thin black tie reminding me of children at funerals or even his two layers of aggressive teeth, each tooth at war with the surrounding ones. He claimed not to know how to sweep. Upon Jamie's insistence, I had to spend nearly *ten* minutes of my life showing a seventeen-year-old how to do the most basic of household chores.

His attitude felt like mockery, and we all froze him out. It wasn't even on purpose. Still, he quit sooner than later.

If things were a little different, if my qualifications were more open, he'd be on my list. Oh, and if I hadn't ranted to everyone at Juniper Foods about him as if I was a drunk on a bar stool at 3 a.m. My frustration helped endear me to the other employees, though. They felt closer to me after that.

I suppose there are a few people like Isaac who have gotten

under my skin. He's not the only one. And that dumb seventeen-year-old was one of them.

By the time I'm done mentally raging about Skinny Tie Brian, Michael and I are in front of the break room's closed door. He walked us straight here. Guess he figured it out.

He turns the door handle, and the music begins. Jamie's timing is perfection.

Sid, Jamie, and Emma all shout, "Happy Going Away Party!"

Emma, a woman from the deli counter I've barely spoken to before asking her to sign Michael's card, blows a paper blowout. It makes no noise. She looks disappointed.

Michael is tearing up. He doesn't seem to notice or care about the noisemaker's failure. "You—You all did this for me?" He's facing me now.

I stand on my tippy-toes and kiss him on the cheek. "You'll be missed." I mean it, too. "The rest of the gang will swap out after a little while of hanging and cake. So don't worry, you'll get to see everyone who's here."

Whenever I'm close to an unsliced cake, the need to feel its innards is overwhelming. I want to bring a handful to my face and smear it on my lips, lick it off. I tingle as the snapshot of me with chocolate cake and white icing turns to blood and viscera. It's all I can do not to touch my face, stick my fingers in some-one's mouth and bring the saliva to my cheek.

I agree with Adela's therapist's views on urges and thoughts being neither good nor bad. She told my best friend this after Adela admitted to having the urge to hog tie her boss and fuck him—with permission. But his wife wouldn't like it. When Adela confided in me about this, all I could think about was that I wished more of my urges could become reality. I bet her therapist would put a value on them then.

Jamie smirks, and I pretend she's psychic just for a moment. It's enough to make me smile back. "I expect you two will do very little work today—even when you're out on the floor—but

Elizabeth is a brilliant negotiator. She got me an extra cake! So clock in now, and we'll pretend your day is the same as always."

Michael fills the space between him and Jamie in two steps and hugs her. "Thank you so much! This was so nice."

"You got me streamers!" His expression is open, vulnerable, childlike.

"I'll clock you in. Just grab some cake and read your card," I say. It's not often I think things like this, but *wow*, I'm a lucky woman. The moment the thought crosses my mind, I picture Crystal's sister talking to Wendell, Chike, and Mel and how they kept me off the board. I should acknowledge it more often.

Michael's voice matches his excited and grateful energy. "There's a card too?"

"With a gift card from all of us in it," Emma says, stretching over the table to tap the card Michael is reaching for. The layer of red frizz sitting on top of her straight hair gets in his mouth as it moves his way.

Jamie's arms are crossed, and she's leaning against the empty prep counter. Her bangs are a little flat today. Maybe she was in a rush. "It's not much, but we hope it will help while you're living the bachelor life," she adds.

It's a $300 Visa gift card. "Wow! This is more than I've ever gotten for Christmas. You guys! You GUYS! You didn't have— No, I won't do that. Just… thank you so much. Come here, you two."

Emma rushes into his arms, while Jamie doesn't move.

"Get in here," he insists, as if he didn't just hug her.

"Alright, alright," Jamie says.

He bear-hugs the two of them, while the computer ticks down the minutes he's supposedly on the floor, helping people who don't care about him. All-in-all, I think I've given him a pretty decent last day. I'll try to stretch everything as long as I can. I'm hoping for an hour or two.

We hear Jamie's name over the intercom. "That's me. But

before I go, I wanted to let you know that you've always got a place here. So if you need something while you're getting established or on the weekends, just tell me what hours you want." She winks and leaves before he can respond.

Emma settles in a chair and skips a song on the playlist.

I bet the bakery is slammed. But the baker is a nice guy, so I say, "I'll go grab Darrel. He should be able to sneak back for a few minutes." I'm going to be dead by the end of today.

26

cheek.

Jamie pages us over the intercom. It's gotten busy. We hid away for an hour and forty-seven minutes. *Not great, but not terrible.* When we leave the break room, Michael heads towards the refrigerator section, and I go to the registers.

Isaac is standing in Aisle 7. I'm stunned. The audacity of him showing up here...

I glance over my shoulder, but Michael is already gone.

Any happiness I've accrued disappears. I pivot before he turns. At most, he'll see the back of me.

"Hey, Lisa." His voice is colder than the freezer section.

My mother told me often that nondescript hair makes it distinctive. For a long time, I thought her saying that was proof of insanity. Just like when she said my *a little prettier than plain* face made me beautiful. Time and time again, she's been proven right. On one account, that is. Sandy loose, baby-soft curls seem to be as identifiable as if my hair were green. It makes no sense.

I know he's talking to me. But I only answer to my name.

"Lizzie. Liza. Bethie. Bella. Betsy. Elizabeth." He's a child trapped in a grown man's body.

Slowly, I turn to face him. "Hi, can I help you?" I say with my customer voice, pretending I've never met him and my blood isn't boiling.

He moves towards me. With each step, he emphasizes his next word: "You. Got. Me. Fired." Isaac's breath smells bad, an unbrushed tongue at a fish market. Stopping *right* in front of me, he adds, "And that's after you tried to electrocute me. Don't think I don't know. I do."

"I heard about that. I must say, you think highly of me. You think I'm capable of electric anything, nonetheless making a wire look faulty enough to fool an electrician? Also, what makes you worth killing, anyhow? Do you think you're the person I like the least? Wouldn't I try to kill someone… I don't know… worse? I had a high school bully that broke my collarbone once. Now that's someone worth giving a hoot about." *Hoot?* I guess I'm a sitcom mom from the 50s or something. It keeps my mind off of the collarbone ache that loves to threaten me with pain echoes whenever I think about that moment, the boy's fists and weak, uneducated attempts at homophobic slurs. *I wonder where that girl is now… What was her name?* I refocus. "There was also this guy at a party… I guess you can put two and two together there." Until a moment like this, when I feel inclined to devolve my life into a list—often to make others uncomfortable—I forget the dark things people have done *to* me. Soon after they happen, I shelve them.

I notice a shopper that's tuned in to our conversation. His head is tilted down, and he's pretending to read a can's contents. His eyes are cut towards Isaac and me. I wonder how long he'll stay.

"I don't know *how* you did it, but you did." Isaac takes a small step back, rocking on his foot, antsy. He clearly listened to nothing I said. I rarely talk that much. So, I'm hurt. "I thi—"

I hold my hand up. "I'm sorry that happened to you. Truly. You got a bad lot with the wire," I start. *Bad lot?* I guess I'm going to sound like anyone but myself right now. "But it was just bad timing. And as for getting fired? You didn't really do your job well and were constantly rude to customers. I didn't make you do that. I didn't even work the day you were fired. I think you need to go home, sleep, maybe get a therapist to talk through some issu—"

I don't see his arm move. I feel the back of his hand on my cheek—a brutal sting as hard as a punch to my loose jaw and fucked nerves. The shock is worse. It's been a long time since anyone has hit me. I don't allow people to hit me anymore.

My eyes water. Isaac sputters. The eavesdropping customer rushes forward and grabs Isaac's arm. The man pins it behind his back and shouts for help. Pushing the back of Isaac's knees with his own, the man lowers Isaac to the ground.

This man knows what he's doing—not an off-duty cop, or he might have cuffed him. Or did it need to be worse than this?

Michael is beside me, staring at my throbbing cheek before I sit down. I tell him it's over as I notice his curling fist.

When I'm on the floor, slightly dazed, I just look over at Isaac. He's in a criminal's position, and it looks painful. It probably doesn't hurt him badly, but for me, I'd be sobbing.

Jamie rushes in, her cell phone in her hand. I shake my head. "Wait," I say.

Though her face is confused, she doesn't hit the call button.

"Isaac, I don't want this. I don't want police or whatever else comes with you attacking me where I work—a place that fired you. I don't want you accusing me of attempted murder for no reason or you being near me either," I say, not mentioning how bad it would be if anyone dug into his accusations. "How about this? You're going to leave, and I'm never going to see you again. If I do, I'm going to take out a Stalking Protective Order against you. You don't want that on your record, okay? For now, I don't want you to come back to this Juniper Foods or visiting Varetta Community Center." I'm not sure if he knew I worked there, but I have to cover my bases. "And if you see me *anywhere*, you'll leave. If you agree to that, you can walk out of here, and I won't press charges."

I tighten my shaking hands into fists, mimicking Michael, and ignore my buzzing insides. It's nothing like the electric pleasure I get from killing. *Why am I so anxious?* On the outside, I stay calm. Adela had to look into Restraining Orders and Stalking Protective Orders a few years ago, so I sort of know how they work. Most of the time, they don't.

At least with this incident documented—and it will be the moment he leaves—it will help strengthen any case against Isaac in the future. Though I have a feeling that won't be necessary.

"Okay," he mumbles into the scuffed linoleum his face is mashed into.

"Louder," I say. Isaac doesn't know why I'm doing this. He thinks I'm being generous. If he knew I was keeping scrutiny away from any of his claims until the Juniper Foods store tapes erase themselves—which they do every 30 days—he may have a different response. It's a terrible policy that should be changed *in 21 days.*

Michael squeezes my hand—a *future police officer* squeezes my hand.

Turning his face to the side, he says, "Okay, I'll leave you alone. I agree to your terms. I won't come back. However you want me to say it. I'm sorry. I just... I lost control. I've never hit a woman before. I don't know... *Fuck.* I don't know what came over me."

I don't believe him for a second, but no good can come of digging into his claims right now. If I ever have to file a report, though...

"Okay," I say, nodding to the customer. "Thank you for handling that like you did. You were great."

I no longer acknowledge Isaac.

After the customer eases him up and slowly releases his arm, the customer cracks his back. Pride beams off of him. Isaac rushes past us towards the exit. His bag of chips lay crushed on the floor.

Michael shakes the hand of the man who took charge, saying, "Thank you. We owe you a great debt. Your groceries are on me today, so stock up. Just tell them it's on Michael." He points to his name tag.

The man sputters a few words about it *just being right*.

"Nope. That could have gotten really ugly. I just want you and yours to be taken care of because you took care of mine," he says in the most Southern and cavelike way possible. Apparently, this situation has us both acting like strangers.

The customer nods and thanks Michael. "That's so generous of you!"

They hug, and the onlookers I hadn't noticed gathering earlier clap at the happy resolution.

"You two go home," Jamie says, as she shifts her pants to the left, using the belt loops. "I'll clock you out at the end of your shift. Love you both too much to have you work through that. Sorry your last day ended like this, Michael. Come visit when you can, though, okay? Honestly, don't be a stranger." She pushes her glasses up on her nose.

Michael hugs her. "Thank you for everything. Going to hug everyone, then take this one home," he says, hitching his thumb towards me.

Holding my chilly hand to an already swelling face, I tell him I'll head home now, meet him there.

27

leaves.

Itchy with irritation my entire drive home, I go on autopilot, trying not to worry that I'm coming undone. The sudden urge to pick a fight is Isaac's fault. The daymare of Michael arresting me as I pass flashing police lights on the side of the highway doesn't help.

I arrive back at my house and immediately change out of my synthetic, primary-colored work shirt.

Michael must have said very quick *goodbyes*. Because sooner than later, I hear his voice. "Knock, knock. I'm here!" he calls out as he knocks.

I hate it when people say an action while they are actively doing it, like sorority girls with *snaps* and anyone with *chef's kiss*. The only exception is *cheers*. Sometimes I believe I was born in the wrong era or culture. Being born wrong isn't off the table either.

"I'm in the bedroom," I call to him, trying to keep calm.

I'm laying across my bed in a worn-in white tank top and soft shorts with a gauzy robe falling off my shoulder. The effect is sexy, I'm sure. It's not for Michael. When he steps into the bedroom, it's clear he thinks it is. While his imagination has gone dirty, I'm picturing myself on a chaise lounge outside with a cocktail in a sweaty glass, ice *tink*ing against the glass as I lift it to my lips. There are clementines and pomegranate seeds beside me on a small glass table. Underneath, my favorite white platform sandals lay unbuckled, speckled with blood from a kill. I'm not in pain, just enjoying the memories of a perfect murder. It's highly specific and what I want right now.

Eyes darkening with lust, I could say the word and let Michael fuck me into oblivion. But right now, I would be far, far away.

"I'm in a bad mood," I say, balling my hands into fists. My fingers crackle like rice cereal.

"Oh." His voice is quiet, and he looks like he's been rejected. I suppose he has been. I suppose it's his prerogative to take it personally. "That makes total sense," he says, as if only just remembering the afternoon and seeing the swelling on my cheek.

"Yeah, sorry," I say, not sorry at all. *Why did I say it then?* I, a secret murderess, am not above the decades' worth of brain-washing telling me—like most women my age—that I should be sorry for taking up space. "I know it's your celebratory day, but Isaac kind of ruined it for me. Do you think I could just nap for a bit? Then we could go to dinner and have some drinks?" I wonder if my face will still be red or bruising.

"Of course. Do you want me to stay and cuddle, or?" The thought of his body curved around me turns into me pulling him apart and tucking myself inside his ribcage.

"I think I'd just like some alone time. Help yourself to anything anywhere, of course." I say it as if he's a new man in my house, not a long-time boyfriend who could ask me to marry him at any moment, given society's arbitrary relationship timeline. "I'll be out in a few hours. You can pick the place while I'm napping, or I can when I wake up." I reach my arms straight forward from the bed and make a grabby hands motion. "Kiss first." I want to say that I want his mouth, but the one time I said it, he made a face that said it made him feel uncomfortable. I'm saving the next few times I say it for when I *really* need or want him to get in *that* headspace.

Michael leans down and presses me into the mattress so hard I sink to the floor, through the wood, and into the earth. I wince with the force. For once, he doesn't notice. "I'll grab you an ice pack, then pick a place," he says. "I love you. Sleep well."

"I love you too."

After bringing me an ever-available soft blue ice pack, he closes the door behind him.

I curl under a cream-knitted blanket and a poofy beige linen comforter and stare at my hanging string of pearls plant. The slotted sun streaks illuminate the round, waxy leaves. Crystal had plants hanging in her window. I never stopped to consider if they were real and would need water. When Crystal's sister ran upstairs and saw a blood-stained comforter on the bed, did she notice wilting leaves in terracotta pots or find a bloated body in the closet first?

To calm my mind, I untuck myself just enough to roll up my sleeves. I open my mouth wide and bite.

Instant regret. Tears spring to my eyes. I unlatch my teeth and wipe the slobber away.

Just a few weeks ago, this was soothing. Today, the pain is unbearable, and I didn't bite hard. I can't think about that now. I don't *want* to. I can't face another disappointment.

Reaching towards my nightstand, I turn on the noise machine Adela bought me after I told her Michael snored when he had nightmares. She told me that beauty rest is important, and if I don't get mine, I look like shit.

28

ready.

Michael knocks on the door moments after I open my eyes. It's still bright outside, but my yellow analog cat clock says 5:39 p.m. That's what happens when you leave work early in May.

I yawn. Existing in my body is horrible on most days. But waking up to a cracking jaw and throbbing cheek is new. Normally, my face doesn't hurt much.

"You up? I'm getting kind of hungry, and I've picked out a place for us to eat. It's somewhere we haven't gone in a while," Michael calls out.

"Just waking up now. Let me change, then we can head out."

Taking my time to get ready, I stretch, wince, yawn, wince, stretch, wince, then crawl out from under the covers. I slide my slippers on with the speed of a hungover Sunday morning. I'm not hungry, and there's food in the fridge, so everything is okay.

Some of my curls smushed during my three-hour nap, so I fix them with the curling wand Michael says is my mini lightsaber.

I floss with minty string *and* a water flosser, brush my teeth, scrape my tongue, then gargle with mouthwash while I mentally sing the chorus of *Pressure* by Paramore. My mouth is clean and fresh and smells like an open tube of toothpaste.

I wash and moisturize my face, which was slimy with drool. The redness on my cheek has all but faded. As with me, more often than not, my pains aren't visible. At the moment, I appear to have had a dental procedure, as my cheek is only a bit swollen. I contemplate blush, decide against it.

A thin swoosh of eyeliner is all I can muster tonight. If Adela was here, I'd let her go ham. I'm just too tired to give much of a fuck.

My mother used to talk about women who focused too much on makeup, on outward appearance in general. She said they had little to do with their life and would make no great impact on the world. I've seen this to be false, but it's stuck in my mind. Once every little thing started taking energy I didn't have, once I started needing to choose killing or makeup, sautéing veggies or roasting them, I began to live more by her creed.

I take a while to choose my outfit. A pink and white floral maxi dress with khaki saddle shoes seem easy and comfortable. I grab my floppy hat in case we go to a nice patio and get to enjoy the last hour of the sun. The weather is perfect; it would be a shame not to. But it's Michael's night, so I'll follow his lead.

Beyond my sunny yellow door, he's shuffling around, slamming cabinets, moaning every once in a while. If I had telekinesis, I'd have one of those cabinets smash his hand so hard his hand bones would shatter. I realize that would keep him home and in need of my help. So no, he's better off just passive-aggressively complaining.

After I grab a tote and a cushion in case we go to a place with hard seats—*shudder*—I join him in the living room. He is sitting, unperturbed or flustered. Seems the cabinets banged themselves.

"All set." I hold on to my accoutrements and try not to laugh at myself. I look like I'm going to the beach.

One day, I'll be close to decrepit, carrying a duffle bag full of creature comforts when I go to a kill. There will be knee pads and a back brace, some cushions, a walker, because a cane can get knocked out from under me easily.

My body will give way with ease as a victim claws at me. Tender skin will peel away like a soft citrus rind, strip by strip, leaving stringy, meaty bits exposed. In the end, I will become the victim of my own crime.

Michael doesn't look at his phone to check the time. His eyes dart in that direction, though. "Great." His voice is clipped. "Can we take your car? I'm low on gas."

"Sure," I say.

This is our most nonverbal conversation in a while. Michael is upset with me. And I don't much care.

29

blend.

Moody and candlelit, Midnight Bistro is not Michael's usual style. His favorite place is called Thriller Burgerz (*with a z*). Everything on the menu tastes freezer burnt and leaves an after-taste of cardboard.

Had I known we were going to a date night restaurant, I wouldn't have dressed so casually. He's wearing nice jeans and a button-up, also not matching the locale.

I can't remember the last time he suggested a place with anything resembling a front-of-house. Yet, here we are. We're told there is an hour and fifteen minute wait.

I'm about to have very verbal feelings about Michael's lack of forethought when I hear a chorus of his name from inside the restaurant.

"We're actually with them," he says, pointing to a small fan club in the corner booth.

Three women and two men wave frantically when they see Michael moving into the dining room. They salivate when he's close and all jump up, filling the entire small walkway space between tables as they line up to hug him. One is so excited that she leans onto a couple's table and knocks their bottle of wine over. The elderly man eating a salad catches it with ease and carries on with the conversation as if his night hadn't almost been ruined.

I want to slice her ear off. *Hm. Jealousy.* New for me.

When the gaggle of humans I've not met settle down, I realize I don't fit at the table. The male Lego-headed friend offers to sit in a chair at the head of the table. I half-expect him to sit backwards. He doesn't, but he does look like he's sitting at the kids' table. The booth sits on a few-inch platform, which makes Lego-Head look small and foolish. I'm almost certain he's used to being the hot jock women go to for a quickie in between boyfriends. His probable embarrassment is equal parts thrilling and upsetting. Upsetting only because I don't like feeling uncomfortable, and men's discomfort still seems to cause a collective discomfort.

I didn't know Michael had friends, let alone female ones. One of them is wearing a sleek little black dress, and her breasts are heaving out for her practice run audition for historical soft core porn. A knife would slide through her thin skin like a sausage casing. She is clearly in love with Michael. It takes almost half the meal for me to realize that Heaving Bosom's boyfriend is Lego-Head, which is yet another thing that makes him look foolish.

The other two women are together. They barely speak to me —too lost in each other's eyes, pretending to read the menu, gushing over excitement to see Michael, or anything that doesn't have to do with me. They act as if they are Michael's closest and oldest friends. Yet, since we started dating almost four years ago —*or is it three?*—I've not met any of these people. It's a *them* problem.

Michael's second guy friend is picturing me naked—if his licking his lips is any indication of his thoughts. He's not trying to hide it, but Michael is caught up in Heaving Bosom to notice. I like what I see too, so I return the favor. Then, he smiles and introduces himself, effectively ruining the illusion. Waves on yellow teeth are secondary to halitosis.

All of Michael's friends blend together. Dressed in similar style clothes in neutral tones, moving only their shoulders when they talk, they become a smear of *human*. They are all *fine*.

I doubt I will remember much of anything they tell me well enough to recount it to Adela. Tonight will be boiled down to "Michael and I met up with some of his friends at Midnight Bistro." She'll ask which friends. I'll tell her I've never met them before. I'll forget to mention their race or sexuality, their unusual head shapes and large breasts, their bad breath and odd noses, their boring clothes. I'll forget to mention the way they look—or don't look—at me. They'll just be people I met the one time for a few hours.

Adela will forget my lackluster story about my night immediately, switching to a vibrant anecdote about a customer or person in line while she got takeout. And that will be that. They will be erased from my memory.

Until then, I must get through the rest of dinner.

They are boisterous, and I hate it. They may visually blend into the background, but audibly, they stand out.

I allow myself to become a wallflower, to observe. I order shrimp fettuccine, a side salad with raspberry vinaigrette, and a Cab. I listen. I smile. I consume a meal no one would write home about. I do not engage, so Michael stays the focus.

When one of the queer women begins discussing how many people claim to be in pain but aren't, I tense. I don't enjoy talking about pain or disability. She must not have noticed my pink poppy-patterned cane. The one I had to hook on my left arm when I shook their hand. The room isn't dark enough for her to miss it. But it's *fine*. Just like she is *fine*.

It's still odd to me, shaking hands with my right hand.

Why must I conform to the norm? I'm left-handed, so I want to shake with my left hand. Then again, that's asking people to conform to me. I'd rather not touch people I don't know and don't want to get to know at all.

Michael squeezes my right hand under the table twice. He always sits on the side that hurts the least. His hand squeezes are our code for *Everything okay?* Three is *I love you.* I squeeze back a *yes* and pick at the wilting lettuce on my plate. It isn't the best distraction since there are only two pieces left.

I can't kill her. I can't kill her.

I've been getting bothered too easily lately. I worry I'll end up a spree killer killed by a hundred of bullets in front of a diner somewhere. Wouldn't that suck?

"What do you think, Elizabeth?" the queer woman who started the conversation asks. Her name is Harriet, I think. But maybe not.

"Huh?" I shake my head and swivel to the expectant faces. I'm trying to buy time, come up with something to say. "Sorry, got lost for a moment."

"About Disability. So many people our age are claiming *invisible pain* these days just to get Disability. I'm just tired of taxes being raised for that shit."

Her eyelashes, caked in black mascara, stick together as she blinks. Flakes below her eyes look like dirt pieces, and I'm reminded of coming home from playing by myself outside. My mother told me that I should make friends, to not be like my hermit father.

I can't make friends with these people. I take a breath and look at my plate, hoping they will ask someone else for their opinion. I'm baffled that Michael didn't veer away from this entire conversation. He knows what I want to say, what I *will* say if they keep pushing me to talk. He also knows that it will look like I'm on a soapbox lecturing his friends. And this, the day of his dinner party.

"Pain is always invisible," I say. "It always comes from your brain, so no one can ever *see* it."

Pausing, I choose my words carefully to not become someone they talk about later. I murder people now. But I can't hold my tongue. I'd be an excellent candidate for therapy if there wasn't that pesky law that therapists have to report you for harming people.

I take a breath in and release it. Then, "For some people, a broken bone won't hurt, but a smashed finger can hurt for weeks. Nerves are complicated. Brains are still being studied because pain is extremely complex, and no one truly understands it, though they are beginning to." I try to keep my words simple, not branch to the medical terms I've learned over the last year. People's eyes glaze over when you do. I should know. "I'm one of those people you're talking about—the ones living with pain every day. I'm not ready to apply for Disability, simply because I enjoy buying stuff too much, and the government doesn't pay enough to rent a room in most cases."

That's not the only reason, not even in the top five, but it certainly is part of it. I don't want to discuss my personal life with the smudge of human that has probably already tuned me out.

Michael nods, encouraging me to go on. It's sweet, but I just needed a sip of wine.

"So I guess my stance—" I start again. "—is that if people say they need it, I'll believe it. I think we all should. There are so many hoops to jump through that most people give up just because it's such a hassle. Of course, there are exceptions, but those shouldn't ruin it for everyone. Otherwise, we shouldn't have any social gatherings for fear of a mass murderer shooting up the place or eat food ever in case it's bad and we'll end up with food poisoning. As a society, we should help; that's why systems like Disability are in place. No one is rigging the system to live in a fancy apartment in New York, thanks to SSDI. They are living with family, friends, and roommates and are still doing side hustles and/or racking up debt." I take a big, deep breath. "And with that, I step off of my soapbox and pass it to anyone else."

I do so hate going on rants. But that was still the cliff notes version, and Maybe-Harriet *did* ask.

Michael's friends have varied expressions, but the median vibe is floored. Michael, however, is beaming with pride. "Well said, love," he says. "What do you think, Joe?"

Who is Joe?

Lego-Head blinks.

Oh, him.

"Uh—um—I think…" His stuttering almost makes me laugh. I didn't say anything groundbreaking. "I think Elizabeth makes some good points." He sits up straighter, taller, trying to compensate for his short straw seat. "Scientists are still doing a ton of research on pain, so who are we to claim certain things aren't real? People will always game the system—any system—so we can't assume people of a certain age will fit that category. I think it's unfair. I mean, none of us could even list a tenth of the illnesses that cause chronic pain, so how can we know what does and doesn't affect people—our age, younger, older, whatever? Right?" He smiles at me. His teeth are straight, with little gaps in between each one, as if they never quite grew into his mouth. I love them. It's my turn to be floored. By his words, his teeth, and his squared shoulders.

Maybe-Harriet nods. "I love debates," she says. Her smile is almost genuine. If her eyes didn't move to my cane, even *I* would have believed her.

"Me too. I need to excuse myself to the restroom, but don't start any new and fun topics without me," I say, disgusted with myself.

What I do for Michael, even knowing I'll almost assuredly have to cut him loose one day.

30

pushy.

Standing in the small stall of the perfume-scented restroom, I text Adela. "One of Michael's friends is the worst."

Before I hit send, I hear a voice. "Elizabeth?"

I click my phone off and toss it in my purse. I don't know why I don't hit send first. "Yeah?"

"I'm sorry. I feel like I struck a nerve back there." It's Maybe-Harriet.

She doesn't understand bathroom etiquette. We are in a public restroom, and she's apologizing through a door that has a smiley face smoking a blunt sticker on it. Even nice places can't escape vandalism.

I flush the unused toilet and step out. Moving to the sink, I allow her to speak. She does, though I barely listen. Buzzwords like *opinion*, *hot-take*, and *challenging* are involved. I let them wash down the drain with the frigid water that's burning my hands.

Why do the taps in public bathrooms never run room

temperature or warmer unless you leave the faucet on long enough to fill a bathtub?

I wince at least once during the process, but I can't tell if Maybe-Harriet notices.

When she stops talking or pauses, I say, "It's fine. I just happen to fit that category, though I'm fortunate enough not to have had to apply for disability yet." The time could come at any moment, and I fear it will be much sooner the more I struggle to restrain adults or drag their limp bodies around their homes. It's imperative that I find a comfortable and effective method to kill people.

Maybe-Harriet's face splotches in the mirror. She turns on the faucet beside me and washes her hands. As she does, her jaw false-starts some apology or understanding coo or anecdote about a friend who also has a *thing*. She flicks water on her flushing neck, and I picture holding her face to the sink and yanking at her tongue with my fingers. With kitchen scissors, I snip at the meat of it. My hands tire before I cut all the way through. *No, that won't work.* Even if I was at my peak, she'd still be too squirmy for me to handle.

I break the fraught silence, and ask, "Do you want a honey butter? I make them myself." I smile with a hint of teeth.

Peeking out of the corner of my eye, I see a trustworthy woman, someone kind, with straight teeth and serious eyes. The bathroom lighting makes me look more exhausted than usual.

Maybe-Harriet's eyes get wide. I get it; it's out of left field. "Oh, that's so sweet. I'm not one for honey. The flavor is odd to me. Thank you, though."

I flash a fake hurt expression. At least, I hope it does, as I mumble, "No worries. Of course… Yeah."

Shuffling my feet, I move towards the door. I'll try poisoning someone else some other time.

"I'm sorry. That was rude," she says. "You know what, I'll try one. I always say to give things a chance, and it's been a long time since I've had honey. I'll try it after dinner and let you know what I think." One side of her mouth crooks up. She probably gives her partner this insincere smile whenever she gets a gift she doesn't like. "I've been wrong before."

"You could try it now? Maybe I'll make a believer out of you. I have a ton." I'm a used car salesperson, all pushy and rude. She'd be inching towards the door if I was a man.

"I haven't finished my food yet, but later would be great." She doesn't seem upset or suspicious, just ready to be done with bathroom honey talk.

This is rash anyhow. I've been rash a lot as of late, and I can't afford to spiral. It's hard to not see what would happen to her. There's not a lot in one candy.

I see her coughing so hard she vomits on her dress, eyes watering as she registers it being my fault. Does she run and tell the group, ask for help, or just stare at me in shock? It could be a failure, and all she gets is some mild stomach cramps she'd attribute to whatever boring food she's just eaten.

"Sure, of course." I open my purse, irritated that I have to give her a normal one because I can't hide the evidence if she takes it with her. "Here you go," I say, handing her a pink cellophane wrapped honey butter from my safe stash.

She regards it with curiosity. I wonder if it's the penny-candy feel of the simple, unmarked wrapping.

No matter. I'll try again another day, with someone equally rude and frustrating. Then I can watch. I would love to have another way of killing people that takes less effort. The more planning each kill takes, the more I see why some women just choose poison. It's easy and still gets the job done.

31

buckets.

Rick's Hardware is nestled in the Warehouse District. I normally shop at Drind's because it's close to my house, but I'm not looking to put up a shelf today. Though the house I was recently hired to stay at has a leaky faucet, I'm not getting tools to fix that either. I'm window shopping.

It seems silly, perusing a store for ideas, but after watching a marathon of horror movies, it was clear I needed to be creative. Many murderers are buff men who can drag two women by their hair while still holding a live chainsaw. Nothing about that is helpful.

The parking lot is full when I arrive. Saturdays are project days. I drive around three times until someone pulls out close to the front. My hip's bothering me so much from merely existing that I've taken the day off. Jamie thinks it's about Michael leaving soon and me wanting to spend extra time with him. *Sure.* Let's go with that.

As I walk towards the building, a woman matches my stride

in that way that makes it look like we're together. She turns and smiles at me.

Blue eyes sparkle as I take in her soft cheeks and stubby top four teeth; they leave a space above the bottom row and give the smallest peek into her mouth and white, gunky tongue.

Neither of us says anything.

Best not to engage. Suddenly, I wonder how Adela is my friend. I must seem like I have drastic mood swings—pleasant and caring about people to aloof and ignoring the world.

Inside, we both turn left. Noticing this, she pivots and goes right.

My mother told me when people do this not to get offended, that they worry I'll start up idle chitchat. Many people do, if not just a quick comment about the weather. I shrug, glad she left rather than be the chit-chatter herself, and take to wandering the aisles.

I survey each object I pass with the same scrutiny, not wanting to miss out on any inspiration.

In the gardening aisle, a sign about May flowers boasts that two brands of seed packets are on sale. I pick up one with two red peppers on the front and tilt it. The sound of rain on a sidewalk follows as the seeds tumble inside.

My cane must have gotten someone's attention because a young woman peeks down from the end cap to look me up and down. This is a problem with being younger and disabled. Being invisible was a superpower of mine for the longest time. I planned to use it to my advantage when I was ready to kill. I waited too long, tried to perfect what I am worse at than I would have been before. And now, I'm more visible than ever. At least I'm not regularly spoken to, just noticed and commented on, pointed at.

I go back to studying the wall of gardening supplies, letting the woman and her eyes do what they will. Beside the seeds, there is a pair of lemon yellow handled gardening sheers with matching gloves. They are eight inches and bowed outward like a capitalized *d* in the center. I pick them up, holding them—as intended at first, then in a stabbing motion. If anyone asks, I'm looking for a movie prop; normal gardeners don't use sheers like this. They cut through the air nicely.

A previous client—a woman in her mid-fifties who hired me to watch *two* dogs—comes to mind. When I arrived, there were five, and the house was disgusting. After a horrible three days, her check didn't clear.

Unsurprisingly, trying to reach her was an exercise in futility. Her number was no longer in service, and her apartment was up for rent. She could have been evicted, or maybe she was a ghost the whole time. Either way, I've not accepted checks since.

That woman had a flat face, thin lips, teeth with rippled edges that I always imagined would hurt like hell if she bit me. She wouldn't be on my list, even if I knew where she was. Still, I jam the sheers into her eye socket. Eyes can be injured without bleeding much. It's the skin around the eye that has vibrant blood. So I stab at her eyelids and the top of her cheekbone, leaving gashes in my frenzied wake. I try to shove the sheers into her temple. They bounce off her skull, leaving her screaming in pain, eyeless. My shoulder dislocates, though, and I'm left scrambling to find something to end her with. *Ugh.* That's too messy and painful. I have to be better than that.

Window shopping is good for me.

Moving through the next few aisles is equally eventful. I find a tool and go through the murder of someone I'll never kill, watch myself fail spectacularly, and stroll on.

No one knows that I imagined sawing an ex-girlfriend in half or taking a weed whacker to my childhood neighbor's stomach. They all just see a thirty-something woman in tight jeans, oxfords, and a multi-layered tank top *clicking* along, considering her purchase options or biding her time until her boyfriend is done shopping—depending on their mindset.

Wandering past the rows of screws, I see four-inch long wood screws. A nice option with requirements. A secluded or sound-proof place to tie someone to a table or chair is a must. Obviously, a sturdy drill can do the bulk of the work for me. I'd still need a new body. That's too taxing.

If only I could take the good old axe to someone's head. But I can barely lift an axe, let alone swing it with any precision. Hammers would be on the table if I had better aim. One inch off, and I'm hitting my hand. With my nerves the way they are, the pain would blind me. My intended kill would run for help while I'm sobbing on the floor.

I want to have good memories to take with me as my health declines, sure. I don't want to speed the process up. I need to find something that works *with* me, not against.

A row later, I see a rubber mallet. It has old country vibes that resonate with the me that visited my grandmother's farm every other year for a few days. I pick it up as I imagine the server that spat in my food, kneeling on the ground, blindfolded and crying. *No.* I don't like that at all. My wrist is already aching by the time I slide the mallet back on its metal hooks.

The next sections of the store are wood and doors and dishwashers. I loop back to the other side and head towards the exit, meandering through the rows I haven't been through yet.

Lightbulbs only remind me that the bulb in the house I sat for a few months ago flickered the entire time I was there, giving up on the final flick as I was packing my bag. After Isaac, I can't even entertain an idea involving electricity. Whether or not anyone listens to him now, if people wind up dying by electrocution, he may sound less delusional.

When I roam through the cleaning supplies, I think of how I could convince people to drink Kool-Aid. Nothing comes to mind.

I hear a couple arguing in a hushed tone about how to get up cat vomit. The man doesn't want to buy the expensive stuff, he just wants to send the cat back. The woman tells him it was only a hairball, and that's part of having a cat. The man reminds her he never wanted one in the first place.

I must turn my head a little because I bump into a paper display sticking out into the aisle—blue shop wipes are on clearance. The couple clams up, then the man snatches the cleaner the woman wanted. As he storms passed me, she mouths *sorry*.

The half-smile I give her will sustain her through the drive home; she'll think that someone cares enough to feel sorry for her. And I hope that's true.

Strolling through the next row is boring. There are no arguments or objects sparking my imagination.

Over the intercom, the back office summons someone named Jerry. The rhythmic beeping of registers, the cold floor, the faulty cooling system, the employees that rush out of earshot as soon as you lock eyes with them, it's all familiar. It's more like home than most stores.

Summer Fun items litter two seasonal rows, unorganized and unlabeled. A little slow to set displays up here at Rick's Hardware, I see.

Inflatables remind me of drowning. Though I've always imagined holding a specific man's head under water, enjoying the knowledge that it's all he can swallow, I'm not strong enough. I will not be that close to being overpowered again.

The sand pails grab my attention, pull my thoughts to a favorite historical figure of mine—Erzsébet Báthory, otherwise known as Countess Elizabeth Bathory, the "Blood Countess". It's said she believed bathing in the blood of virgins would keep her young, but there are debates as to the validity of that. Either way, plenty of letters document her crimes. If they are accurate, they are some of the sickest in history. Most too dark for even me to entertain. But bathing in blood is enticing. I crouch to see the buckets available.

A woman named Veronica—a high school principal, if I

remember correctly—hired me to house sit a few years ago. She had long white-blonde hair and beautiful teeth. I've thought of her once or five times when Michael's tongue was swirling and dancing along my clit. I imagined it was her lips that kissed my thighs, not his. She seems decent, maybe good even, given how she handled the insanity of the Hockins' case when one of her teachers was accused of murdering the other. On top of that, she can't possibly be a virgin. Yet, it's her neck I slice open, her blood I watch pour into the plastic green bucket meant for collecting shells and building castles. It's her teeth that let me put aside her goodness. That and the fact I'd never touch her never *hurt* her, that is.

I picture putting my hand in the bucket, grabbing at the liquid as if it's solid. The warm blood is thick, dark, silky. Like melted chocolate, I want to cover myself in it or suck it from my thin fingers.

That does it. It's calming, comforting, and comes with a tingle that's half arousal and half dropping from the highest peak of a rollercoaster.

Hello, self-awareness.

The child's toy bucket will not be enough. I suppose I will need a pulley system. *How the fuck do I get one of those?*

I'll have to find something else, some other way to sate myself and protect my joints. I don't see renting a container where I can drain a person like cattle being in my future.

With knowledge, excitement, and disappointment, I leave with nothing.

Several people watch me go.

32

clementines.

Jamie's voice rises over the bakery phone. "Do—don't answer that," she sputters.

I can't remember the last time she told us *not* to help a customer.

Her face is red and splotchy, and her bangs are inching towards her sweaty forehead. Our baker, Darrel, is leaving us. He's spent all day boasting about his new job at *a real bakery*. Those words have Jamie upset. If his opinion mattered to me, the implication there is something wrong with this job might hurt. Luckily, it doesn't.

Yanking at her ear, Jamie mutters a half-hearted congrats to Darrel, then turns on me. "Elizabeth, isn't it about time for your break? Please get off the floor." She's an angry extreme couponer the day after our expiration window has passed.

Jamie stomps off, disappearing into the aisles before I have a chance to snap back. She's in such a mood, I think I'd take an early lunch just to avoid her.

I shrug and wave, leaving Darrel to decorate a birthday cake with blue icing that tastes like it looks.

Exhausted and in pain, I shamble more than walk. As I near the break room, I see Jamie coming from the bathroom. She pauses, and I worry she sees me and is in the mood to talk about those feelings she's having.

I notice a new dusty rose lip liner drawn just a little above her lips, filled in with color just one shade lighter. Whenever she dips back into the early aughts, there's a reason. Either she's getting Glamor Shots or she's meeting with a person of import—for business or pleasure?

It's nice she won't have time to lament about losing a second employee in a matter of two weeks. Considering most branches of Juniper Foods have a high turnover rate, she should just be proud this one doesn't. Sensitive as she is, she takes every person leaving as an attack on her managerial skills.

She waves and rushes towards the double exit doors. They open, and her coifed hair *whooshes* backward. Since she's leaving now, without stopping to tell anyone, my guess is it's a lunch date that she's worried won't go well. Maybe another setup from her worried mother. If I were her, I'd kill mom, put her in a rocking chair in the attic, take over that rambling ranch house she has on the edge of the Dead Lands, and call it a day.

The break room is a much-needed escape from other people's baggage. I crumple into the chair nearest the door. I'm scrap paper, a first attempt drawing or poem, used and tossed aside. *True* relaxing often causes extreme pain, so as usual, I cannot fully unwind. I pull myself up by the shoelaces of my favorite oxfords and move like a marionette to the refrigerator.

Every muscle I shift for the next ten minutes is calculated. My joints scream as I reach or bend or sit or breathe. I shouldn't have taken a break at all. I need a new job. I want to kill again. I'm tired. I—

Sid cracks the door and peers in, saving me from thinking

about all my wants and needs that will go unmet. "Can we come in?" they ask.

"We?"

"Me and my girlfriend."

Didn't they break up with their last girlfriend—someone they supposedly loved very much—three weeks ago? Or is this the same person? That second of curiosity is about how far my caring goes.

I say *yes*. Nodding will hurt too much.

I don't remember eating my sandwich, but the bag is empty save for a smear of red jelly and two dots of peanut butter. The break room is like that for me—a space where I lose track of time and space.

Now, it's time for my clementines. Michael says it's unnerving to watch me eat fruit, that I pick at it like I'm a curious animal tearing apart its prey. He's not alone. I've gotten comments it looks like I want to have sex with the fruit, that I'm searching for gold, and some ask me if I'm going to eat it or just play with it. A few years ago, I started eating fruit when no one was around. There's a sense of self-preservation in the decision. The fewer people think of me when weird or uncomfortable or dark things happen, the better.

Only Michael and Adela have seen me eat fruit in over three years. I've gotten good at hiding my need to rip, poke, touch, suck, *then* chew. And now, Sid and some girl are threatening to ruin my streak.

Ce la vie.

Sid shows off the woman with them as I tear into the leathery flesh of the small citrus. I'm tempted to ask if it's Bring Your Significant Other To Work Day.

"This is my girlfriend, Sally," Sid says, swinging the door open with dramatic flare.

In steps a woman, tall enough to be a pro-basketball player. Freckles cover her face, dainty and everywhere. Long, dirty blonde hair is shiny and matted at her scalp. She has yet to give me more than a closed-mouth smile, which emphasizes her plump lips, so I don't know the state of her teeth.

Sid is a child in stature beside her. Unlikely pairs make for longest-lasting relationships.

"Nice to meet you," I say. "Sorry, I can't stand right now. I'm on my break."

Sid chuckles. "Elizabeth takes her breaks very seriously. Like, she gets food and tries not to move much otherwise." Something about the way Sid looks at me tells me they know more about me than they're letting on. I've always wondered what they see, what they notice.

Sally nods. "That's smart thinking. You've got to conserve your energy for the walking and the talking to customers bit." Even when she speaks, I can't see her teeth. For a fleeting moment, I imagine slick gums with gaping holes where they once were—a trypophobia nightmare.

"Sally gets it." Looking up at Sid, I say, "I like her." I lock eyes with Sally. "I like you. How'd you two meet?"

"May I?" Sally asks, gesturing towards a chair across from me.

"Of course." My neck would appreciate it.

Sally sits and launches into a story. Sid sits beside her, watching her every movement. They are smitten. My focus bounces between Sally's story, Sid's glowing face, and my unopened clementine—mostly my clementine.

Sally gives an Adela-sized retelling of Sid coming in to pick up dry cleaning for their elderly neighbor weekly for almost a year. She says she and Sid had been flirting for months before she asked them out.

No longer unable to wait, I jam my thumb into the center of my clementine. I nearly moan as the peel gives way.

Sally snorts when she laughs, and she finds whatever part of her own story she's telling me amusing. I smile to pretend I'm keeping up as I strip the fruit slowly. The rind pieces make a nice pile beside the three untouched clementines.

Sid adds a comment about Sally looking perfect the day she asked them to the movies.

"Aww, that's so sweet," I say, encouraging them to continue. This next part is when people think I'm strange, so if they're talking, I won't have to hear about it.

Peeling the white pieces of rind that cling on soothes me. For some, it's cleaning a dirty surface or unveiling a finished work of art. With each removal, the clementine grows more vibrant and exposed, juicier and supple.

Sally notices my meticulous de-stringing, as I have always called it. "I do that too. People hate it because *it's not bad for you.* But like, it tastes so much better when it's gone. Who wants to eat bitter white string, am I right?"

She smiles with teeth this time, and they are pearly and straight, with a chipped canine I need to run my tongue over. I want the story behind it. I want *her.*

I laugh with her, I think. I hope I do.

Before I can respond, she continues on with her story. She's describing their first date at an arcade and bad hot dogs. She won so many tickets that—

Sally has pinned me against a pinball machine. My skirt is up, and I'm aware of people walking by. Her fingers dance their way down my cotton underwear and touch and tease. Her neck cranes down to meet me, and she nips at my lip. Our heavy breathing is in sync. She slides two fingers into me. Her chipped tooth snags on my skin, and when she kisses me, the tinny taste of blood mingles with the ketchup from her hot dog. It brings me over the edge. I scream out her name.

Then I remember Michael. And Sid. I remember that I'm in the break room, and Sally is here for Sid. The throbbing arousal I'm feeling is invisible, as I've been told I rarely even blush. My breathing is normal. All the while, I've still been picking at the clementine.

Almost raw, it's so spotless, I pull apart each piece one by one, then line them up beside each other. Rarely do I display signs of Obsessive Compulsive Disorder, but it's clear here. I just have hints of it. Nothing like my father when he was around. But I don't talk about my father much anymore. He was weak and died early.

I choose the clementine slice to my far right first. I slip it into my mouth and let my eyes roll back, as they always do. Along the outside of the clementine slice, my tongue feels the almost unnoticeable groove of the silky sides, the rougher back. I wish this was Sally I was tasting. I push the fruit back and sink my back molars into it.

I know I moan this time. My eyes are closed, so I don't see Sid or Sally squirm.

I relish the citrus flesh shredding between my teeth, the juice bursting from inside. After three chews, I swallow and open my eyes.

Sid is still staring at Sally. Sally is smiling at me. She's stopped talking, I realize.

"You just made that clementine look like Heaven itself," she says. "Are there any more in the fridge?"

"Yeah, help yourself," I say.

As if I broke the spell, Sid stops gaping at Sally. They reach for their bag and begin rifling through it for something.

Sally's eyes take a moment to roam. She seems to take in my face, my shoulders, and land on my breasts, smashed under the same red shirt Sid is wearing. Her gaze meets mine, and she bites her lip. "I will, thanks."

When she stands, I do not look at her anymore. Sally is a complication waiting to happen. I want it, but I don't need it. More importantly, I can't have it.

33

splashes.

Michael spent yesterday packing for Police Academy, which starts Monday, so I had to pretend to be supportive and fold clothes. I was a cartoon witch by the end of it, my hands seized in achy, curled claw positions. He had to pause everything to microwave a rice heating pad. We watched a movie while my fingers became their normal, shiftable selves.

After the movie, he asked if I was okay. I wanted to tell him *no*. This has made me realize that a lot of my plans have to change. What I thought I could do is now unpredictable. I'm pretending too much. My hEDS is worse than I thought. Pushing past it will only work for so long. Tonight's marathon folding has shown me I need to be kinder to my body.

Those memes about disability have been right all along.

I'm glad tonight is another movie night. My hands still feel bruised. I don't know if I have the mental or physical energy to do much beyond facilitating conversation and correcting.

Last Thursday's movie night went well. We ended up talking

an hour beyond our class time. I had nothing to do, so it was fine by me. A few students even said this kind of learning would have helped them when they were younger.

I smiled and thanked them. I did not tell them I had no patience for small, screaming things that wanted to touch everything and needed to be walked to the bathroom. Pets were hard enough.

Tonight's movie is fairly intense, which I love. It's also suggested for ESL classes, so I'm still being responsible.

I notice that Jemma is not here again today. She's just going to be one of those people, and that's okay. I've got far too much going on to worry about one woman, no matter how much I want her mouth.

I shelve that thought and go through the list of content and trigger warnings. No one gets up again. Licia shifts in her seat, but that could be from the fact that hard plastic is uncomfortable to sit in.

Drive is one of my favorite movies. A classmate of mine in college has a replica of Ryan Gosling's jacket, and it took a lot out of me not to go all *Bad Seed* on him. "I told him I'd hit him with my shoe if he didn't give me the jacket!"

I hit play, and settle in to watch the film with the class. Planning my next kill here isn't wise anymore, so I may as well enjoy myself.

It's not long before I hear Wendell shout, "Ryan Gosling!"

"Ms. Dauphine's celebrity crush," Anita, the aspiring actress, purrs.

The class gets a good laugh at this but settles as the music tenses. I don't believe anyone says anything after that. Only the occasional gasp or pen scratch interrupts the quiet, intense, moody film. Even during the splashes of violence, no one stands to leave. Some lean forward.

Once the film is over, we have an intense conversation about Ryan Gosling's hair, moody films, what makes suspense suspenseful, unfamiliar words the students have learned, old cars, and one final swoop back to Ryan Gosling's jawline.

The podcast trio stay behind after most of the class leaves.

As it does whenever I see them talking, my heart races. They still seem so polite. It can't be me.

Instead of staying to talk to me, they agree to follow one another. *To where?* I miss that bit.

After almost two weeks' worth of them excitedly chatting, I still don't know the case they're working. I really should ask about the name of the podcast next time I see them.

34

overexposed.

Driving to work, I'm hunched over the steering wheel with sunglasses and a sweater. It's an energy of hungover with a body in the trunk that should get me pulled over.

Once I clock in, every customer gets maimed, slaughtered, coated in their blood or the blood of the person waiting behind them. It eases my stress a little.

I crush a stout man's face. He's wearing pajamas, stinking of morning breath and cigarette smoke. His basket is filled with freezer meals, soda, and sour cream. If I was strong enough, I'd try this in reality. I'd take the rubber mallet from Rick's Hardware and swing it at someone's nose. It would be satisfying to feel the cartilage give way. Would the skull crack? Cave in? Explode into tiny bone fragments that would end up in nooks and crannies of the magazine and candy displays?

The man pays with a card that has an American flag and a bald eagle on it. He leers as he waits for the receipt. I see him as one of those people with a mouth full of teeth—no ridged pink roof, just more rows of enamel.

Two women carrying a half-empty hand basket between them are too busy laughing to speak to me. They pull out two bottles of wine, three kinds of cheeses, two multi-packs of crackers, and a bag of grapes and place them on the conveyor belt. One of the women is short with a matching canine tooth that's small enough to still be a baby tooth wedged between the rest of her adult teeth. She rambles about how the book they chose for their book club. They're normally better than this.

Beep. Beep. Beep. I scan their crackers and grapes and push her off the roof. *Beep. Beep. Beep.* I scan the cheeses and look down at her broken body and the blood pooling under it. *Beep. Beep.* I scan the wines, and the computer prompts me to confirm that the customer is 21+. I ask for ID for no reason other than boredom.

They laugh.

I stare, waiting. They stare back, then make an *oh* sound.

The taller woman pulls her wallet out, grumbling. Under her breath, she says, "Honestly! I thought you were being sweet. Clearly we're over twenty-one. This is just a waste of my time." Her voice is raspy.

I push her off the roof too. This time, she has a noose around her neck. Getting so lost in the sounds of bones crunching in my head, I almost forget to tell them how much they owe the store.

On and on it goes—lambs to the slaughter. People come for groceries and leave victims of my imagination. Everyone is just temporary relief.

When I step out of the store, it's after 9 p.m. Yellow light washes over our still bustling parking lot. People in work clothes jog towards the front, deep circles under their eyes. They're desperate to get home. Others in pajamas stroll, as if they've got all the time in the world.

A warm breeze, like exhaust from motel ice machines, caresses my arm hairs. I stand by the car, leaning on my cane more than I'd like to admit, and inhale deeply. For a moment, my attention is on something other than irritation or pain or the future.

With no conscious thought, I'm going for a drive. One moment, I'm heading for my house, aware that I need another house sitting job to pay the rent. The next, I'm miles from the city. Amber streetlights become sparse as I end up in the Outskirts, meandering towards the Dead Lands.

Breathing easier, I turn off my air conditioning and roll the windows down. Warmth rushes in as I take advantage of the quiet.

Soon, only the moon and stars peek through the tree line and illuminate the two-lane road. I flick my brights on. A short strip of the road in front of me becomes an overexposed photograph. The rest of the world gets darker.

Up ahead, I see the shape of a person. I could hit them. They're walking on the wrong side of the street. There are no lights. I'm on my way home as far as anyone knows. It's fortuitous. It's a gift.

Speeding up feels natural. Right hand tensing around the steering wheel, I brace myself for the impact. My heart tries to break free of its already sore ribcage.

The figure becomes a woman. The woman turns, becomes aware of me. I slink down in my seat some. The brights must blind her. She holds her hand in front of her face for a moment, leans forward a little.

It's too late for her. I'm not stopping, and she's not moving quickly enough.

The thrilling thought of seeing her body hit the windshield causes me to press harder on the pedal. She dives to the right and into a ditch, escaping me. I whizz past her and shake. I flick the lights off, thinking of my license plate.

Oh. Oh no.

What have I done? That was rash, impulsive! This... this is how I get caught.

I take the first right I can, then the next right and head back towards the highway. The speed of traffic is almost twenty over the speed limit, and it's keeping my nerves at buzz-level. *I did it again.* I was thoughtless.

I can't try to kill people on a whim. I have to maintain a healthy boundary between my normal life and my nightlife so I can sustain both. My needs are more important than my wants. I must live in a preservation mode of sorts.

All I want to do is grab some frozen pomegranate seeds and pour myself into bed, forget my mistake, my almost mistake with Maybe-Harriet, my close-call with Isaac, and forget that I still have feelings.

I waffle between hoping the woman is dead, slipping into the ditch and hit her head on a rock, to hoping she is alive, terrified, and ranting online about some drunk driver who ran her off the road.

I'd be disappointed if she died without me there. I'm disappointed enough that her small frame didn't bounce off the hood of my car.

My phone lights up somewhere during my train of thought; it's Michael. I glance at the blinding notification. "I'm on my way over. Text me if you need anything. I love you."

I forgot he was coming over. I'm glad I told him 11 p.m., not 10 p.m. Juniper Foods is low on staff, and I wasn't sure if Jamie would want me to stay late.

It's fine. I'm closer to my place than he is, which is perfect. I don't want to explain where I was.

35

problems.

By the time I'm parking, my heart has calmed to a normal pace again. Michael isn't here yet, which is good. It would have been suspicious had he arrived before me.

I unlock my door and feel heavy. My fingers itch to text Michael, "Hey, I just tried to run a woman over on the side of the road and it didn't go well, so could you come over tomorrow when I'm a little less frazzled?"

I remind myself that he's about to go to the Police Academy. *In two days.*

I'm not sure I'm cut out for a long-term relationship. I don't see how I can risk it.

As I step into my home, I feel safe. My sanctuary, my happy place. Part of me wonders what would happen if I didn't answer the door when Michael comes over, just lock the deadbolt, put the chain on, and not answer the door. *What would he do?* Call my name out, try the key, call 9-1-1. It could get messy.

I've only just slipped my feet into my fuzzy bunny slippers when I hear the door.

I answer it, expecting an eyebrow wiggle or grabby hands; he's leaving on Monday, after all. Instead, Michael's shoulders are rolled forward so much he looks like the waitress I house sat as she was telling me this would be her first vacation in two years. Bags under his eyes that weren't there hours ago may as well be bruises in the blueish glow of my porch light.

"What happened to you?" I ask, hoping I can get him in such a frenzy he won't ask how the rest of *my* day has been.

"Wow, what a greeting," Michael says, with no hint of a smile. *Rude.*

"I'm sorry, you just look exhausted. It's only been a few hours since the last time I saw you, and you look like you've been through hell."

He sighs like someone who has actual problems. *I* could sigh like this, with pain, subluxations, dislocations, worries of getting caught, but Michael is doing *just* fine.

"My day was a mess," he starts, walking me into my own kitchen with his hand on my lower back. He opens the refrigerator and sticks his head in. "First there was traffic, then there were lines, then there were rude people, and—"

I zone out for a few moments, accepting my mind's insistence to drift back to the woman I almost hit. So reckless.

"—he told me they were out of soap," he says, closing the fridge door. He's holding a soda I never bought. "Can you believe it?"

I nod, having no idea what he's talking about.

"And then—" Off to the races again, Michael continues on to describe near accidents on the highway, cold food, and not knowing where something was in the mall—thus "having to walk the whole thing *twice.*"

I love the man, but his problems are privileged and irritating. Michael would be on my list if it wasn't for him being Michael.

"It sounds like it was a very frustrating and very long day," I murmur. Compared to mine—and honestly, most people's—his day was a cakewalk.

As if my understanding was all he needed, he sets down the soda and reaches for me.

Seconds later, he's taking both of our minds off of a stressful day and the uncertainty of Monday.

36

spittle.

The vacuum cleaner *whirrs* as it moves across the floor. I watch it bounce into furniture, see the marks left behind from years of the same banging day-after-day.

I think of Michael leaving marks all over my life for years. He left for the Police Academy two weeks ago, and now his absence has left me listless and questioning.

Adela's been busy, so I have no one to occupy non-working hours.

Juniper Foods has been wrecking me, and I wonder how long I can stay there. A year, two tops. I'm waiting to hear about one house sitting job, but I need more to afford my rent.

I've tried not to think about my next victim, but how's that possible? So many people can wait a year or more, biding their time. I'm ready to get back out there. I'm pretty sure I know who's next. But first, I need to clean.

Despite not being home often, my house always seems dirty. And despite Michael not living with me and being gone for so long, *man* still lingers in unexpected places, as well as the usual suspects.

The kitchen is my first order of business. I loathe ants with a passion I've never had for any person or place. It's easy to have lone scouting ants just crawling in between dishes, in cupboards, on the floor beside the refrigerator. So, I scrub and dust and sweep.

I gag when I open the vile dishwasher. Often I wash dishes by hand to destress and avoid bending down for every plate I own, but it seems Michael used it. He stuck two bowls of half-eaten cereal right side up and closed the lid. This is what draws the ants that plague me a few times a year—sickly sweet cereal and spoiling milk in a damp space. I empty the bowls, imagining what it would be like to smash the faux-porcelain over his head. It doesn't break easily, so it may just bounce off. I doubt I'd be strong enough to knock him out if I really wanted to. *I don't.*

After throwing the kitchen cleaning towels in the washing machine, I collapse onto the couch. I need thirty minutes of rest, maybe an hour.

Three hours later, I creak up from the supine position to finish what I started.

I suck cookie crumbs from my carpet, trying not to be annoyed that I haven't eaten cookies in weeks, but I *have* cleaned since. I polish Michael's fingerprints from the tables.

My room is next. I dust, I pick up clothes, and I rehang the ones that have fallen from their hangers in the closet. Michael's in here too, though why, I'm not sure.

I can't get to the bathroom before my hip subluxes and takes me down to the floor. I lay there—half-in and half-out of my bedroom door. Cheeks burning, I'm embarrassed. No one is around, yet I see more to this. One incident means two. Two means three. Three means I will have to stop killing sooner than expected. More means I will need that help Michael always mentions when he talks about us living together. I'm in pain and angry at my body's defiance.

Under the bed, I see a dust bunny. I decide to leave it and climb under the covers, sweaty and sore. I'll wash myself and the sheets later.

I wake at midnight, realizing that I forgot to eat for almost a day. Clicking joints into their anatomically correct place makes my eyes water, and I scream *fuck* a few times. Then, I get up. I can't sleep on an empty stomach.

I reach for my dying phone and text Jamie. "Can't come in today/Saturday. The pain is too intense. Sorry. Should be okay by Monday."

Within seconds, she messages me back. Must be working the late shift. "No problem. I hope you feel better. Just let me know about Monday as soon you can so I can get someone to cover your morning shift if need be." Then she adds a sun with sunglasses emoji. Jamie does not have a good emoji game.

"Thanks for understanding," I text back. I don't care, but pleasantries keep me in her good graces. This is the life of someone with Hypermobile Ehlers-Danlos Syndrome; my body is unpredictable.

Twenty minutes later, I'm able to heat myself a frozen pastry. It's gone in three gobbles, and I feel a little more human.

Before I go to bed and sleep until noon, I want to finish cleaning. It doesn't have to be a good clean. I'll just hit the highlights—orangey circles in the sink, spittle on the mirror, dirty toilet bowl.

I move extremely slowly and carefully. I have to save some of myself for killing.

Every time I look at anything I wonder, *Does this really need to be cleaned?*

Three small breaks, two glasses of water, and another frozen pastry later, my body has declared me done. I now have to accept that my home is as clean as it will be for a while. I take quick stock in all I've done and realize Michael is now gone from not only the city but also my home. Suddenly, it's like he's never been here. It's that simple.

It's almost 3 a.m.—the perfect time for being sad. But I'm smiling because I no longer have to deal with Michael's face shavings behind the toilet or half-eaten sandwiches left in plastic baggies growing mold while I'm house sitting. That is, until he comes back as a police officer.

Then what?

I waffle about Michael once again. After he becomes a cop, it probably isn't wise to stay with him. I should have broken up with him before he went to the Academy. The moment he became a Cadet. *A Cadet.* Honestly…

A life without Michael means a lot of things—sleeping alone, having no sex, fewer conversations, and no longer having anyone to help me on bad days. But it also means one less person to care about, allowing me to create a murder board—which I believe would be helpful in mind mapping my journey. And no one would be around scrutinizing me, my body, or my actions.

Like the day Michael asked me about my shiner. If he wasn't in my life, I wouldn't have had anyone who cared enough to push for a story.

There's something to be said about being alone.

baggage.

I sleep in until my room is feverishly warm. The fans have no effect on the June afternoon. I arrange them to blow around only me, so I cool down. The remainder of the day I spend choosing my next victim. By the time the sun disappears behind the neighborhood, my bedroom verges on chilly.

On my bed, wrapped in a blanket, I have an ice pack on my knee, a heating pad tied to my lower back, and a heating rice pack on my neck. Sprawled in front of me—all within arm's reach—are notes, photos, and the box of my house sitting Polaroids.

If Adela was here, I'd have her take a photograph of this with my Polaroid. The lights are dim, so it would come out dark and eerie. On the white part under the image, I'd write *working* or *plotting*.

Most of the photos on the floor are of Olivia's photography, some still dripping as I hold them with tongs close enough to the light my camera could pick up their contents. Though Olivia is no longer mine to kill, she cannot go on as she is.

I snap on gloves and wipe my fingerprints off of each print. I'm slow about it, not wanting to smear anything so they can pull a partial. But I'd also hate to ruin the print itself.

Devoid of me, I stick the photos—one of which has her name, address, and *peeping pedophile* written in shaky handwriting on it—in a wiped-down envelope. In the same handwriting, I write the address of the police department on the front. I stick three stamps in the corner to cover my bases and call it done.

Tonight, I'm going for a drive. I've got a seed to plant. I'm going to try my hand at setting up someone else. I'm a woman on the verge. I won't be eating or fucking my way through a country, but I've still got plans to find myself without a man.

Before I leave, I flip through the box and pull out the images from Crystal Keaton, Cora Stone, Olivia Penn, and my soon-to-be victim, Marian Jefter. I choose one of each from their selection—the more obscure one from each. A blurred photograph of Crystal's chipped stairs, the corner of Cora's broken picture frame, a pink smear on Olivia's glass table, and the foot of a metal bed frame in Marian's gray guest room. Those are the only ones I'll keep. I touch the others, petting Cora's lamp and Olivia's windowsill, Marian's broken mug handles and Crystal's clown sheets. They are too identifying. If I want to keep doing this, I can't have proof lying around my house.

I set them aside to melt them when I get back from my drive.

Tonight, I try giving the police a suspect. Both Olivia and Marian will get what they deserve—more or less. I hope that will encourage the police department to close the case quicker than usual.

Marian seemed fine when I first met her. Her teeth are straight enough, white enough. She has a sliver of a gap so small it barely counts, but it's hard to find gaps at all.

She was gone for two weeks with her husband and two children. Their idyllic home is large and screams *rob me*. I was there to make sure the lights and TV were on and a car appeared in the driveway often enough the home didn't look vacant.

At the end of those two weeks, she came home alone. She had one bag, and her car was no longer littered with multi-colored toys. I asked if everything was alright.

"Well, no, not really, Elizabeth." She tossed her hair back off of her recently tanned shoulder. "My husband rented a motor-cycle while we were at the beach. Some sort of manly thing or recapturing of his youth. Anyhow, he got in an accident." I remember being ready to give sympathy, but she didn't stop. "The fucker shattered some stuff. I'll be honest... Once they told me he'd never walk again, I stopped listening. I mean, I can't possibly love... What am I supposed to do? Take care of another child? He's my husband! We won't even be able to fuck the once every few months we were doing. Honestly, it's just not in me. So I left."

I probably blinked a few times, but it's possible that my eyes got stuck open. Even I didn't understand what she was saying, and I was still trying to learn how to commit the perfect murder. "Where are your children?"

"Oh, with him and the nurse. The nurse was eyefucking him like all she wanted was to be with some cripple. *Fine.* If that's her kink, she can take his baggage."

I wanted to kill her then. Only disabled people can call themselves *crippled*. Also, who dumps their children with a nurse?

"I want the house, of course. Before I left the beach, I went ahead and called my lawyer to get all that ugliness started."

There was lipstick on her teeth, according to my notes. The conversation feels pretty fresh, but that bit I would have forgotten.

"Oh."

"Yeah, I know. What a trip, right? I was wondering if you

could stay another two nights? I met this guy at the airport… He just moved in downtown, so I was going to go see his place."

I was so broke—*am still broke*—that I had to say, "Yeah. I don't have another job for a week."

"A week, huh?" She seized the opportunity. "Well, I'll pay you double if you stay and don't mention anything if you're called in by his lawyers."

I nodded, but I was crossing my fingers behind my back. There are only three people alive that I'd lie to the police for, and Marian Jefter did not make that list.

Her house is exactly as I remember—looming, excessive, white. The lights are all off at this hour. I don't bother pulling over. I open her mailbox, gloves still on, and slide the letter in.

As I drive away, I've never felt so good about a murder. I've never set it up so well, so far in advance. Once someone discovers Marian's body, there will be a connection between her and Olivia Penn. The post office person will have seen the distressed-looking letter being mailed to the police. They'll keep it in mind. When they see police surrounding her house, they'll have something to share. As long as Olivia wasn't in custody at the time of the murder, she'll be the prime suspect. And with just a few pictures, the police won't arrest Olivia. They'll have a little more digging to do first.

I head straight home, thinking I'm good at pointing the police in a certain direction. I just need to get better at the actual killing.

Or else I could be a vigilante. But where's the fun in that?

38

dining.

Adela texts me at 11 a.m. wondering where I am.

Shit.

We have a brunch date at Farmington. It's a nice dinner place that has brunch on the third Sunday of the month—and no other time. Adela put us on the waiting list a few months ago, so I *can't* skip out.

I message her back with an apology, saying it's been a rough morning, and I'm on my way. I freshen up and throw on the nearest clothes I have. I smooth my half-mushed curls into a stubby bun that's more messy than cute and don't look in the mirror again. I'm able to leave within six minutes of my text.

Turning right breaks my neck, turning left shoots an arrow through my shoulder, pulling up short to avoid someone who doesn't know how driving works is an onslaught of slap bracelets —only my back is the bendable plastic and my cream lace top is the rainbow leopard fuzzy fabric. Cleaning didn't use to hurt like this *a day and a half later.*

As I park in a miraculously available handicapped parking spot, I see her. She looks flawless, all modern in her white and turquoise floral jumpsuit with slicked back hair. Her scrunched face and the crazed swiveling of her head tells me she's been keeping track of the time. She's normally the one who runs late, so this anomaly will be something we laugh about sooner than later.

When I slam my car door, she turns to me and brightens.

"Elibet!" She waves wildly before rushing into the restaurant, leaving me to catch up. "We haven't lost our table," she shouts, half of her body inside Farmington.

I almost yell back that we might lose it if she keeps it up, but I just mosey along. The *click* of my cane gets lost under the *vroom* of an old Nissan with no muffler. *Sad, sad, sad-sack.* With a chastised-looking wince, Adela closes the door with her on the inside—at the request of one very flustered host, I'm sure.

After another moment, the obnoxious car is gone, and I'm opening the door to Farmington.

The ballroom-sized space is as chic as Adela made it out to be. Glittering glass, polished wood, bright white walls. It's loud, filled with the chatter of thirty filled dining room tables and servers moving like Pong pieces.

I glanced at the prix fixe menu. Brunch costs $68.

"You look gorg, my dear!" Adela says, spinning me around.

"And you," I say, wiggling my eyebrows. "Seeing someone after this?"

"Nope, just for you."

"Well, aren't I special?"

An irritated thirty-something with a starched white shirt and tie cuts her eyes to us. "This way."

"Thank you for waiting, dear," Adela coos.

"Sometimes it's hard for me to get going in the morning." I shift my gaze down to my cane, hoping it earns us enough points not to have anyone spit in our food. That's surely paranoia again. In case it's not, I'd rather be safe than sorry.

She softens a little and nods. "It's fine. I wouldn't care, but it's our policy—all-or-nothing parties. Just glad you got here when you did. I wouldn't have wanted to give your table away."

"Well, we really appreciate it," Adela says again, her fake smile plastered on.

Maybe it was the word *appreciate* or the smile; I'm not sure. She veers us from the empty table in the center of the restaurant to the booth in the corner. My smile becomes genuine when she winks at me.

"How's this?" she asks.

"Perfect," both Adela and I say at the same time.

She gives us our menus, pointing out the drink menu and suggesting a fruity cocktail that pairs well with pancakes. "Enjoy your meal!"

We settle in, and Adela smiles. "I was worried you forgot."

If this was Michael, I could lie. Men are so easy; women less so, which has been a bonus of being with a man this time.

Alas. "I had." I rifle through my purse, making sure I go in the safe zipper pocket, and pull out a pink cellophane wrapped honey butter. I hold it up as I say, "Sorry. My alarm didn't go off, and I didn't know what day it was. I cleaned a lot on Friday, had to call into work yesterday."

Adela gives me a reproachful look but takes the candy. "Calling in, huh?" She *tsks.* "When are you going to quit?"

"Um, when I can afford to do that."

"So, when Michael becomes a detective, then? That could be a while…"

I stay quiet, take the napkin from the table and place it on my lap. She notices, but thankfully, lets the conversation die —for now.

After we make our choices from the *this* or *that* menu, she jumps right in to telling me about her date from Friday night.

I listen and nod, happy for her.

She looks around the room, sniffs the sweet scent of waffles and strawberries. I know her, and she's practically drooling.

It's hard for me to think about that. In mere hours, I'll be killing Marian. I'm so close to trying something new, and Adela's dating life is just… not important.

When it's my turn to talk, I tell her about my boring life since Michael left. She thinks I'm devastated. Sure, I'm missing him already, but I'm seeing benefits.

I mention the podcast my students are working on, and to my surprise, she's heard of it. "I like to stay informed about local goings-on."

"I forgot to ask them what it's called, so I haven't heard it yet," I say, trying to stay calm. But if I'm as pale as a ghost, I wouldn't be surprised.

I didn't know that about Adela, my sweet, wonderful Adela. Perfect teeth, lips, hips, thighs. But I've found a negative. She listens to true crime podcasts. Honestly, those people are… a lot.

"It's pretty good," she says, not telling me the name of it. "Their latest case is—"

The waitress comes up with our food.

"So fast!" Adela says, eyes matching the size and shape of the plates in front of her. "Thank you so much!"

"Anything else I can get for either of you?"

Leave us the fuck alone when Adela is giving me important information. "No, thank you."

"We're good, thank you!"

"You were saying?" I prompt.

"Right," she says. Her face flickers with disappointment at having to talk instead of eat. "Some woman named Pe—"

Perfect. I no longer care.

39

uneven.

After brunch, Adela and I go shopping. She buys me a new purse that *matches everything I own*. It's not the best design for my life. I can't keep two types of honey butters in it, for instance. Only safe honey butters from now on.

She gives me a long hug before we part for the day. I know what pity from my best friend feels like now. She says she's here for me at the drop of a hat. Someone has to replace Michael, she says. I don't tell her she's better.

The moment I get back to my house, I pack to visit Marian.

Now, I'm here.

I've never felt so prepared, so confident, so ready. My younger self would be so proud. It's taken us a while, but we're here now. I tug on my new mask and glance in the mirror. Lime green painted eyeshadow begins above my eye and extends past drawn, wild eyebrows. Drawn hot pink lips are so wide they almost cover the lower half of my face. A squiggle over the bridge of my pantyhose-smashed nose obscures the shape, and three old-age stage makeup lines on my forehead complete the distortion.

Pleased with my reflection, I slip from the car and reach for my cane out of a newly formed habit. I stop, realize what I'm doing, and curl my fingers back to myself. I see it now: ground matter coating the bottom, indentions in the ground, imprints on the floor, maybe sounds that wake Marian and make everything messy. *No. Not today, Satan.*

I pop the trunk and smile at its near emptiness—a box of tissues and a medium-sized bag sit in the middle. Along with plastic bags and rubber gloves, I brought pliers. It seems high time to try collecting.

I stretch like an 80s mom work-out video, bending and reaching in the dark. Stars above me make the movements feel graceful, though I've seen myself in a mirror. I'm a backup dancer giving birth on stage. But I must be limber for my evening's activities. I cannot dislocate and tear something every time I kill. I have to continue to improve, like my ESL students.

It's 1:17 a.m.

I step into white, disposable protective coveralls and slip on a plastic face shield, both brought to keep me from needing to shower or try to clean blood off of more clothes. Tonight will be messy.

Marian living in the country makes this easier for me in most ways, but harder in one: early risers.

I've parked smack dab in the middle of Marian's property and her neighbor's. Nestled in between two large trees and a cluster of bushes, my car teeters on the edge of a ditch and a side street that connects to the main road. As long as no one drives down it, my wheels should stay on the right side of tipping over. *That would be a disaster.*

The sounds of the night cover most of my clumsier footsteps. The uneven ground filled with small divots and thick clusters of weeds shows me how tired I am. Halfway to her house, I lean forward on my knees to rest. Michael not being around to help me is turning out to be more problematic than I thought.

I'm worn out before I've even started. I can't reschedule this because I've sent the letter already. If I wait, the police might find her, knock on her door, and they'd quickly realize she knew nothing about it, thus crumbling any thought of Olivia being the murderer. Also, Marian's boyfriend is out of town. More importantly, I really don't want to. I have a good feeling about tonight. I think it will go well.

A bullfrog calls for a mate and reminds me I've been hunched over, my hand pressing into my thigh, for several minutes now. If I don't straighten, I may hurt more in the morning. Not to mention time is ticking down.

I continue my trek to her mud room's door.

My foot slips on a large, round rock. I curse the lone stone laying abandoned in between the grass and the flower beds as my ankle gives and cracks to the left. Though it's nothing new, it still fucking hurts. I breathe through the pain and click it back into place. For once, I'm grateful I have hEDS.

Limping and exhausted, the thrill and bravado I had getting out of the car has waned to nothing but pain. But no floodlights come on, illuminating the slow-moving female CDC employee with patent leather isotoners hiding in the bushes. I take it as an omen. I'll push through, just like I do at Juniper Foods every day I work or the many times I've showed up for friends and lovers despite hurting or not caring enough.

I've pushed through pain before, and I can do it again. Especially when it will sate a hunger.

40

marian.

I see her mud room door just up ahead. I'm about to get to the fun part.

When I reach the door, I pull out the old key and a lock-picking kit I bought two weeks ago. I assume with Marian dropping her family like a bad habit, she'll have changed the locks.

I've been practicing with a simple little kit I bought online, mailed to my neighbor's address, using a credit card taken out in my ex friend's name. She was sickly for a time, so I had access to her social security number and past addresses. I kept it all *just in case*.

I slide the key into the lock. Much to my extreme surprise, it clicks. I'm actually disappointed. There's no need for me to waste time picking the lock since it's open now, but I hope I get to use the skill sometime. People rarely think about changing the locks. It's shocking.

Stepping into Marian's mud room is surreal; it's nothing like before. The children's tiny rain boots, her husband's camping gear, even the family beach towel set is gone. The shoe bench is the only remnants of her old life. There are five hangers instead of eight which now hold a cashmere sweater, a rain jacket, a sun hat, a purse, and nothing. The last feels telling of what I'll find throughout the rest of the house—that is, if I had time to take it in.

Slipping my shoes off right outside the door, I decide not to look around much anymore.

I spent too long making my way to her house, taking so many rests. It's already 1:29 a.m. Twelve minutes from the car to the house. I think that's a time the tortoise would be proud of.

The mud room leads into the kitchen, and I'm pleased to see that the once brand new knife set I'd banked on using for tonight is still here. When I first saw it, it begged to be used. It's still shiny enough to show it hasn't gotten much use. I'll change that.

Gloved hands grab the meat cleaver. It's heavier than expected. It's basically a fat knife. *And yet.* I can tell that with all the work I'll be doing, I'll need both hands or I may dislocate a wrist. Trying not to be frustrated by my lack of physical prowess, I continue towards the bedroom.

Walking through the living room, I remember the massive gilded frame that held a print of her three smiling children in their Sunday best that hung over the mantle. It looked heavy enough to lodge deep in her skull if I brought it down hard enough. But it's gone now, replaced with more nothing.

Everywhere I bother to glance, I see more emptiness. She deserves this—bare walls, missing color, dust outlines of a family that loved her. Marian's choice ruined lives. She deserves what I'm about to do. With any luck, her family can move back into the house that her ex-husband almost assuredly paid for when he was the breadwinner.

I shove my pain and tiredness aside as my hand touches the banister. There is a familiarity that feels *good*, like I'm finding my footing. I'm getting a Crystal redo—upstairs with a knife, now upstairs with a cleaver. This time I won't come home messy, and hopefully, my legs will hurt less. This time there will be a suspect without podcasters providing one.

My hips burn as I traverse the silent stairs. I grit my teeth to hold back a whimper. I'll need a good long rest after this.

Marian's room is at the end of the hall. I push the door open, and it's soundless.

No one is close enough to hear her scream, but I don't want to hear it. It grates on my nerves. Loud sounds have also been known to rattle my head. I'd hate to get frazzled and lose my grip. Tonight, I am in control.

I sneak across polished wooden floors at the speed of a teenager sneaking out.

Marian doesn't stir. Her silver sleep mask, with a design of one eye open and the other winking like it knows what I'm about to do, is too large for her scrunched pug-like face. I had forgotten to write about how funny looking she is in the spreadsheet. I was remiss. Now it won't matter. She will be nothing but a memory soon—a memory, a Polaroid of a nondescript bed frame, and a single tooth. I've already fully deleted her from my computer, burned her three identifying photos when I came back from hand-delivering the police a suspect, and I'll throw her key from my car window as I drive home.

For a moment, I watch her breathe just as I did Crystal. Marian's chest rises into a shaft of moonlight and falls into darkness. Without meaning to, she has made her last moment a thing of beauty.

I stand above her, remembering botching Crystal's murder, focusing on how I can do better this time.

Taking a deep breath in, I clasp my gloved hands around the meat cleaver. It loses its heft. Now, it's an extension of my arms.

Her flat nose is my bullseye. When I'm done, her face will be erased, just as she erased her family's faces from her life.

I close one eye and raise the weapon up high, needing the

momentum. I slam my arms down. The cleaver slices through the air. The blade gouges into the bridge of her nose, and I gasp with pain. This way should have hurt me less. But it's worse—*much worse*.

Marian gurgles something incoherent. Her hands grope towards her face. She doesn't scream, but I bet that's coming.

The cleaver sticks a little as I yank it back. Her sleep mask comes with it.

Everything moves at a warped speed, both lightning fast and honey slow.

I swing again. Blood splatters on my face covering. Leather gloves slick with dark liquid would only make it worse, so I leave the crimson dots, allow them to obscure my vision more than the pantyhose mask already does. This must be an average morning for a person with shitty vision.

She doesn't roll away like Crystal, nor does she flail like Cora. Marian doesn't move, as if struck still by my presence.

Her face already looks mangled. But *her teeth*. I can't break a tooth.

I switch locations and aim at the base of her chin. Thinking of her neck as a chunk of steak, I chop. There's resistance. What little strength I have is failing me. Marian still squirms enough that I press on the dull end of the cleaver and jump, putting all of my weight into my hands as I land.

She stops moving. It's so very anticlimactic. It took *work*, but it didn't take *time*. I'd rather spend hours with someone and spend less energy on it. That may be why I dislike guns. The lack of time feels like it's a lack of care, but I *do* care about what I'm doing.

From my neck to my ankles, every part of me hurts—my hands especially.

Marian's lips are mush, gone the way of gooey. Her neck is an exploded hand pie, with golden brown still visible under the burgundy ooze that's leaking from inside. A minor cut has turned large, as if the slit for the pastry to breathe has become a gaping hole for the insides to go out.

I pull rubber gloves on over my bloody leather ones and grab my pliers. I put one knee on the bed for stability.

Opening her mouth with my fingers is a surreal sensation. Delusional though it is, I'm worried she'll wake up and bite me. Shaking, another part of me is thrilled by the instrument of collection in my hand. I see her sucking on her own blood, grabbing the pliers with strength she no longer possesses and leading the pliers to where they work best, pointing, winking, giving me the *okay*.

Latching onto the tooth is harder than expected. Slippery with blood and saliva, the small pliers slide off the tooth and snap shut. They pinch at her tongue, the inside of her cheeks. They grasp and grasp. I try another tooth and another. There's a sound akin to scraping a pearl against glass—a sound I recall from the moment before I smashed my friend's mother's necklace into a patio table for calling my mother a whore because for a short time before she died, she had no husband. A lot of dark secrets hid in our home, but whoring wasn't amongst them.

My shoulder aches when I bang into a tooth, trying to grab another. It's grueling.

The tooth beside the right canine is longer than the others. I gain purchase on it and pull back. Nothing happens. I wiggle like I remember my mother doing when my tooth was loose for three weeks but wouldn't fall out. Marian's tooth is more stubborn than mine was; it doesn't budge.

I tighten my grip. There's a loud clicking in my fingers. A burn follows. I've pinched a nerve. With all the pain I've put myself in, there is no way I'm *not* getting it now.

For almost an hour, I try.

I'm panting from exertion. With one odd twist, I yank my shoulder out of its socket. I don't have time to put it back in, so I just leave it.

I manage to chip two pieces off no larger than something one could break while eating a particularly hard banana chip.

The sun is coming up.

I know now that I won't be able to have her teeth—her teeth or anyone's. That's just another thing I can't do, can't have. I'm forever having to make concessions. First a cane, now no teeth.

I've decided not to cover anything up. I guess I want to see what happens if I just *don't*. Will they make connections between her and Crystal, given they both died bloody in their bed? Will they connect a house sitter from years ago? Or can I go about my business and save some energy?

I can't imagine Marian won't make the news, with or without me trying to buy myself a day or two worth of time covering her or rolling her under the bed. This became more brutal than planned. Or at least, it *looks* like it was. She was gone long before the worst of it.

If only I had a partner. We could hide this, clean it up, and dump her body elsewhere. But with Michael becoming a police officer, it feels unlikely I'll ever be able to count on him for that. And Adela wouldn't in a million years; she's too squeamish and just *too good*. I wouldn't want to ruin her.

Oh, well.

I step out of blood-spattered protective coveralls and take off the bloodied plastic face shield, wrap them and my rubber gloves in a plastic bag and shove that into my duffle.

On my way out, I check the mirror to make sure no part of me can be seen. I'm still just a person with an obscuring panty-hose mask and no shoes.

As I slip out of the mudroom once more, I grab my shoes but leave the mask on. I wobble back to the car that… hasn't been tipped into the ditch. An immense relief. I toss the bag with the hazmat suit and both masks into the space with the extra tire and pour myself into the driver's seat. *I can drive home without passing out.*

Despite the extreme disappointment of not getting Marian's teeth, by the time I'm halfway home, I'm ecstatic. Turning off the part of my brain that tells me my body will fail is usually hard. But I killed Marian, no one saw me, and I hand-delivered Olivia to the police. That was a motherfucking success, a home run, perfectly al dente pasta. It's proof I can do this, that my practice is paying off. A *big victory* if ever there was one.

Turning onto my street, I yawn. I have time to take a nap before work, which is much needed. Maybe, while I'm sleeping, I'll dream of what I want to try next.

41

high.

Going back to normal life has been like pulling teeth. Probably because that's partly why I hurt so badly. It's been almost a week and a half, and the inside of my shoulder burns and subluxes if I move quickly.

I go to Varetta Community Center extremely early because of my snail speed. When I arrive, I see a newspaper on the front desk. Marian's face is in black and white, splitting the front page with Olivia's. I don't smile, because that would be abnormal. Skipping would also not be great. I got away with it. I knew I would, but there's something to be said about seeing it in the papers.

The only thing keeping me from floating on Cloud 9 is the fact that killing Marian is still physically clinging to me. It's worrisome. I'm not thinking about it. Just like I don't think about what kind of job would be better suited for someone who shouldn't be on their feet for hours at a time. In the end, neither answer will lead to a change in my life.

Putting the usual paperwork and snacks on the desks for my students today hurt less than it did last week, but I would swear bull riders' hands feel like this regularly.

Now, I'm trying not to move any muscle at all so they will calm themselves. Today is a reading day, but I'll be sitting in the chair behind the desk anyhow.

Wendell is finishing a story about a young glass blower who wanted a refund because the leather apron wasn't melt-proof.

He swivels his head back and forth between me and Licia as he recounts, "I said, 'It wasn't *explicitly* said, no, but it's leather. Animals can melt.' They left and said I would get one star."

Explicitly was in last week's poem. Though he'd heard it and understood it already, the pronunciation has been hard for him. We worked on it for a few minutes after class. He thanked me *explicitly* on his way out. Seems he's incorporating it already.

Licia laughs. "Stars. Why we care? Arbitary things." *So close!* Licia blows a raspberry, then laughs. "Only one person. You did good, Wendell."

"You did." I chime in from the front of the class. "I'm proud of you for using the poem's words already. Speaking of... Licia, it's *arbitrary,* not *arbitary.*" I emphasize the *r.*

She waves me off. "I know, I know. Licia knows these things."

I smile. My students are so good, so pure. I meet so few of these people in my everyday life, people that bring joy to the world and their families, offer hope to new generations that a brighter future is possible if you put your mind to it. I can't imagine killing any of them. It's not that I can't picture it, because driving an ice pick through Wendell's skull has flitted into my mind. But I would never choose them. If everyone were like these kind adult learners, I wonder if my urge to kill would have never appeared. Did it come from irritation at stupidity? Or is it my DNA? Nature versus nurture—the eternal chicken and egg question.

I remember not having many scruples as a child—when I first

thought killing might be worth exploring. There was a lot of darkness around me, and I wanted to get it out. Now killing goodness gives me pause.

Everyone is settled. Even Licia and Wendell have slid into their seats. They are all looking at me expectantly.

I wonder how long we've been like this—having a stare-off I didn't know about. It's my turn to talk, so I should fix the awkward silence.

Recounting Marian's murder has almost slipped out of my mouth at least five times since I killed Marian. This moment is no exception. *Ugh, I'm tired. My body hurts because committing the perfect crime is hard work—especially when you are physically disabled.*

I start with my usual *hellos.* I tell them about the poems we'll be reading from and ask them if they have questions before we get started.

As usual, they don't. They're the group who asks as they go, not the group that pretends they can anticipate what will come next.

I start the popcorn reading, ignoring the curious looks I get when I don't stand.

I'm still on a high despite the extra pops and snaps and *better not move*s. Killing again, capitalizing on my momentum, that's what I want. That's not how killing works. It's almost the opposite. I've got to lie low or ruin my accomplishment. I also need more rest. So hard to do that when I'm seeing improvement. Like asking the people in the course to not use their new words yet. Wait a while, let it all sink in. Feels impossible.

Just like avoiding the local podcast ended up being impossible. I could only hold out for snippets for so long. I was making myself sick. I finally gave up, started listening.

They are still looking into Percy Reece. Apparently, her mother hated her from the get-go. Poor thing had the name Percy, *then* someone carved a heart into her cheek.

I expected a switch to Marian, given the splash the case is making. But their prime suspect is Olivia Penn—*who would have guessed it?* She's being investigated for multiple counts of child molestation, child endangerment, child pornography, the list goes on. Seems open and shut.

Let's hope the police believe that too.

The students move seamlessly from one to the next. So far, no questions. I'm on a roll.

42

watching.

It's been three weeks since much of anything has happened in my life. I've been on the same damned schedule. It was bad before, but now I'm *hard up* for money. At the drop of a hat, I get a call. There's a gig that will pay for the next five months of my rent. It's a two-month job, which is extremely unusual for me, but not unheard of.

A wealthy older man needed someone to watch his nine-year-old chocolate lab, Choco, and five-year-old tabby, Taffy. He decided to *take a trip*. If he'd said he was traveling to eat people meat, I would have just asked for a doggy bag. No big deal.

Choco and Taffy are both plump. They eye me from their respective curled up positions in the living room as I walk over the threshold. For once, animals *are* a good judge of character.

The house is uncomfortable, all sharp edges of dated steel and glass furniture with no cushions or blankets in sight. Someone has watched a few too many 80s movies about the wealthy. I drop my bag by the door and wander.

I didn't meet the homeowner or come to the house beforehand. He contacted me by recommendation (as most of my clients do nowadays) and offered me an ungodly amount of money to start immediately with no haggling or asking my rate. He told me about his wanderlust and said he had to follow his gut.

It must be nice to be able to follow a midnight travel craving.

A lot of things I can imagine, but honestly, that's not one of them.

Five closed doors, a living room, two bathrooms, a kitchen, a pantry, a screened-in patio, and a backyard with a pool—that's his house. If I was a different, more social human, I may be inclined to have a party.

I wonder what he'd say when he saw that. He has cameras everywhere. Little blinking nanny-cams hidden in odd places and tucked behind sculptures no sane person would risk touching. I know they're there, even though he didn't tell me about them, because the eerie feeling of being watched follows me throughout the home. It's especially prevalent in the museum-style living room. Its white walls and aboriginal art lit by small overhead lights should not make my skin crawl. And yet.

I have the urge to grab a kitchen knife and stab at the walls. The plaster would bleed, as if it was a living being watching me, not some HD spy camera.

It would be challenging to stay here if I didn't need the money.

There's no *don't ask, don't tell* agreement like with the Vickersons. I can't flaunt a bloodied shirt or dispose of a pantyhose mask speckled in blood in his garbage. I want to convince myself that someone watching me isn't creepy or sexual, that me in a bathing suit won't end up on some porn website as a teaser for what goes on in his house when he's home, but I can't. No part of me will be able to relax. Already sore and angry muscles constrict and cause more pain, thinking of my breasts bobbing in cool, chlorine water while some man behind a screen jacks off wondering how much I cost—because to him, everything is for sale.

I rarely worry about men like that. I seem to have less fear than the average person. But a healthy dose of paranoia and the illegality of my after-hours activities change that.

There are a lot of possibilities for my four Polaroids here, so I need to investigate before I can decide what's worthy.

I start with the kitchen and pantry. It screams *rich bachelor*, filled with booze and takeout menus.

The first room is a stock movie library. Books with red spines serve as a backdrop for leather, shiny wood, and a fireplace. Sadly, he's forgotten the globe and bar cart.

A guest room across the hall is littered with replica master paintings and statues.

When I open the next door, a wet dog accosts my nose. It's Choco's very own room, complete with a small primary-colored dog jungle gym filled with enough toys he can wear himself out. I'll usher him in there when he gets rowdy. But Taffy has not been left out. Her room is next door. It has a kitten smell, even though she's grown and the litter boxes are clean. It, too, is an absurd-colored haven.

Whatever may or may not be going on with the man who hired me, he loves his animals. Too much, I think.

The fifth and final room is locked. His bedroom, I assume. I want to take photos of what's inside his closet, look for dirty secrets or the hidden dark parts of him. But eyes linger on the back of my neck.

I go back and grab my bag to do a minor unpack in the guest room. Though my stay is two months long, I don't plan on getting comfortable.

Thirty minutes later, I make a grocery list and feed the pets. They don't jump up or pester me while I fix their food because they don't want to be in the same room as me. I like them.

When they do finally ease into the kitchen, they eat slowly and silently.

Once they've finished and curled back under their respective tables, where clandestine beds lay in wait for good animals who blend in with bad aesthetic, I pull out my Polaroid camera.

Number one is the crack between his door and the floorboard —a reminder of the hidden secrets I slept near. I maneuver my way to the floor to take the photo. On my stomach with my legs contorted like a frog, I look as if I'm trudging through mud under barbed wire.

Hm. Making an obstacle course for my victims could be entertaining. *Saw, Hunger Games, Squid Game, American Are You Scared Yet.* There is already a blueprint.

I think of the energy I'd need to accomplish something like that. *No.* I doubt I could finish all the shopping. Add in the setup needed to make it good enough, *hard* enough, and I'm dead before they are.

Getting up from the floor involves a lot of *oomphs* and *cracks.* I stretch for a few moments before I continue.

After a complete investigation of Choco's stinky room, I photograph a claw mark dug deep into the wall. Like my first kill, it has a raw, frenzied energy—an unintentional, but unavoidable consequence of letting oneself go.

One of his bachelor's kitchen drawer is my third Polaroid. It's a pile of ketchup and soy sauce packets, two plastic forks, a metal spoon, and three steak knives. An ex-girlfriend had a kitchen drawer like this, but under the remnants of to-go orders and mismatched silverware, she had a plastic bag full of flash drives. Each contained incriminating photos of a different prominent member of our community—from politician to deacon. At any given moment, she would get a text with an address. I remember two times she interrupted dinner so we could go back to her place and grab one. We dropped it off on a dumpster in an unlit alley. I broke up with her when a soup kitchen coordinator committed suicide. There were reports that someone threatened to expose her for giving marijuana away to houseless people in pain. I told my ex that I couldn't be with someone who blackmailed decent people. She thought I was too pure. I thought she was weak. She should have taken a hit out on half of the people she had flash drives for. I haven't thought about her in a long time.

As I shake her away, I snap my final photograph of a statue of a nude woman clutching a sheet. Her scuffed face shows the brass is a façade. It makes me wonder how much of everything else in this house is too.

I order Cantonese food, because I didn't know I could have that in Janes.

Semi-settled on a semi-soft sofa, I open my laptop. It's been a month since Marian, and I'm itchy, hungry for a new kill. I haven't seen Michael, haven't had police officers bang on my door. I wonder if I really need to wait any longer.

I think I've chosen her—a woman named Yasmine Morales. I still have research to do, and maybe I could try for slow and steady this time. Who knows, maybe I'll love that? It will give me time to make sure I cover my bases like I did for Marian. I can commit the perfect crime twice, three times, for an entire lifetime, should I want that. Which, of course, I do.

I wish I hadn't thought about being watched. Now I worry he'll see Yasmine's name or photos of her and her girlfriend, her girlfriend and her girlfriend's husband, her address and car make and model.

Instead of risking anything, I pull up a movie I've been wanting to watch and hit play. Tomorrow, I'll spend some time at my place. I'll feel free there.

43

notes.

A bottle of wine and large espresso mug in hand, I'm ready for an early afternoon at home. The pain has been getting to me a lot lately, so I need to relax a little away from possible prying eyes in one of the few ways I can.

Juniper was slammed all morning, so the fact it's only three in the afternoon and overly sunny is not a deterrent from me finishing this and at least one other bottle I bought on clearance last week.

Just as the vinegar scent of cheap red wine hits my nose, I hear three knocks and a voice at my door. "Surprise!"

It's Michael.

He's home. He's visiting. He's actually here—here because I sent him texts about the weird vibe at the house I'm sitting for, and he took that as an opportunity to come see me.

My heart skips a beat. It's not just for the sound of his voice. Right now, there is a stack of true crime books on the couch, a photo of Yasmine in the window of her house with her girlfriend on my kitchen counter, and sticky note ideas of ways to kill people strewn in a semi-circle on the floor. My hopes laid bare are the antithesis of why Michael and I will be at odds in our relationship today, tomorrow, *eventually*.

Whether or not he's happy waiting, I make him. I stack the books under the kitchen sink, silently cursing as I knock over a half-open wood glue bottle. I foresee an impossible mess when I come back. Quickly, I gather the sticky notes and photo.

"Elizabeth? Is that you? I'm using my key in ten seconds!" he shouts. I see the shadow of his shoes under the poorly insulated front door.

I'm glad he counts down. Shoving the notes and photo under the mattress, I call, "I'm coming! I'm coming!"

Rushing to the front door, I hold my stomach and hunch forward. Without looking at anything in particular, I unlock the door, pull it towards me, and walk away as he follows me in. Out of the corner of my eye, I see his arms outstretched. I'll hug him after we settle, after I lie.

"Sorry, love," I say. "My stomach has been acting up, so I've been on the toilet. I heard you shouting, but I couldn't exactly respond. I was trying to text you, but I couldn't even do that."

He pulls me into his arms, the scent of french fries and aspartame clinging to him. "So sorry to hear that. Sounds like a rough day. Let's go lie on the couch." Michael's voice is laced with disappointment, but when I look into his eyes, he hides it.

I'm smart enough to know his tone was a choice. I let it slide, as I have no interest in engaging more than I have to.

"We'll just stay in," he coos at me, as if we officially decided to do *anything* together, as if I said I'll try to rally for him. "I'm here for you, after all," he adds.

At the same time, I'm mumbling, "Yeah, I'd planned to do that." Mentally, I motion to my pink tank top and soft shorts with moons and stars on them—my favorite pajamas.

He surprised a girlfriend with a chronic illness, so any

outcome, including, *"Um, that's fine, but I can't be touched or jostled,"* should be expected. No illusion of wellness lives between us. I've kept him in the loop of how I've been feeling. Sure, he doesn't know that killing Marian is *why* I feel worse. Michael knows I'm not doing well is what it boils down to. Most days, I appear normal—to the world, to him, to myself even. If I'm honest, I'm just not. My hEDS makes itself known more and more with every long shift, every drive, every kill.

Michael slips his arm around my waist and leans in to kiss me. After three dry kisses, he walks me to the couch and plops down, patting the seat beside him.

"I've missed you," he says.

"Me too. It's been weird without you."

The sentiment pleases him, but as I settle, he eyes the dusty side table, the two bottles of wine, the large cup, a discarded cup from yesterday I haven't washed yet, then me.

I remember to clutch my stomach. Easing myself onto the sofa is only partially for his benefit. A lot of me aches. Once I'm beside him, there's a rush of panic. I've been getting better about calming panic and paranoia. I've been on Cloud 9, despite my pain, because Marian's murder was a smash hit.

Thing may have just gone sour.

"So…" he starts.

I'm having trouble thinking. If I tried to speak, it would come out in fragments of thoughts that would probably give me away.

Stuck to the bottom of Michael's running shoe is a mini orange sticky note. It could say anything: *Serrated knife to the throat from behind; Bricks in a lake; Zodiac reenactment; House fire* —or any of the other twenty-three ways I came up to kill people, most of which are bad, too hard, and would have Yasmine overpower me or get me caught easily. There are no bad ideas.

I must stare at it for too long. Like many people who get caught, stupidity is my downfall.

Michael looks down at the floor and sees the note. "Oh. What's this? Didn't mean to step on a project or something."

There is no visible project, so he knows he hasn't. *What's with him today?* I think I should have asked him about the Academy by now. Didn't I tell him I felt bad? Lie or no, that should have gotten me off the hook. I rarely force myself to rally for him—even when I feel good. Why would he expect fanfare because he's visiting?

The party. Maybe I set new expectations of how I would support him with the going away party. Well, damn.

Before I realize it, Michael is reaching for the sticky note. There are some people who wouldn't read it, some who would ask if the person whose house they were at wanted it back or if it was trash, but I've only heard about those people. Michael, Adela, literally everyone I work with does not fit in that category. They are nosey. They're like me.

He pulls it from his shoe and flips it over. The ocean roars in my ears. *This is it.*

"'S.O. too?'" he reads, his eyebrows raising in question to the question.

"I was brainstorming a birthday party for Jamie. She hasn't said anything about a significant other yet, but she is on a lot of dating apps now. And last week, she left the store all done up—lip liner and mascara. So maybe she's seeing someone on the sly for now." I couldn't be happier that I was lazy and didn't write *girlfriend.* Jamie is only interested in men, so this could have gotten more complicated.

"When is her birthday?" His hand reaches for mine. When we interlace fingers, he squeezes.

"Not for two months, but I've been bored since you left." I do not know when Jamie's birthday is exactly, just that it's early fall. The timeline is close enough.

He nods, releases his death grip on my hand, and kisses my temple. *For fuck's sake.* I think he was imagining me and someone other than him tangled in my sheets, making inhuman noises while I jostle a dislocated hip back to where it belongs and orgasm at the same time.

"I'm sorry you've been bored. I should text more." The way he says it reminds me of his apology when I told him about the dishes in the dishwasher, the reek of rotting food and spoiled milk. It was equally underwhelming.

"I understand. You're busy. Why don't we just go get a bite to eat and you can tell me all about the Academy?" I smile as brightly as I know how.

His face screws up. "But your stomach..."

"Things seem to be okay at the moment. I want to stretch my legs and hear about your adventures." I pat his thigh—watch his eyes roll back in his head at the motion, an exaggeration if ever I've seen one—and stand. I'm a skip away from asexual at the moment with the noise in my head and the pain in my body, so all it does is irritate me.

"Yeah, if you're sure. That would be great. I have *so* much to tell you." He stands and stretches. His navy polo rides up to expose his stomach. *Does it already look more defined?* When he notices me looking, he winks. "Stories first, sex second," he says, already forgetting about my fake stomach problems. He's probably wishing I'd jump him right now.

Instead, I rush to the bedroom and swap pajamas for a white summer dress. In minutes, I'm leading him to the front door.

44

petulant.

In no shock at all, we end up at Thriller Burgerz. Since my stomach is supposed to be hurting, the fact I can't eat anything here shouldn't be problematic. Authenticity to my IBS flare-up comes as I get slightly nauseous from burnt flesh and ketchup.

Michael talks and talks. Eats and eats.

The electronic rock dubstep nonsense that's playing over crackling speakers isn't enough to drown him out, but I feel like an elderly person wanting to scream at their grandchild to *turn the racket down.*

Unenthused by Michael's story about getting a nod from a fellow student, I switch my attention to the other patrons. A fat man is ordering a salad and ten burgers for a table of eight, and a woman in a business suit is chomping on a hunk of meat covered in cheese with no bun—she's using her hands. The loudest sounds in the restaurant by far are three kids with no parents in sight squealing about being out of school—or is it skipping school?

Michael better not expect me to remember any detail he's giving me right now. I'll pretend it was the stomach stuff, not my lack of caring, as to why I can't remember stories about nothing. The other Cadets have uninteresting lives—or at least Michael doesn't tell me the good parts. Everything Michael does there is as dull as his classmates. I'm trying to pay attention. I am. *Okay.* I am starting *now.*

First, he tells me about reading books. Then, it's stories of how much work he's put into PT. Next he regales me a tale about decorating his simple box of a dorm room with two photos of me and a poster of the movie we watched together on our sixth date. I don't ask if he keeps a journal. No one is around to congratulate me for that. He moves to how much he misses me, where I interrupt to tell him I miss him too. His eyes glint under the neon glow of a sign that says *Burgers with a Z.*

He's made friends with two people—a woman he runs with and a man that goes to the gym with him. He's been there a month and a week. I expected some flashier stories by now.

I want to know what's really happening there, what he's learning, who he's making connections with. There are benefits to being with a cop if he knows the right people. We could get married. The police chief of wherever could give a speech about Michael being an upstanding man. Then, if I was ever suspected, I'd have a cop beside me and a slew of them behind me.

Realizing I've checked out for the third time, Michael asks me if I'm okay.

"Yes, sorry. Just not feeling great." I look around the restaurant, and I hope he thinks I'm looking for the bathroom.

"I saw the wine," he says, with a face full of french fries.

"Okay."

"And the two cups."

"Okay." I nod, if not for something to do.

"Who were the two cups for?"

It's almost as if the entire one-sided conversation we just had didn't happen. Our 180° turn is not completely unexpected, though.

"Me," I say, more than a little miffed he's actually asking. I have to remind myself that he will be a police officer. He's going to be more inquisitive now.

He sits up straighter in the discolored, glittery yellow booth. He's got a smear of burger grease on his cheek from inhaling it like a vacuum. "Why two?"

"One was from two days ago. The sink was fu—"

Cutting me off, he asks, "Are you having trouble keeping up without me?"

"What?" I sputter my water with a hint of orange soda.

"Full sink, bottles of wine, sticky notes on the ground, being bored but not able to clean up, sick to your stomach—and when was the last time that happened? You'd been handling it. Not to mention—" He kills his own monologue like the cow he's eating —abruptly and before it's time.

"I'm fine," I snip, swiveling my head around once more. There is something about this moment that makes me feel like another Elizabeth—a *normal* one—who is passive aggressive at the dinner table and doesn't kill on her days off.

"Are you?" His hands find mine across the table, elbow knocking over the pepper shaker in the process. "You're planning a birthday party months in advance... Do you... Do you..."

I tug my hands from his and right the shaker. As I wipe the pepper in my hands to roll up in the napkin, I say, "Out with it."

"Do you resent me for going?"

Yes. "No. Don't be crazy." I dust my hands off like an annoying man pretending to be done with a conversation. I really wish there had been more than three napkins on the table.

"I'm not crazy. I just see my girlfriend falling apart, and I'm worried. I love you, you know."

"'*Falling apart*'? I'd like to go home now." It's a petulant move, but it will end this conversation quickly.

Hurt flickers across his eyes, but he nods and waves to the waitress.

She saunters over from the window, an empty tray in her hand. With a smile plastered on her face, she asks, "What can I help you with?"

"Can we get the check and two more Coaster Burgers to go, please?" *He's kidding, right?*

"Of course," she says. "Oh, and sir... You have a little grease on your cheek."

Michael's face flushes, and he snaps back to me. "You didn't say anything."

"I thought I did," I lie.

"Oh, fuck!" His voice panicked. "Are you having memory problems?"

"Jesus Christ... No, it was just one of those things. I love you too, by the way. I'm sorry about this. I'm just not feeling well. I guess I'm not myself."

"Without you, I'm not myself either," he says, reaching for my hand once again.

I don't know how we got to this place.

Today I was going to delve into how to kill Yasmine Menick, the abusive nanny. Now, I guess I'm going to end up cuddled on the couch with Michael, putting his guilt at ease.

Michael is staying the night. I tell him I've got to take care of the pets I'm sitting, so he comes with me. Most of the drive there and back, he's talking and I'm nodding.

After, I insist on us staying at my house. "We'll have to go back in the early morning, though," I tell him.

I can't sleep with Michael under the possible watchful eye of cameras.

At my place, I tell him to get something to drink and sneak

into the bedroom. I remove the notes from under the mattress, sliding them into the shoebox with my Polaroids.

Once I've hidden my secrets away, I put on a nightie and open the door. "Remember, I wasn't feeling well earlier," I say. If I didn't say it, he would remember in the middle of the night. He'd wake up, shake me, and apologize. And no, he's never apologized for waking me up.

Though we both get off, the sex is *careful*.

Instead of pounding into me with my legs hooked over his shoulders, he moves slowly while I hold my left leg as still as possible and wrap my right one around his torso loosely. That position is short-lived, and we end up having the most vanilla sex. Still, he has an orgasm because it's been a while. I fake it because no part of me is sexually stimulated—call it too much pain, stress, or being a woman, which is complicated.

I know he wants to talk more about my health, prod about why I'm in such bad shape with a sick stomach, loose hips, and more pain than usual. Right after sex, though, that question doesn't go over well. So he knows better now.

Having talked and sexed himself out, he falls asleep quickly.

45

glowing.

Michael's gone back to Salem—back to a dorm room filled with other potential problems for me. I miss his presence and the space he filled up already, and I feel the joy of his absence all over again. I know I don't love him like he loves me, but I love him more than I've loved anyone before.

Yet again, I'm filled with confusion and frustration about Michael. I allow myself to wallow in that for long enough to feed Choco and Taffy. They make sounds like the slopping in Marian's mouth as I worked around blood and saliva to gain purchase of her tooth.

Once they're nearly done, I head back home.

It's a quick process, pulling the materials out of their hiding places, rearranging them on the floor around me. Settled in, I plan my night. I have a lot of recon to do before I can say that Yasmine will work.

Already, she's a little off my mark. Her teeth are less than ideal. A canine is too long for the rest of her mouth and bulges her lip. Brown lines from copious coffee types have stained three of them—*just three.* Worst yet, she has no gap. *I'll miss that gap.* But my list has shown me it's hard to line everything I want up perfectly. I scrolled past two women with gaps in order to choose Yasmine. The abuse just clung to my ribs.

It was like Marian. I wanted to snuff her out because she was awful. I find myself wanting to kill people more when they are shitty. There is a moral superiority I feel knowing that the women I've murdered will no longer be a burden or a thorn in anyone's side. *You're welcome, world.*

My mother would be beaming right about now. *See Elizabeth? You are finding your footing. This is the Elizabeth you are supposed to be. You're going to be another one for the books.*

Four glasses of tea later, and I'm grabbing my keys.

Yasmine lives in the center of the Dead Lands. Light Sunday evening traffic makes the trip take forty minutes. Dark and angry raindrops beat my windshield as I drive fifty, both hands tight on the wheel. I've got the radio turned down low. A concerto I don't recognize is an anticipation soundtrack. When it builds, my excitement does too.

She won't see me. She won't know I'm there. I could give into temptation, break in tonight. I haven't chosen how I'll kill her, so it would be purely improvisation. At my healthiest, I was best when I was peak stressed. Now, my brain may shut down and activate one of those many co-morbidities that will have me on her floor thrashing around. Not sure that's how it works, but if it's possible, during a murder seems like a rational time for it to happen.

Her little orange house glows bright in the darkness, alone in a sea of forest interrupted by only a cracked two-lane road. She's got a lot of lights on outside, despite it being past midnight. Is she still awake, or is this to keep away the monsters that go bump-in-the-night?

Flicking off headlights, I park at the edge of the darkness.

No lights are on inside the house that I can see. That means little. Yasmine could be watching a movie in the dark. She could be asleep, but her girlfriend isn't. They didn't live together when I house sat, but I don't know their status now, except that they are still together and happy with no visible ring—or so says social media. And really, that means little to nothing.

I pull out binoculars I bought for this kind of occasion. I've purchased seven little gadgets as of late, having to stretch them out over months so I can afford food and rent first and foremost.

Nothing seems to move in the house.

Scanning the perimeter of the house, there are only flowers and vegetables and *Yasmine*. She's in her backyard, crouched low in full rain gear. Her yellow shines in the mini flood lights, while her dark green coat and slick pants blend in with the muddy earth she's kneeling in. She is digging or stabbing at the ground with a small tool. Glimpses of it rise above her folded knees every few arm movements.

Yasmine gardens in the middle of the night. Living all alone with no nearby neighbors allows for that, I suppose.

I make a few mental notes about the house entrances and exits, as I can see them from where I am. Slowly, I back up, make a five-point turn, and drive home.

46

yasmine.

The last Friday in July isn't usually this muggy, but I'm sticky with sweat. If I wasn't going to wear my painter's slash CDC getup, I would worry about getting DNA everywhere. I'm more worried about passing out or vomiting, which I suppose would get also DNA everywhere.

The itch is in full-force, though. So I can no longer wait.

I'm a shark who's tasted human blood. Fish—or, in my case, fruit—will never be good enough again.

According to social media, between last Sunday and now, Yasmine and her girlfriend split up. It couldn't be more fortuitous. I don't have another person's schedule to contend with. I can make an educated guess she'll be alone at two in the morning.

So, here I am. With only one car in sight, the night is starting off well.

Like my last visit, I park out of the light's grasp. I've spent the last week thinking through all of the possibilities, all of the ways this could go wrong. They all stem from me walking *around* the house, easily seen in her peripheral. Whenever I walk *through* her house, things go better. That is, if she has an easy lock to pick.

It's 1:38 a.m., and Yasmine is in the backyard again. I know nothing about gardening aside from *hole, seed, water, grow*, but I do wonder how there is this much to do. So many busy people have successful gardens without spending hours every night working on them.

It's not raining, but she is still wearing her yellow hat as if in anticipation of an unpredicted storm.

As long as she stays there, I'm in a good position.

I set the binoculars on the top of the car and grab my new mask. It's got a lot of squiggles on it and some dark purple eyeshadow—very creatively lazy, this one. It obscures my features, which is all that matters. I slip on my leather gloves and zip on my white hazmat suit.

I'm exposed. The two-lane road isn't huge, but there's a glowing house with an illuminated person beside a car parked out of view. It's… not great. I hurry.

My cane is further down the side of the driver's seat than I thought. I tug and my purse comes along with it. I forgot it fell down in the void when I swerved to avoid some truck who didn't believe in stoplights. The bag tumbles onto the ground. I heave a sigh and drop my cane back in between the side of the seat and the floorboard. I made the right call at Marian's. *Just leave the cane.* I may need it today, but it only causes a mess.

Luckily, I have very few things in my purse. It doesn't take but a moment to stuff the contents back in. It's so new, I keep forgetting the closure is different. I do not like it, but Adela brought it, so I'll deal for a few months.

I toss the purse back onto the floorboard and ease the door closed.

In the trunk, I grab my bag that holds some plastic bags, a change of clothes, and the unusual weapon I bought for tonight.

After I kill Yasmine, I'll tuck the brick in with the stack beside the small grill. I close the trunk slowly.

Step one: complete.

Step two: get to Yasmine without being noticed.

I peek through my binoculars one more time and zip them into the duffle bag. She's still on her knees, head bowed, facing away from the house.

Hip be damned, I take off towards her front door. Racing anywhere isn't something I've done in over a decade, so I tire quickly. My breath is uneven, and I regret trying to play the *you can't see me if I'm fast enough* game.

Still, I run. It's too late to stop.

My knee locks. I'm in the center of her lawn. Bright yellow lights highlight me. This is Crystal saying my name all over again, knowing me. I'm sure I'm done for.

Half-dragging my leg, I move as quickly as I can to get out of the light.

I hear the rumble of a car. There's no way of knowing how far away it is, but it's on this road, and it's close enough that I'm at risk.

I fall to my stomach and slide into a bush beside the three-step staircase to the front stoop, knocking the wind out of myself and subluxing two ribs at the same time. My vision blurs, and my stomach turns.

The car drives by at a snail's pace. It slows as it sees my car, maybe looking for a person—or persons—inside.

Minutes later, it's quiet again. Yasmine has probably resumed her gardening, if she ever stopped.

To get out from under the shrub, I shimmy backwards. Pain makes me gasp as I try to stand. Three landing steps, then the door.

Crack, pop, crack. I step from the stairs to the door. It's locked as expected. I pull her key out of my pocket and try the lock. It doesn't budge. The lock picking kit is in the pocket of these coveralls. Guess it's time for Plan B.

Another car is coming down the road. This time, it's fast. *Really* fast.

There's no way I can keep doing this back-and-forth thing. I'm not quick at lock picking. Around the house it is. I move to the right side of the house, hugging the orange siding.

The inside of her house is still dark, empty. I pass the kitchen and remember her Polaroids. The speckled yellow pot filled with stew on the stove came first. The fist-sized hole in the wall above the dinette table was second. I chose that because it was a carbon-copy of my childhood neighbor's wall after her husband tried to punch her. She had told him dinner was going to be at seven, not six, because her daughter and I had a late lunch. A cracked aloe vera plant was the third. Water had created a brown amoeba around the based that looked like spilled coffee. And a red stain on the sunflower bathroom *carpet* toilet mat was the fourth and final Polaroid. I wonder if she still has those things.

I reach the back of the house. Her long, voluminous curls are pinched under her hat and forced into a large tube between her shoulder blades.

Can you feel my eyes on you, Yasmine? Are your hackles raised?

Unchanged, she continues to do whatever it is that she's doing. I step away from the not-quite-safety of the home's skin. There is no darkness for me to hide in.

Brick in hand, I begin to walk. She has to know I'm here. Steps can only be so quiet this close to someone. Only a bird and an occasional hot breeze make another sound.

"Hey," Yasmine says. "I hoped you would come."

I don't speak. I just keep walking.

"Listen, I'm sorry. I love you, you know. Did you get the flowers I sent? They came from here." Her shoulders droop. My shadow overtakes her shape. "Why bother coming if you won't even talk to me?" Yasmine asks.

She leans back on her heels and dusts her gloves off.

Throat going dry, I clutch my left hand around the brick.

Yasmine begins to stand, begins to say something—begins to, but I cut her short.

I bring the brick down on the back of her head. She stumbles forward onto her knees. I wait for her to scramble forward, to fight back, but she doesn't. She's still.

Her yellow rain hat is now scuffed and discarded beside her. It was useless before she died anyhow.

Loud breath is as hot as the surrounding air, as stale as day-old bread. Anyone driving by could see me standing over a lump with a brick.

I lean forward to check her pulse. The mask shifts and tugs my eyelashes with it, disorients me for a moment. Yasmine wrenches her head back towards me as I'm blinking.

Eyes caught in a state of contortion, I focus on Yasmine. I hit her again so she can't hit me. I learned my lesson with Cora. My forefinger smashes between her skull and the brick. A splintery feeling shoots up my hand, settling into my knuckle.

I shift my finger out of the way, and it's as if the brick does the work for me. Every following strike is a shapeless brand on my biceps, burning deep into the bone.

The motion tears at my fingers until they feel like mangled lumps of flesh dangling from the stump that once held a brick. But somehow, I'm still holding it, still slamming it into her head.

I stop when her skull resembles the watermelon I bludgeoned in the fourth grade, all caved in with white, pink, and red showing.

Suddenly, it's done. She was there, kneeling and thinking I was someone else one minute, and now…

Glancing around, I see there are many spots I could bury her. I'm fighting a wave of nausea and more pain than I've felt in a long time. Digging doesn't seem likely.

Not far off, a forest filled with tall trees like a mouth of sharpened teeth stares back at me. I'll hide her, shove her behind a tree and let the animals have their fill. I'm doing good for the environment.

In theory, it's so easy.

If I had trouble lifting Cora, I'm a toddler dragging a crate of intact pumpkins with Yasmine. A slight woman who weighs at least ten pounds less than me has me in a tailspin.

I'm gasping by the time I've tucked her behind the largest tree.

I collapse beside her, lay my head on her shoulder, and fall apart. If I could come up with a good lie, I'd go to the hospital. But my fingers are clearly broken, and that doesn't happen easily.

Somehow, I'm finding myself thankful for having hEDS again. When I wrap my hand up, no one will find it odd. I can still use my cane, still function with only one hand. I'll just blame a spontaneous dislocation.

An hour later, I'm up and cleaning up the area. I grab her hat and cover her shattered skull. I toss dirt over the blood spatter. Then, I head to my car.

I take off the bloodied suit and mask. Everything is slow, painful, draining.

Yasmine's murder was a success because I wasn't seen, but I'm a wreck. It'll be hard to look back fondly on this one.

Few cars are on the road at this hour, so I get to my temporary home in twenty minutes. I pour myself out of the car and all but crawl into the house, heading straight for the shower.

Real life crashes into me as I take my clothes off—no blood in sight, thank you very much. I'm going to have to call out of work again, at least until my hand is a little better. I better look up how to handle a broken finger in case that's what this is. And *oh, fuck.* Planning next week's ESL graduation is going to be rough.

solved.

It's been nearly a week since I murdered Yasmine. I'm back at work now—starting on an abnormal day. I never work Wednesdays. I've been monitoring the self-checkout area, so I'm able to sort of rest my hands. They could use another month, if I'm being honest. I'm out of sick leave days, though. And Juniper Foods has a rule about working once a week or you'll be let go. Fucking corporations.

I have a few months' rent taken care of, which is great. But it doesn't afford me the ability to quit a job. So I'm working.

Yesterday, Jamie apologized for not being able to give me extra sick leave, as if the worker's abusive rules are her fault. She's been trying to make life as easy as possible. Normally, self-checkout is a position given to our older workers, the ones on pensions that don't support them. I guess having a chronic illness that has me regularly calling out has moved me to a new category of worker.

After watching six people in a row have issues with the same machine, I flick off the light. My time is better spent doing just about anything other than entering a code to override every other weighed item. No one needs that.

I sit on a bar top chair and cross my legs, getting as comfortable as one can get in an environment like this. It's settling in to be a regular workday.

The moment I think about that, I see Wendell and Mel. They are in the line for the self-checkout.

I flush, picturing them coming to Juniper Foods to confront me. Yesterday, we had a decent class. After, they must have figured me out. They couldn't wait another day to accuse me of my crimes.

But there would be police with them, wouldn't there? In spite of myself, I'm looking around, checking the exits, glancing at hips and chests for holstered guns.

At first, they don't seem to see me. I could be overthinking this. I'm just another worker bee in a red shirt. That's all they see, and they aren't looking for more.

Could be my hair or face or the pink lace patches on my white leggings, but they notice me.

Both are smiling by the time they reach me. Wendell's teeth are angry in the fluorescents. A fresh purple stripe in Mel's hair gives them a pop punk vibe. The two seem to be in a very good mood. I wonder where Chike is.

"Elizabeth!" Mel says first. They roll to me as Wendell checks out.

He's buying a platter of subs and two bags of chips.

"Hey, Mel! Fancy seeing you here." I smirk a little, show them I'm joking.

They laugh, and their accent gets heavy enough for me to miss the first two words of their next sentence. The gist isn't lost on me. They are glad they ran into me. They have good news.

Wendell is tapping his foot loudly as the machine runs

through the prompts for checkout. Impatience isn't something I've seen on him. It's a funny look.

"What good news?" I ask Mel.

Wendell shouts that he's coming, to not say it yet. So Mel waits.

Number 3 flashes. "One second," I say.

A young person with barbed-wire teeth, a bulbous pimple on their narrow nose, and wide eyes pokes the screen repeatedly. I ask what's the problem, but I don't listen to their answer. I skin them alive. Every strip I pull from their body is long and thin. I lick it, chew it, eat it.

"Excuse me?" they say.

"Sorry." I raise my left hand. "I'm a little out of it today. Can we start over? What's wrong with the machine?"

Mel and Wendell are waiting for me off to the side. The cheese on their sub sandwiches is getting sweaty, and the bread is getting hard. They don't seem to mind.

Once I've helped another woman with a coupon and settled back into my chair, the words practically pour out of Mel. With animated, bright eyes, they boast that the three of them solved another case.

Wendell corrects them by saying it was at the same time as the police, so *they did, but they didn't.* His words.

"Oh?" I try—and fail—to sound casual.

No one has banged on my door yet, come to arrest me for murder. Yasmine hasn't even been found, looks like. Still, I cross possibly broken fingers.

Mel doesn't mention the victim's name. They launch into the story of a woman bludgeoned. Everyone assumed it was her boyfriend. He has proof he was out of town. They moved to the neighbor, the best friend, the ex. They've run the list down.

"So, where did you find a suspect?" I ask through a dry and scratchy throat. *Is it hot in here?*

It seems there was a receipt at the scene. No one thought

much of it because she was found at a bar. *It's not Yasmine.*

Mel continues. The woman had two amaretto sours at the bar. There was nothing special about that. It wasn't until they (the police and the podcasters, separately) did some digging that they found out the woman left through the back door before the second amaretto order was placed.

Her husband is a mean drunk and doesn't like the word *no*, apparently. When the police asked him where he was during the time she was driving home and ordering a drink at the same time, he raged. They said they had footage, and he changed his tune, sang like a canary. They never said what the footage was of. He sold himself out.

Wendell is laughing so hard at this point. "Something so small solved it all," he says.

I chuckle. "It usually is, right? That or a video camera catching it all. Murderers aren't that smart."

They both agree with my assessment of people like me.

"Graduation is next week. So sad," Mel says. They cast their eyes down into their lap and tell me they love my class.

"I love having you all in it. It'll be sad not seeing you twice a week, but you've improved so much! And it will be a fun party."

Wendell leans forward, and his arms start to shift like he wants to hug me. I don't move to meet him. I'm not sure it's appropriate, and I don't enjoy hugging much. On top of that, I'm in so much pain, one too-tight squeeze, and I may be down for the day.

I tell them I'm looking forward to seeing them for our last class before graduation next week.

They beam at me and wave. Mel says Chike would say hi if he wasn't setting up for filming, so hi from him. They are recording their case wrap-up episode.

That explains the sandwich tray.

"Well, have a great filming session," I say, my chest a little lighter.

48

wrappers.

When my break comes, I feel I've been working for days, not hours. I grasp my cane tighter than I'd like as I walk. I need to change my tampon *and* my pad before lunch. Often, I don't have much of a period, but this week has been atrocious. It's my victim's blood, and it's pouring out from between my legs, desperate to be seen by others.

It takes far longer than it should to go from self-checkout to break room to bathroom, but finally, I'm sitting on the toilet. Wet toilet paper sticks to my skin, and I regret not paying more attention before I chose the bigger stall.

I unzip my purse and reach for the tampon bag. It's a mess in there, and I remember it tumbling out at Yasmine's. I haven't reorganized it since.

A massive wallet filled with plastic, receipts, and loyalty cards takes up most of the room. Two lip glosses, honey butters, some bobby pins, keys, empty wrappers, tampons, two pads, and my cell phone fill the rest of the space.

I find two dried leaves and a small pebble at the bottom of the bag. Those go straight into the little metal trashcan meant for feminine products. I collect the pink cellophane into one hand, prepared to mush them down into an open pocket, but Wendell's words nag at me.

Something so small.

Like a candy wrapper? I almost laugh. My left leg is going numb, signaling me needing to get off of the too-low toilet, so I put paranoia aside.

I shove the pink wrappers into their pocket, grab a tampon and pad, and finish using the bathroom.

Stuffed with cotton, I'm a taxidermist's work in progress. In my mind, I waddle to the sink with bowed legs. I turn on both faucets, waiting for the water to Baby Bear itself.

Something so small.

I wash my hands. Standing with my cane between my legs, I use the loud hand dryer and think back to putting honey butters in my new purse. I put an even ten in. I gave one to Adela, so I should have nine. I can put my overactive mind at ease by counting.

In my purse, two remain. I pull out the balled up wrappers and count. Seven pink pieces of cellophane. I relax.

I toss them back into the mouth of my bag without another thought.

Reaching for the metal door handle, it dawns on me: I gave Adela her honey butter *when she bought me the purse.*

I put ten fresh candies in *this* bag.

I am one wrapper short.

Blood rushes to my ears as I play out the worst-case scenario —the wrapper on Yasmine's body with my saliva, my fingerprints on it. The police find her and all they need to arrest me in one fell swoop. How would it have gotten there? Fuck if I know… Stuck to a shoe because honey is sticky? *Plan for the worst*, my mother always said.

Calming a rising heart rate takes effort, but I remind myself it could have fallen out anywhere. The most logical place for it to be is my car.

Trying not to use up too much energy, I propel myself forward towards the parking lot. I hear my name but don't turn. I'm going to pretend it's another Elizabeth being called. I'm not the only one.

My car is fairly clean. It's always been that way, but I've tried to be better since Crystal. There's nothing on the floorboard. I check the sides of the seat, the seat itself, the trunk, the spare wheel compartment.

Nothing.

But a missing pink cellophane candy wrapper could mean nothing too. I've worked. I've been to multiple houses. I don't even know if I lost it before or after Yasmine.

With no mention of her on the news, no *wow, some stupid woman left her DNA on the body* update, I'm probably still in the clear. But I want to go back, to check her body, her garden, where I parked my car on the highway—the most likely place it would be, of course. But revisiting the crime scene isn't wise. After watching all the documentaries I have, I know better than to do that.

The police may be lying in wait for me, hoping I'll go revisit her. That sounds gross, seeing her body all bloated or stiff or whatever stage it would be in when I visited her. *No*, when I leave, the thrill comes with me. I don't need to go somewhere to tap into a memory. That's weird.

Even if it fell out at Yasmine's house, I parked on the edge of the property. It could just be on the floor of my bedroom calling to ants.

With great restraint, I go back into Juniper Foods. Though my throat is dry, my mind on fire, and my heart is convinced I'm running, I still have to eat lunch before the second half of my shift.

49

spiced.

We did it. Well, *they* did. It seems like it's long overdue and has come too soon. I'd gotten so caught up in my personal life and lost track of the time until Yasmine. Killing her seemed to reset the clock, slowed life back to normal speed.

This last week has been hell. I've been babying my hand, not knowing if I bruised it, fractured it, or if there's an actual break—my assumption. I'm still pretty frazzled about Wendell's offhanded comment. Sleep has also eluded me most nights.

So, I ended up outsourcing a lot of this party.

At the beginning of the course, I asked them all to write a small paragraph about their favorite ways to celebrate, including foods and drinks they love. I use those to design the party. It's like a potluck they don't have to bring a dish for. In this cohort's case, I had Adela do some cooking and shopping for me.

When she saw my hand, I told her that hEDS is a bitch, and she asked no more questions. She's been super understanding and attentive while giving me the space and autonomy I need to commit homicide. Thanks to her, today is what I wanted. Another *little victory* for me.

Our "graduation" celebration is in full swing. Even though no one needed to bring anything, almost everyone brought a snack or treat; one student brought homemade hard candies and children's Valentine's Day cards that have dancing ice cream cones and chubby-faced ice cream sandwiches declaring us *cool*.

It's the biggest graduation I've had. These students tried harder and practiced more than most I've had before. Their work is already paying off, as they discuss movies they recently saw, politics, and the latest ridiculous policy changes for local high schools in *much* better English than when they arrived.

Today is their tangible reward. They have foods that remind them of their homes, their mothers and grandmothers, their childhoods, and happy memories, and they get to taste the foods that do that for fellow learners from other countries.

This is *my* reward—watching them feel pride in themselves and celebrate each other. It's in their success I find my happiness. For the average person, there aren't a lot of times in life when one can say they made someone's life better in any significant way. I get to say that often.

Licia's Italian accent rises above the low hum of conversation. "Elizabeth!" She still doesn't say the *h* in my name.

I'm trying to be more present. This matters to me.

"Sorry, I spaced. What's up, Licia?" I ask, stepping towards the center of the room where I had a few Varetta Community Center volunteers push the desks together to set up the massive spread of food.

Half of it was divvied up before I sat down at my desk again. Now, some of the white platters only have dark smears reminiscent of Crystal's bedsheets.

"I made a plate for you, so you rest," she says, motioning to my bandaged hand. "Little of everything."

Licia sets the first plate in front of me on my desk and

motions to the others she put off to the side on a nearby table. Three paper plates are piled high. Chunks of pink and silver fish touch one of my favorite Greek desserts—and one of the only foods I recognized from the students' favorites list—galakto-boureko. One of Adela's contributions was a spicy Indian curry with falafel. It oozes into the fish and dessert, coating the bottom of the plate to the point of being soggy. An imprint of sauce remains when I lift the plate.

"Thank you." I smile and grab another plate to double stack it as she flits back to the group.

Licia moves through the world like a social twenty-two-year-old, and I love it. This plate of mush, however, turns my stomach. I set the first plate beside the other two, which are equally disgusting. A garlic heavy dish mingled with a puff pastry filled with some sort of berry compote and cheese combination. Either she eats everything in one bite, or she wasn't paying attention. The thought was sweet.

Wendell sidles up beside me, frowning. "Oh. I did this, too," he says. "The desserts are together." He presents a plate fit for Sofia Coppola's Marie Antoinette. "And spiced foods. And sauce dishes." Those came on four plates, spaced out so very few foods touched at all. "And finally, yeast."

He, like most of my students, came in with good English, but now there shouldn't be a person who can't understand him. He's clear as a bell. Some people may claim to have a hard time, but I'll preemptively assume those people are just racist assholes.

Chike walks in as I take a heavenly bite of something green and spicy with okra and stewed tomatoes in it. He smiles—no teeth—and gives a half-wave, though I'm not sure to who.

"Hey," he says, his intended target still unclear. "Sorry I'm late!"

It's so uncommon for him. I almost ask him if everything is okay. The classroom interrupts with *hellos* in various forms— from casual to formal, English to their native tongues.

"Welcome," I say instead. "Licia made you a plate." She's out of earshot, so her feelings won't get hurt by the lie.

His eyebrows raise, but he says nothing. I point to the lined-up food mess, and unlike me, he seems grateful.

"Okay!" I raise my voice to garner everyone's attention. "Now that everyone is here…" Chike blushes behind his forkful of multi-colored mush. "I wanted to say a huge *thank you*. You have all been wonderful to teach, really. I know that teachers and reality hosts say this all the time, but you honestly have been my favorite class to date. I beg of you not to tell the other students that. You have all improved so much, and I'm so proud of you." It feels weird to say, though I've said it many times before. Even with Michael and Adela, I'm not good at expressing my emotions. I could blame my parents like every other adult does, but like hEDS, it's genetic coding. "It really has been a joy. I hope you enjoyed the class as much as I enjoyed having you in it." I smile and wave at them. "Alright, enough of that. Back to your food. We have the room for another hour, so eat until it's gone. And whatever you do, don't forget your goodie bags!"

The bags Adela filled have safe honey butters from my reserves, a college prep workbook, a list of some of the best movies to help them with conversations and conversation starters, as well as a secondary list of some of the top movies that are quoted regularly (so they can understand the pop culture refer-ences should they want to), a handout with five more poems, and a small notebook and pen with the note "to keep track of new words or phrases" attached to it.

I print handouts by the hundred and buy everything in bulk, so it's not very expensive, but it means so much to the students.

Everyone loves goodie bags. And there is nothing like free stuff to encourage people. Really, it's all about getting them where they want to be without paying for college courses or making them feel small by being the eldest in a room full of judgmental children.

The food disappears from plates, and the class raves about the offerings. One-by-one, the students find their way to me. They thank me, give me presents and hugs. All of them ask how I'm feeling and point at my hand. I smile and tell them *better*. It's half-true.

The podcast crew takes their moment. "We saw you subscribed. Thank you!" Mel says without a single misstep—not that they needed much help to begin with. Their accent is still heavy, but I hope it doesn't go away too much.

They wheel themselves back and forth in place. I think it's with excitement.

I wonder if I end up in a chair, will I be able to have so much life, so much energy and joy? Will I still be able to kill? That seems like a life limited to poisoning people, but I could adjust, I think.

I'm already having to cross off so many ways to kill because of my body. What are a few more?

"I did, yes. You are very good at podcasting." I smile at the same moment I have a spike of knee pain. The smile warps into a grimace.

"You're a great teacher," Wendell says. "See you soon!"

"Thank you so much! And I hope so."

It seems highly unlikely. I have so much going on, after all.

50

eggs.

It's been over two months since I killed Yasmine and my ESL cohort graduated. Michael has had a busy time, and I haven't been able to be absent for any of it.

He graduated from the Police Academy. The ceremony was long and boring, but his smile was radiant in the early autumn sun. Adela kept me company during it, but even she felt a little dozy in the unusually warm weather.

He moved back to Janes and started working under Officer Ericks, who monitors everything he does. The two of them do very little in the way of exciting police work, but I've still heard recaps of every second of it. Officer Ericks likes her coffee black with two stirrers. She has one teenager, a bastard ex-husband, a decent boyfriend, and two blind dogs that slobber a lot.

Michael has been staying over as often as possible, following me to house after house, with me having very few valid reasons to stop him. The more he sees me, the more he sees my physical problems and how they've worsened. I've allowed him to think nature is quicker than expected. He's been trying to convince me to quit my jobs, let him support me.

It's been a trying time.

I've realized how much I need the release of killing. Before the pain got too bad, at least I could bite myself. Now, all I have is murder. I've been planning another... slowly. Her name is Holly Sylvester.

Wendell accidentally had me in a tizzy for weeks, thinking about the missing honey butter wrapper. I found it last week on my bedroom floor under a pile of books I was about to donate. It must have gotten kicked under the nightstand until the vacuum sucked it back out. I don't have to worry anymore. I'm good at this. I haven't gotten caught, and I won't. I'm careful.

As if *thinking* about killing summons him, Michael appears beside me. I'm in the kitchen. It's early morning, and I'm standing in front of a heating pan.

He kisses my neck, nestles in like a furry creature. "Morning, love. Have I mentioned how great it is when we are at your house?"

"Once or twice." I step away from him. "Eggs?"

"Please, and thank you." Plastic *click-clicks* to my right. He's making himself a coffee.

I grab another three eggs from the refrigerator and whisk them in with mine. He mutters something as I pour the egg-milk mixture into the pan. I'm too busy stirring and thinking about Holly to pay attention. It's been so long since I've been in her house, I barely remember much of anything.

Michael's cell phone rings.

"This early?" I complain. "Who is it?"

"Goode," he says. I hate that he's started answering the phone with his last name. I didn't know people really did that, but it drives me nuts. "Ericks?" A pause. "Seriously?" His voice is laced with surprise, and his face brightens with every passing second. Waving his free hand in front of him, he says, "No, no, that's great. I know about where that is. I can be there in—" He taps his face. "—twenty or thirty?" His voice squeals as he thanks Ericks and hangs up. He wraps his arms around me. "Elizabeth!" My name comes out all breathy, his usual cadence when he wants to have slow sex.

I keep stirring the eggs. They're almost perfectly cooked. His arms aren't worth ruining my breakfast.

He kisses the back of my head. "You won't believe this. There's been a murder about twenty minutes from here that sounds pretty gruesome. Looks like Ericks has been called in because they need help securing the scene. So… that means I'm getting called in too!" Michael reaches for the brewed coffee, his hand shaking.

"Oh?" I say, meaning *that's nice, but you don't need coffee.*

"It's in the Dead Lands, so you know, a bunch of people with massive plots of land worth a lot of money. I'm sure you've house sat for someone out that way."

I still. *Dead Lands?* Surely, it can't be *her.* Surely, they found her already, and she just didn't make the news. The women I'm choosing are not people the public would rally behind, after all. Surely, he's not getting called to 804 Entley Hwy.—the dumbest name for a road ever. *Surely.* "She didn't say much over the phone except that she's texting me the address and to be prepared for a long day." Michael is now bouncing on the balls of his feet. He's no longer trying to drink his coffee, which I appreciate.

"So, no eggs then?" I ask with great restraint. Keeping cool is important right now. There are only four Polaroids that connect me to Yasmine Menick.

"Better not. I'd hate to vomit at my first big crime scene. Is it horrible that I'm grateful Janes Police Department is too small right now?"

I don't answer. I can't. I'm shaking, and shallow breathing is shredding the muscles around my ribcage. Doesn't take long. He hasn't noticed because he's already rushed back into the bedroom to change clothes. It's me making popcorn, waiting to hear about Isaac all over again. Only this time, a woman is dead.

I scrape the burnt eggs onto a plate and zombie walk back to the couch. The scent has me on the verge of getting sick myself. Michael is right. Eggs are a bad decision this morning.

He comes out of the bedroom and his voice is far away as he says, "I'll take a coffee and a granola bar to go in case I can stomach it."

I try to ask about the address, work my mouth into a shape that's bound to push a word out. A small guttural animal being kicked sound shutters out.

He rushes over. "Are you okay? Should I stay home?"

I nod or shake; I'm not sure. He furrows his brow. I must have given mixed signals.

"I'm staying."

"No," I gasp out. That will only look worse for me. At least this way, he can tell me what he saw, what they know. Information is power.

Michael stands over me, hemming and hawing for another few minutes. I don't say anything else. I just stare off into space. I'm making a mountain out of a molehill. I know I am.

Finally, he kisses me on the forehead and puts the phone by my hand. "If you need anything—*anything*. I love you so much. I'll call you in a little while to check on you."

I nod and force thin, dry lips into a kissy shape. It will stave off some of his worry. I need him to focus.

After he leaves, I'm left with thoughts. *Has time travel been proven real yet? Can I race to the scene before Michael, in case they haven't made it to the outer perimeter of Yasmine's house yet? Should I bomb her house and everyone there? Where do I get a bomb? Do I have time to pack up the life I've made and run?*

The most important question will hang over me until Michael comes home: *What if it's not Yasmine at all?*

51

pastry.

In jeans and a sweater, I'm almost shivering. Standing by the front door, I've got the car keys dangling from one curled finger. I spin them. They are precious commodities now. I've been here for five minutes now, trying to tell myself this is paranoia. Blowing my life up isn't necessary because I've been careful, gotten good at this. And so what if they find a candy wrapper? There are over 20k reviews of the exact ones I purchased, and all pieces of pink cellophane look the same.

I drop the keys back in the bowl beside the door. Pacing, I think about packing, about watching TV. I think about drinking or calling Adela to come keep me company. I'll go for a drive. If I happen to drive to the scene—or past it—so be it.

Traffic is picking up in certain parts of the city. Churchgoers are going to pray and ask to have their sins washed away so they can have a clean slate for sinning this coming week. Restaurants that serve no-reservation brunch are getting early lines that remind me of the one time my mother and I spent seven hours waiting for tickets to watch a popular boy band. They were called something ridiculous, like Hot Boyz. Maybe the man who opened Thriller Burgerz used to be a member.

No one I see is wearing the *I may be arrested for murder* face. No one except me when I glance in the rear-view mirror. Stormy blue eyes read angry, resigned, done with it all. Light crow's feet have developed around them, along with dark circles underneath. I wonder when all that started.

My stomach grumbles as I drive by the police station. I don't know how I ended up here.

The first place I come across that doesn't have a line out the door is Little Good Pastry. Street parking means I end up two blocks away.

I grab my cane, toss an extra jacket on, and brave the unsettlingly cheery morning. Does no one care this might be my last day of freedom? *No? Just me?*

Most of the people milling about have large purses and dresses or nice, crisp shirts and shiny shoes. I only get glimpses of their teeth as they laugh at stories that aren't funny. So few people are really funny, yet there is always laughter.

One man, strolling in the opposite direction, has coifed, supervillain hair and a blue pinstriped suit. He's alone and smiles at every person he passes. Wide teeth flash at woman after woman, couple after couple.

A homeless teenager is sitting, knees curled to their chest, on the sidewalk. Their back is touching a building-high window. The glass must be freezing. The man veers towards them. With a big, toothy grin, he kicks the teenager's ungloved hand into their shin. They don't cry out, but a steady stream of tears slips down their cheeks. The real Wolf of Wall Street is back to wandering down the sidewalk without a second glance back.

No one but me notices. As he passes me, I stick my cane out a few inches. He stumbles over it. I wink at the teen.

The Wolf spins towards me and snarls. Watching it all,

amusement plays on the teenager's lips—a temporary distraction from pain and cold, and pain in the cold.

"Oh, I'm so sorry, miss!" The Wolf says. It's for the man in the yellow sweatshirt, the woman with a bagel, the couple who couldn't care less, the squirrel by the trashcan. Anyone but me.

I imagine I go further and swing the pink poppy-patterned cane at his kneecaps. He goes down, letting his mask fall. On the sidewalk, I wallop him. I stop when his blood obscures my cane's pretty pink poppy pattern. I take the teenager out to lunch on the Wolf's dime.

His teeth are sharp now—fangs ready to sink into pure flesh. "Hope you have a killer day."

My mouth goes dry. If a Wolf's gaze makes me nervous, what does that make *me*?

He moves past me, doesn't wait for a response. I glance over my shoulder, and he's whistling to himself. He stops at the edge of the sidewalk and looks both ways down the street. His hands in his pockets propel him forward, and he jogs to the other side of the road.

I realize I'm in front of the bakery. A quick glance through the smudged window of Little Good Pastry offers me little more than a bustling room of person shapes. It just rained, but they should still clean the muck off sooner than later.

A small bell chimes as I open the door. Fresh bread, icing, and strong coffee greet me.

I fall into line. The tailor-suited blonde in front of me taps her heels incessantly. That will not speed the wait up.

Taking in the decorations that surround the chalkboard menu, I see the bakery has the style of a college student desperate to grow up. Japanese toys line beautiful wooden shelves. The artwork is a collection of hanging farmhouse kitchen utensils, snarky signs, and framed graphic novel covers.

The line moves.

I inspect the case of pastries. The varieties are standard fare for bakeries.

The words *homicide case* float above the chatter, and it's all I can do not to run out.

I'm on the news. There's a TV out of sight, and reporters on every channel are pointing to my face, declaring me a murderer. I shouldn't have left the house.

The line moves again. Now there are two people behind me. "Next!" *That's me.*

A kid with a frizzy hair and a split lip mumbles that I must be new because he hasn't seen me around.

"I'd like a black coffee and croissant to-go, please." Familiar pressure builds in my neck.

The kid looks hurt I haven't engaged in conversation. "Right, sure. Um, did you want the croissant warmed up?"

"No, I'm good." Already, this is taking too long. I tilt my head to the right. *Crack.* To the left. *Crack.* The release makes me a little dizzy, but my neck doesn't feel swollen anymore.

Another snippet of conversation is about a robbery. I sneak a glance at the voice the comment came from. It's a police officer. Beside her table, a male and female seem deep in conversation. Steam fogs the woman's glasses as she holds a drink near her lips. Her suit jacket is open, revealing a badge and gun at her hip.

Across from them, a man with a gun slung over his shoulder slaps the table and reaches for a breakfast sandwich.

Pretending to stretch, I scan the bakery. Too busy holding my shit together, I didn't notice. Every person is wearing a suit, carrying a gun, or in blue.

I am in a fucking cop hangout.

52

nothing.

Yanking the coffee from the to-go counter, I almost burn myself. It's so full it sloshes through the mouth hole. I half-wave, then head to the door.

Tension and fear grips my shoulders so tightly, I can almost feel their individual fingers.

"Miss?" It's a man. *Oh.* He's grabbed my cane-free shoulder and planted my feet on the sidewalk.

Why did he put his hands on me? I don't trust myself to speak. My eyes meet his, and he softens.

"You left your croissant," he says, holding up the unmarked brown paper bag. "Just thought you might not want to start your day off on the wrong foot."

He's young, nice-looking. His teeth are perfectly uniform, which is odd and cartoony.

I remind myself how close I am to a hoard of police, and say, "Thank you." Holding my cane between wobbly knees, I take the pastry from him. I tuck it in the crook of my left arm. "It's already been a pretty weird Sunday."

He waits, expectant. Of *what? A tip? My life story?*

"Bye."

"Want some help?" His voice is kind and even-keeled. "I could walk you to your car." The gun on his hip would give anyone pause. For me, it's a hard pass.

"I've got it. Thank you, though." I'm holding a coffee and carrying a paper bag like a sack of groceries on my left. On my right, I've got my cane and purse hitched over my shoulder. *I've killed struggling people and dragged their bodies to hide them*, I want to say. *This is nothing.*

"Sure, of course." He runs chewed fingernails through greasy hair. "Have a great day."

And then, I'm gone.

The drive home is much worse than the drive there. Visiting that bakery has assured there will be no unwinding for me today.

53

mark.

At home, I feverishly tear at the croissant. It's a mound of yeasty fluff when I'm done. I eat the buttery cushion foam piece by piece.

The coffee is cold by the time I touch it, but I'm a live wire. Like Michael, I don't need it. He won't be home for hours—all day, probably.

With time to kill, I get out my Polaroids to enjoy for what could be the last time.

I perch on the edge of the couch, not able to get fully comfortable. My left foot is a buoy, bouncing my leg up and down. Opening the boxes is bittersweet.

For the next two hours, I'm lost in memories.

So far from my current worries, I'm able to enjoy reliving the moments. Nostalgia is powerful. Nostalgia about *being* powerful is intoxicating.

When my fingers caress the smooth film, it's me brushing hair out of their faces. I want to see my handiwork. I was the worst of us—the huntress, the murderer. But I was not alone in my darkness. If the women I killed were different, they would be cuddled under blankets in the yellow Sunday morning light.

"They were strong and loving, brutal and kind. They were what they needed to be to make it in the world, just what I want you to be, and they did what they needed to do to make their mark, just like I want you to do."

I've done what I needed to do to make my mark.

Putting the lids back on the boxed is a gut punch. I may never see these photos again. Adela's mouth, my teeth's evolution, reminders of my crimes, memories of my childhood and trauma. They may all be evidence. Knowing this, I still can't bring myself to get rid of them.

After they are tucked away, I collect the crime books—both fiction and non. I keep three and put the rest in four boxes.

Over the next hour, I deliver the books to used bookstores around town. With sunglasses and the jacket with a fluffy hood, almost everyone in the Pacific Northwest owns, I'm another busy woman who only has time to drop books as far as the front door. I'm irritating, but I don't stand out.

When I get home, I'm less stressed.

As I make lunch, I torch notes about Holly. She will always be my woulda-coulda-shoulda.

Once I've eaten, all that's left is to stay busy until Michael comes home—alone or with friends.

54

forensics.

Excited raps on the door shatter the careful illusion of a normal day off.

Whatever words I'm about to hear may change my future—or take it all away.

On a normal day, Michael would unlock the door now. The knocking is a heads-up, so I'm not scared (his words). We've come to the place where he no longer has to wait for me, and I no longer have buffer time to hide myself. If this was before, I would glance through the peephole first. I would expect two officers behind him, maybe a SWAT team with guns trained on the house at every exit.

But this is now, and Michael lets himself in. No one is with him. "It's me." His voice wobbles as much as my legs do.

I stand to greet him.

His face flickers with a mush of emotions as he walks towards me. I read his knocks wrong. They weren't excited. He's hard to read now, though.

I recognize plenty of the feelings overwhelming him—love, exhaustion, fear, even anger. But some I don't. I'd swear disgust and horror hide behind them.

He knows. And that's that.

"Hey, how was it?" I ask, trying to keep my voice steady. "You've been gone all day. Are you okay? Did you…" I let the unasked question hang in the air for him to fill in. *See the body? Solve the crime? Get along with your fellow officers?* Already, I've asked more about his day than usual.

He's not stepped far into the kitchen, and he's not kissed me. But in a game of chicken, the murderer always wins.

"It was harder than I expected." He's normally busting at the seams right now. After a moment of silence, he opens a cabinet. Glass *tinks* against glass as he pushes three cups aside to grab his favorite.

I lean against the back of the couch as he pours himself some milk.

Fingers clutch out of sight fabric. I am a bomb. My heart is the timer. I'm just ticking down. *Tick, tick, tick.*

Slowly, he drinks the milk. The sound of it going down his throat seems loud. Once he's finished it, he wipes a hand across his mouth. A small smudge of dirt becomes mud on his chin. He sets the glass on the counter, and a few drops he missed ooze back down into the bottom of the cup.

"I guess I didn't know what to expect, really," he finally says.

"Oh?" I'm small when I say it.

"Yeah, I thought it would be a lot of me standing around. But Ericks walked me through it—" Michael seems to loosen as he gives me a blow-by-blow. From pulling up, parking, and helping with… something about the perimeter to meeting new people, drinking bad coffee, and picking up lunch for everyone, he has stories. I relax into his voice. "I saw her—the body, I mean." His eyes meet mine.

Jolted by his words, I have to move. I go to the couch and sit. "You did? Are you…" Again, I just drop the question.

Michael stretches the usual four steps across the kitchen into eight. I'm not sure he's blinked yet, but he's not stopped staring at me. The last time he did this was during a staring contest at work.

He eases himself down onto the couch, as if he's ancient and barely holding himself together. His fingers reach out for mine, but he pulls them back. "It was pretty fucked up."

Blood rushes to my ears, waves of crimson I can feel but not see.

"Even so," he says, clearing his throat. "I think I'll really enjoy being a detective. I think I'll be really good at it."

We are moving beyond this, which bodes well. "That's great, honey," I say, reaching for his hand on instinct. I don't even want to touch him right now. But here we are.

Michael's face crinkles as he accepts the gesture. It feels different, distant, uninterested. "Mmm, speaking of honey…" He drops my hand and taps his cheek. "Do you have any honey butters left?" Even in this vacuum of silence, I notice his voice is louder than it was moments ago. It's growing taut and nervous. "I could use a little sweet right about now."

His neck muscles become ropes as he gulps. Still, he's somehow keeping his eyes from going cold or angry. After that initial moment full of feelings, he's trying to stay himself—regular old Michael.

My palms sweat, and I'm glad he's no longer holding them. I'm standing in front of my Developmental Psych class trying to give a presentation of the lifespan of humans all over again. I failed that test, and I will fail this one. I was wrong. The honey butter wrapper must still be out there somewhere—or now, with the police. I allowed myself to get cocky, and here we are.

"Of course. I've got some in my purse. One sec," I say.

Legs buckle under me the moment I stand. Where is all of

this weakness coming from? I slaughter women, and I can't stand and walk a few feet?

"Are you—" Michael starts. All the tension from a moment ago turns to worry. *All you need is love.*

"I'm okay," I say. "Just been pretty weak today. I ran a few errands, and they wiped me out."

On shaky stilts, I move towards the door. The keys are in the bowl where I left them. They are right there; I am right here. Shoes, purse, car keys… But Michael parks behind me.

I grab a honey butter from my bag and hold it up.

He knows. He knows. He knows.

Goodbye, life as I knew it.

Settling back beside him, he unwraps it and pops it in his mouth. "Damn, these are delicious. Thank you, love."

"You're welcome. I'll be making more soon," I say. "So you can have your own stash again if you want." On our second date, he told me they were too tempting to have more than three on him at a time. *"I'll eat all of them at once. But these are candies you should savor. So it's just another reason I'll have to keep seeing you."*

"No, no. Still too dangerous." His closed-lipped smile barely reaches his cheeks.

"Well then, you'll just have to keep seeing me." I pull a known trump card—romantic recitation.

"Where do you want me to put this wrapper?"

"Oh, I'll take it. I compost them."

Michael plays piano on the empty seat beside him. His fingers walk their way to my thigh. We're about to melt away from this candy and police talk. I scoot closer to him.

"So, when I was getting out of the car today, I found one of these," he says, holding up the pink cellophane honey butter wrapper.

I'm careful. "What? A candy wrapper."

"Yep." His jaw clenches.

"Hm."

"It was at the crime scene," Michael clarifies.

"Oh. That's random."

"That's all you have to say?" His voice raises enough to be noticeable; in a party, people would turn, but probably not stare.

I shrug, trying to play it cool. "You found a candy wrapper at a crime scene. That's kind of random, maybe a little weird, but you said something about going near the Dead Lands, right? It's pretty trashy from what I remember, so not terribly unexpected, I guess." I just built my defense, should I need one.

"I remember Yasmine Menick..."

I go numb. Before he said her name, I could pretend his crime scene had nothing to do with me. Now... I can't fuck this up. I'm a step away from ice cold as I ask, "Is that who died?"

"*Murdered.* That's who was *murdered*," he corrects with emphasis. "*Gruesomely* murdered."

There are no right words in this situation. Silence, it turns out, is just as wrong as saying *I did it.*

"Nothing? You've got nothing to say?" His anger is clear. "You knew her! Don't you remember you said it smelled like lemons or something?" He's probably just thinking about what it smelled like today. Yasmine's house was filled with the aroma of robust tomatoes and roasting potatoes. "I slept over one night. We sat out in her backyard garden."

Fuck, really? I'll be honest, that may or may not have happened. It's hard to remember *everything* I've ever done.

His voice grows loud, his tone lower. "She left you a pie or something in the fridge? Nothing? You don't remember her at all? So you weren't, maybe, visiting her a little while ago?"

I expected something else more explosive, but he's a passive guy.

"I don't visit the people I house sit for. We have a working relationship, nothing more. What's with the third degree?"

He pinches his nose, then slides his fingers to press them into his eyes. Ignoring my question, he poses another. "So the fact that a pink candy wrapper was found by her house is a coincidence?"

"It's pink? Well, that is weird," I say, thinking it will help. It does not.

"Yes, Elizabeth. It *is* weird. I'm not trying to… It's just… Were you *really* not at her house?" Michael is baffled. "The wrapper is partially decomposed. I don't know enough about it, but it could be from around the same night she was murdered." His eyes roam my face. "In the compost, it would be nearly mush by now. But it was half on dirt, half on asphalt."

Don't gulp.

"Forensics—"

I encourage my eyes to brim with tears with a hard pinch to the back of my right knee. "Get out," I say, turning my attention to the floor. Two words made more meaningful by my voice's quiver.

"Oh, God! Elizabeth, Jesus Christ. This sounds all wrong. I don't know wh—Obviously, you didn't have anything to d—I'm s—so so sorry! Can we start over? Hi. I had a rough day at work and am feeling kind of craz—" Michael backpedals, struggles, stutters.

"Get out." I'm firmer now, allowing my fear of being caught to turn into anger at almost being accused.

So this is how we end? Me watching a stray ant collect a cookie crumb and wondering if smashing it would look like I didn't care about this conversation? And Michael… Well, he's trying to fix the unfixable.

"You're just looking for something," he says.

"What?"

"You're just pushing me away. Is this because I'm here so often? I thought you liked it." His eyes plead.

"This is because you are making me out to be some sort of liar. And bringing up forensics? What is going on with you? Is there something else you want to say—or ask, perhaps? I have been nothing but supportive of you wanting to be a police officer. The first chance you get, it's *you* who's inventing things. You want to catch a bad guy? Then go find out. I was never going to push you away. I figured you'd move in soon," I add for an extra gut punch. "But I can't have the person I love *questioning* me like I'm a criminal."

"You're… You're right. I'm s—s—"

"Go."

His footsteps fade as he walks towards the door. Righting my head, I see that he's staring at me, his hands by his side. "I don't know what possessed me—" he starts again.

"No, me neither," I say, cutting him off. "I can't have your job affecting our relationship. You aren't even a detective yet, and this —" I motion to him, me, the honey butter wrapper. "—is happening. Leave my key."

Actual tears stream down my face as I watch him pull the keys from his pocket. With shaky fingers, it takes five tries to get my key from his ring. Eventually, it's detached. He palms it and closes his eyes.

Michael's head is slowly falling. "Please don't make me do this. I don't—"

"Don't. It hurts too much. Leave the key and go." I can hear my uneven breathing, and I wonder if he can too.

Michael starts to cry.

Unable to watch him, I turn away. "Goodbye, Michael," I say, leaving him in every sense of the word.

Metal bangs angrily against wood, and the door opens and slams closed. He is gone, and I've crushed him on the way out. I've imagined doing this a hundred times over. I figured it would feel good. I was wrong.

I inhale a shaky breath.

As I exhale, I curl into myself, becoming a hunchback in the name of a deep back stretch.

I wipe at my cheeks.

Michael thought it. He actually thought that his loving girl-friend could be a murderer. He was struggling with the words, but they were there on the tip of his tongue.

It will all be okay now. Without me admitting to anything, a candy wrapper is nothing but trash. Through a bone-cracking sadness, I can still eek out a smile. I'll miss Michael, but I don't have to stop killing.

newscaster.

I spend Monday alone.

Michael texts nine times. Each message contains either an apology, an explanation, backpedaling, or swearing I misunderstood him.

The fifth text is where I give up reading them altogether. He blames the entire ordeal on being stressed from his first crime scene. I mean, just *wow*.

Michael may be heartbroken now, but what if that turns to anger? My kicking him out felt like self-preservation, but now I'm wondering if it would have been safer to pull him close.

I only send two texts out.

The first: "Michael and I broke up."

Adela messages me back within minutes. "I love you. Address for tomorrow afternoon's dwellings?"

The second: the address to my latest job outside the city—a bougie widow's home.

My communication skills are lacking at the moment. I'm still frozen in a stasis of *what ifs*. At any moment, the police will bang down my door. They'll be holding an evidence bag containing one small piece of rotting pink cellophane, and I'll be off to prison. So I'm grateful I set this house sitting job up a few weeks ago.

Mrs. Youngstein requested I meet her at a butterfly garden thirty minutes outside of the city. When I arrived, she was wearing a multi-shaded green caftan, a head wrap, and real mink. From her purse, she pulled a flask and, before meeting me in the eyes, told me she always wished she was a young woman in the 20s.

She talked a good deal about her late husband—her reason for buying an estate in Janes—and reminisced about their daughter, who died a day shy of her fifteenth birthday. Eventually, we talked about the house sitting, and she said she couldn't dream of leaving her remaining family—two Pomeranians—with a stranger as she and her friends enjoy a two-week-long trip to France.

My only job is to water the plants and let the cleaning staff in.

The job couldn't be more ideal. It's out of the city, so I'm harder to find. It's also got a garden that still looks lush in October in both the front and back of the mansion. I plan to enjoy a drink amongst the flowers and forget about the world and my problems for a bit.

I arrive at Mrs. Youngstein's before Adela and take my suitcases inside. Up the spiral staircase, on the second door to the left, is my room for the next four days. Mrs. Youngstein had the room set up for me. Air that should smell of mothballs is a bomb of lavender. A fresh bouquet sits beside a dried one. There's even a room spray on the nightstand. It's suffocating.

A luggage rack leans at the foot of the freshly turned-down bed. There is no mint on the pillow.

The en suite bathroom is clean, with a hint of lemon and

bleach. I look forward to soaking in the tub that sits in the middle of the bathroom with a lovely skylight right above it.

The doorbell rings.

I call out to Adela but walk down the stairs slowly, as they are deep. How an elderly woman traverses them is beyond me.

"Hey, you." I open the door to let in my best friend. Her smooth face is pinched. "What's wrong?" I ask.

She drops an unexpected suitcase and opens her arms. "I'm here. How are *you*? I'm worried about you."

"Yeah, I figured you would be."

"Do you want to talk about it?" she asks me as I step into her arms.

Her tight embrace is so soothing I want to take a nap. I hadn't realized how tired I've become over the last few months, how hard it was to keep the secret *and* my body together.

"No, I don't. I'm just glad you're here. Let's make some popcorn, watch some TV, then we can snoop—I mean, check out the house. But right now, I just need something mindless," I say.

"Of course." Her tongue peeks out from the gap in her teeth as she beams at me. "I'll handle the TV. Just point me in the direction of a remote."

We have to find it together. Mrs. Youngstein and I didn't do but a quick walkthrough after the butterfly garden. I know little to nothing about the house.

After depositing Adela in front of a small movie theater screen, I head towards the kitchen. I pass by one of the many mantles in the house. Two simple silver bullet urns sit in the center alone. Unlike much of the house, there no dust surrounding them. Her daughter and husband.

They will be my first Polaroid.

Once I'm in the kitchen, I locate the hidden microwave.

At about the ten seconds between each *pop* mark, I hear, "Oh my God, Elibet! Come check this out."

I wait the extra few seconds, pull the popcorn bag open, and slow-jog into the living room. "What am I looking at?"

Adela wildly gestures at the television screen where Phillip Greaves, the most well-known local newscaster, is rushing through his own words. "—DNA isn't on file. There were no cameras near the scene, but if anyone knows anyth—"

I've all but shutdown, but I'm still holding the popcorn tub. *Little victories.*

She hits mute. "Can you believe it? They have the sono-fabitch's DNA now! Do you know about the Menick case? That's what I was calling you about, just to hear it. It's crazy. This nanny was murdered while she was gardening in her own backyard. For months, her ex thought she was gone, maybe visiting someone or taking a trip because it was a pretty messy breakup. But I guess some long-lost aunt or something came to deal with her house and found her while she was roaming. The woman was hidden in the trees right behind her garden. Can you believe it? I didn't know they had a lead until you came in."

I choke down retort after retort and end up saying, "Yeah, Michael was at the scene before we—"

"Oh, God. I'm so insensitive," she cuts me off. I know she wants to hear what Michael saw, what he knows that isn't on the news, if anything. But she's Adela. "Of course, you don't want to talk about things like that right now. How about some trashy TV, maybe something with hot leads and a lot of sweaty leaning? I got you."

Yeah, let's do that. I don't want to think about me behind bars. I look terrible in orange.

But I can't help but wonder if they really have my DNA. If so, in the form of what? How? I was so careful... And how can I make sure that I never get put into the system? I can't get caught through DNA if I stay a ghost... Right?

"How's this?" Adela asks, switching to a rerun marathon of *Castle.*

I've never liked this show, but I tell her it's great. She can't know I'm panicking.

"Hand me some popcorn, and I'll turn it up," she says, smiling widely.

If ever I decide to run, leave my whole life here, and burn Elizabeth Dauphine to the ground, I *will* lick Adela's teeth before I go.

She pats my hand as if she knows my dark thoughts. "You just tell me when you're bored or want to go exploring around this wealthy woman's house. I'm here for you. I'm here until you tell me to go."

"Thus the suitcase?" I confirm, hoping she *will* stay. I have time to spend with her before I need to focus again.

She nods. "Thus the suitcase."

56

support.

Getting out of bed is harder than trying to extract Marian's teeth. Today, I cannot do much without my cane. Crawling out of bed being difficult has less to do with exhaustion or my desire to stay in this incredible bed I may kill to own and everything to do with my left hip.

My cane is in the car, so I use the wall as my support as I gingerly walk to the bathroom. The wallpaper is satin against my arm. With each step, I consider texting Jamie. I have a place to stay for a little while. But rent will be due soon enough, and there have been too many weeks without a job for me to use the two-month rent cushion I've built up right now. My car also needs an oil change, and I'm running low on toiletries. *Work it is.*

Adela's gone off to work already, but the scent of her shampoo still lingers in the bathroom. I breathe it in and force myself through the motions of getting ready. I limp out of the house later than planned.

Stop-and-go traffic makes the drive horrible, and I'm exhausted by the time I get to Juniper Foods.

Almost ten minutes late, I *click, clack* into the store. The first person I see is Jamie. She looks at my cane with concern, my flat, greasy curls, my wrinkled shirt and baggy leggings, my *tennis shoes*. Lines tent her forehead as her face folds into what I call a *pity puppy*. "Oh, Elizabeth! I'm so sorry!"

I nod, not wanting to discuss how I physically feel. Not addressing it allows me to stay the course—work, kill, spend time with Adela, photograph, rinse, repeat. Without Michael in my life, Adela can have more of my time. Without Michael, I can also rest some, recoup energy from my kills.

Since flashing lights haven't woken me up and police officers haven't busted into my house to haul me to jail, I feel safer. Michael must not have told Ericks about me. The DNA can't identify me. Really, I have to keep living my life. That means killing and mending from killing.

"How are you holding up? You're better off, honestly! You're too good for him. I've always thought that… especially if he—" Jamie glances at my cane once again as she breaks off her thought like a Kit Kat bar and envelops me in a hug.

Oh, God. She's talking about Michael, about a *boy* who she thinks did something, not about my body breaking down quicker because of my inability to control another adult while they struggle.

"Thank you. I'm…" I hedge, wanting to make sure I don't engage. "Okay."

A swift, kind pat on my back feels like I'm being beaten. I feel awful today. Yesterday was a day of rest, too. Adela and I watched TV and ate pasta until we felt sloshy with sauce. And yet.

"Of course you are," Jamie says. "You're a strong woman who doesn't need anyone. You'll be fine without him, just like you were fine without What's Her Name. You are amazing." Jamie believes this is a pick-me-up speech, and that is upsetting for her. Bringing up another failed relationship doesn't make someone feel better.

Luckily, I'm more grateful than sad we ended when we did. Or so I tell myself.

"Just glad to be back at work. I need the distraction," I say, pointedly.

Jamie pulls back immediately. "Of course! Let's get you something to do, shall we? Hop on a 10-or-less register. I wish I could put you on self-checkout, but Warren is here today and just got set up there." Jamie shrugs as if to say that *old white men gotta get theirs first.* "We started a school special today, so expect a lot of moms with lunch meat and fruit snacks. It won't be fun, but it will keep you occupied. Oh, and we got a new baker," she says. I watch her lip liner move in odd shapes as she enunciates the word *baker.*

"Another one?" Since the *fiasco* where a man wanted to better himself by getting a job at a bakery not a grocery store, we've had three, all staying for a short time.

"This one is much better. She hasn't misspelled anything since Tuesday and no one's complained." Jamie's whole body rolls forward. "The bar is low, but what can I do? We need someone." Her sigh is loud and says there is a lot more going on than just a few failed bakers. I don't ask what that *more* is.

"Yeah," I say instead.

She stands up straight again and tugs at her slightly twisted shirt. Forced and awkward, she tries to smooth out her face with a smile; her makeup has already creased. "Right. Just holler if you need anything. Let me have your lunch. I'll drop it in the break room and clock you in for the beginning of your shift. Just head over to whichever register you want."

"Thank you, Jamie. You really are a great person and boss." Fluffing her comes easily at this point. To her, it's a huge deal that I get to pick registers. Seems small, but it's trust.

"Thank *you* for saying that, Elizabeth. You've always been my favorite." With one final smack on my shoulder, she goes to the break room to clock me in.

Sid is at Register 3 with no customers. It's still early, so most people rush through the self-checkout to avoid morning chitchat.

Sid raises their hand a little but refrains from a full wave. "Hey," they say. "How are you holding up?"

"Was that the question you were all told to ask?" I say without thinking.

Hurt flickers across their face, but they shake their head. "Sorry, you must be tired of answering that. How's your morning going?" they rephrase.

"No, you were being kind." I still work with Sid and everyone else here three to four times a week and have a face to maintain. "I'm fine. I'm just talked out, I guess. Michael's gone in every sense of the word, and nothing has changed for me except for his absence," I say, surprising myself with my honesty. Mentioning the nasty business of candy wrappers and murder will only ruin my carefully built image. "And this morning has been… painful."

Sid steps from behind the register—a big *no no*—and comes to me. For the second time in ten minutes, I'm in someone's arms. This time, it's okay. Sid is nice. Sid's girlfriend pops into my mind. *Sally.* I wonder what she's doing right now. "I'm sorry you're having a rough time." The hug is soft, brief, nice, even.

They go back to their station before I can move my arms or respond. They were truly trying to offer me comfort and wanted nothing in return.

I choose Register 2 so we're closer together. For the next fifteen minutes, we talk about the latest TV shows and movies. I've become adept at pretending I've seen the popular media, picking up enough words or headlines from the checkout line magazines so I can carry on a conversation. Often, if someone brings up a topic, they probably want to talk about it themselves.

Maybe they want your input, but it's highly unlikely. It's easier to get by than most people realize.

Just when it seems Sid may actually want to know how I felt about the season finale of a show called Sacrificing Home, the Moms arrive.

Jamie is right; the sale will clean us out of nearly expired kid lunch items.

About an hour in, and I'm rethinking assault rifles. If I mowed everyone down, I could go home early.

It wouldn't be so bad if it wasn't for the coupons. There are two coupons that work with our sales, which meant a lot of *this is multiple orders*.

Eventually, my break does come. My wrists are burning from all the subluxing they've done—every gallon of milk seemed to cause it today.

The break room is Heaven. There are no customers, I don't have to lift anything, and I've got a browning salad with strawberry vinaigrette and crumbled feta that has a little blue on the edge of a few pieces and some pomegranate seeds.

The food ends up tasting like nothing, but the texture is nice. I feel a little better after eating it, but the cheese may change that later today.

The baker comes in as I'm leaving. She introduces herself, as do I. But the moment the break room door closes between us, I've already forgotten her.

A blur of scans and entering quantities and checking the clock like an impatient teen in their last class occupies my next few hours. When my shift finally ends, it's the last day of school, as every employee comes to find me to give me their condolences. I broke up with a boyfriend, not lost someone. My victim's friends and families deserve this more than me, and that doesn't make me feel much of anything.

I'm just so fucking tired.

57

snout.

Life goes back to normal, as if that horrible day two weeks ago never existed. If it wasn't for my not being with Michael, I could almost convince myself it was a dream. I've worked three days a week at the store, slowly coming to grips with my new norm of wearing tennis shoes, no matter my outfit. I've been counting the days until I get a new cohort of eager ESL students I can focus on. Adela went back to her place. Before she left, she asked if we could make honey butters. I told her *no*, that they were Michael's favorites. In reality, I melted the wrappers with a small bathroom trash can fire and threw them away at the post office.

To her, I'm still sad and mopey.

I've had Holly picked out for almost a month now, but everything is getting in my way. This is why I started in the first place. I knew time and my physical body would eventually try to thwart me at every turn. Here we are.

It may be too soon. The incident wasn't that long ago, and I've been having a flare-up—a phrase my doctor told me means that my body is in a freak out mode and needs to *get its shit together*. Until it does, though, I'm in a loop. I can't stop thinking about it.

Customers are victims, passersby are victims. I even pictured Adela's chest splayed open as I was falling asleep last night. I'm worried I'm running out of time. I told myself I'd be happy with one, then two, then getting it right, but I know better. It's who I am. And now, a part of me I've just unlocked is getting snatched away. It'll be any day now that I have to switch jobs to something less taxing. I can't keep going as I am. With this level of pain and exhaustion, I can't account for problems like I want. One wrong push, and I'm in jail. One missed swing, and I'm in jail.

I've only found one way that seems doable in my present condition, and I'm attempting it tonight. I have a feeling Holly will be my last. Heart-wrenching as the thought is, I don't want to enjoy her murder any less, so I'm trying to stay in the here and now.

She was on the Nopes list, but my pool of potentials is limited. Up close, Holly has irregular, polka-dot agate teeth. My notes say her breath smelled of oil and vinegar chips, and she forever had a bit of saliva in the crook of her smile.

But I can handle that. She'll be asleep in the dark, after all.

She's petite—around 5' tall. I remember towering over her and wondering if it was comforting or scary, being that small in a world filled with darkness. That's a bonus when it seems you're getting weaker by the day.

With a lack of any affectation and smiles that come one second later than seems normal, she's a four on the personality scale.

What's put her on my list is a photo. Once I found it ended with the mysterious disappearance of a young girl, I knew she was the one. Bad teeth be damned.

In the photo, she and some sorority sisters are standing in a line together, smiling. There are streamers caught in motion, falling from a ceiling net. The girls are wearing tight dresses that hug their thin yet curvy frames. An overweight young girl with a shirt that says *PIG* is tied to a chair. Smudged makeup and a plastic snout obscures her face. That photo became one of my Polaroids, along with her bathroom counter all lined with peach and cream hair products that reminded me of the afternoon my mother decided to teach me about hair care, a scratched fan blade, and a broken window.

Hazing is gross, but hazers who brag about it five years after graduation on their kitchen island deserve people like me.

It wasn't until recently that I dug into her. She and some of those toothy-grinned sadists were involved in an accident straight out of the CW. A late-night summer beach swim with five girls, four girls come home. The one who didn't? The girl tied to a chair in Holly's prominently displayed photo. There is something poignant in the idea of a murderer being murdered, I think.

58

holly.

As the sun fades, I become a *thing* thinking only of my next moves, the thrill of what comes next.

I've got a new pantyhose mask, painted like an overdone stage Marie Antoinette tonight, as tonight's method is highly theatrical. Hidden inside my plastic-wrapped trunk, I've got my usual bag that I've added a flathead screwdriver to, a chunk of rock I collected from the side of the road in the middle of nowhere, and a gallon of our store-brand orange juice. Seven hit their expiration date, so Jamie had to give them away. It's this act of kindness that sparked the idea of how to murder Holly. It's unusual, it's gross, but it may be kinder on my body.

Whether or not Holly is my final kill, it will be an interesting night.

Driving to her house is a held breath. Parking three blocks away and gathering my stuff makes already tense muscles ache. Tonight, my purse is in the glove box, and I don't bother reaching for my cane. I need it, but I won't be making the same mistakes twice.

Holly's neighborhood has an unexpected Miami vibe to it. Smack dab in the center of Janes, OR, there is this two-block radius of homes that all agreed to change it up. Her modest two-story condo is a light bubblegum pink that basically matches everything I own. Tonight, I'm a cat burglar in black clothes I haven't fit in for a while now. I feel a bit like a sausage.

Creeping to the back of her house, two dogs bark loudly. A man's voice calls out in the night. I hit the ground like a sack of flour. My lungs constrict, and I watch some of the orange juice drip from the broken seal. Her direct neighbor is out of town and the one across the street should be sleeping deeply because he just came back from a long shift at the hospital. I guess he's a lighter sleeper than I planned for.

No lights come on. A dog whines, and I grind my teeth. I wish I could kill men. I'd take him out now, coming back from hospital work, and all.

After waiting another moment, I gather what's fallen from the yard and jog on a newly twisted knee. The gallon of juice is a lead weight, and the rock's sharp edges threaten me through the leather of my gloves.

I should go, but I'm so close to the safety of Holly's home.

The kitchen window is ajar. When I was here a year and seven months ago, Holly's kitchen window wouldn't shut all the way. She said the screen was enough of a deterrent for criminals, so she never bothered fixing it.

I grab my screwdriver to pop that screen from the window casing. It takes longer than expected. I'm a tightened garrote between clenched fists as I ease the window open slowly, just waiting for a loud creak or some resistance. None come.

Slowly, I unzip my backpack and remove my protective jumpsuit. Walking through a neighborhood with it on would have made any car stop, so I put it on now. It crinkles more than its usual quiet rustling—*or is that just my imagination?*

Most of her house is carpeted, so I slip out of my shoes and leave them tucked in a bush a few feet over from the window.

With strength I barely have, I hoist myself up. I crawl through it, knocking over two glasses full of water in the process.

I catch one, but the other clatters on the kitchen counter. I drop to the floor. Hidden, I realize that I've left the orange juice and rock on the counter.

Jesus fuck. What is happening with me today?

Any minute, Holly will come out with a gun or baseball bat, and I'm done for.

Her bedroom is on the bottom floor, along with the kitchen. The bathroom and living room are on the top. It's inconvenient and awkward when she has guests, she said, but it was the only place she could afford. Renting was off the table. I did not ask why, despite my curiosity.

I sit crouched behind the kitchen island and wait for minutes upon minutes. If I hear sirens, I'll just dart out. But the house is silent.

I wait until I can't anymore, then I stand and grab tonight's tools. Heading further into the house, I'm holding the rock and orange juice close to the center of me. Dropping them would basically be an alarm after my kitchen tumble.

I square my shoulders to regain composure. Holly doesn't know I'm here still. The loud thudding is my wild heart, not hers.

Socked feet sink into the plush carpet as I move towards the bedroom. The door is open. Holly steps out. We are face-to-face. I freeze. *As if that will make you invisible, Elizabeth?*

She hasn't screamed yet, hasn't rushed back into her room and locked the door, asked who I was or why a person in a hazmat suit has a gallon of juice and a rock in their hands. Her eyes are still closed. I don't think she's awake. Holly turns right towards the stairs.

She's sleepwalking.

I could follow her, wait for her to stop moving, but I'm exhausted. I'd have brought my cane to lean on if I wasn't worried about it tracking trace evidence on her carpet.

Carefully, I set the orange juice beside my feet. I straighten and raise the rock above my head. Towering above her feels *good*. Using my core, I thrust taut arms down. Gravity does the rest. My tensed held breath *wooshes* from me as a sharp edge of the rock connects with her skull.

Her eyes open. She's not sleepwalking anymore.

"Wha—" she starts to say, as she wobbles, stumbles.

Blood oozes from the head wound.

I shove her to the left. She tips into the wall and slides along, landing on the carpet. Disorientation won't last long. I throw the rock onto her head, relieved to have the weight out of my arms, the stress off of my shoulders. It lands on her cheek. *Crunch.* She gasps.

Holly writhes on the floor. Her hands are pulling at the rock, trying to push it off of her face. I leave her for a moment. I reach down and grab the orange juice. It's heavier now than it was.

Another relief sets in; I only have to carry an empty juice jug back with me.

Avoiding the blood pooling to her left, I stand beside her and pop the broken top of the juice jug.

Crouching to her level, I hear three successive *pop*s and almost scream with the burning in my knee. Twisted before, broken and mangled now—or just shifted out of its socket.

With more effort than expected, I roll the rock from her face. Her cheek is caved in, and she's got a gash on the right side of her mouth. Holly seems relieved, which I don't like. There's a pang somewhere in me, but it's small enough I don't look inward.

I take one more glance at my feet, making sure the only part of me that's gotten bloody won't give away my shoe size and, therefore, possibly my gender.

I pour the entire gallon jug of orange juice on her face, focusing on her slightly open mouth. It splashes up as she gurgles and flounders. The scent of orange soda and cleaner fills the hallways, and it makes me nauseous.

By the time the last drop drips from the jug, she's not moving.

I clean, I strip, I collect what I'm taking with me, and I leave.

59

park.

The knock is hard and angry. I picture Michael on the other side of it with a furrowed brow ready to tell me I've made him wait long enough, it's time we get back together. Then I remember that he promised not to bother me anymore after a slew of late-night texts lead me to text him, *"Stop harassing me."*

So if it's not Michael, who is so aggressive with their knocks?

"Ms. Dauphine. Please open the door," I hear a female voice say. "This is Detective Park from the Janes Police Department."

I die of blood loss—right here, right now. I grow cold and pale and die. But no, blood is just rushing to my head, making me see large blurry dust motes.

If only they waited two hours, this wouldn't be happening. In a few days, my neighbors would tell me the cops stopped by, and I'd know to run. But I'm here, at my house.

I call out to the detective. "Coming!" *Did my voice shake?*

Grabbing my cane is an instinct; I want to appear feeble. A weak person can't do whatever it is they think I could do. No one who needs a cane to move around their home could possibly murder someone.

In soft, pink cheerleader shorts and a silk cream tank top, I answer the door. My curls are wild and poofy. I look like one of Holly's friends from that photo, all grown up and exhausted.

"May I help you?"

"Ms. Elizabeth Dauphine?" the detective asks. Frizzy black hair is loose around her face. An indention in the middle of it makes it seem like she took it down for just a moment—*for me?*

A tall ginger model stands behind her, and I can't tell which of them is more attractive. He says nothing.

"Yes, that's me." I lean on my cane in an almost overacted way. "Can I help you?"

"We just need to ask you a few questions," she says. There's a paper in her hand, so I don't believe her.

"What kind of questions?"

"Where were you on the night of July 21st?" Detective Park stands so still she could be a wax figure of herself.

"Um… What day of the week was that? You know what? Hold on, let me get my calendar." I shut the door with them on the stoop and clomp to grab my cellphone. The more cooperative I look, the better. When I open the door again, both detectives look more annoyed than before. "It was a Friday, and I don't work on Fridays. I don't see anything else on my schedule, so I assume home." I lift the pink poppy-patterned cane up. "I'm home a lot when I'm not working. Why?" I expected this eventually, but not now… not yet. *Which woman is this about?*

Wendell, Mel, and Chike pop into my head. Did they do this? Stumble into another kill and point to me?

"Can anyone corroborate that for you?" Detective Tall, Red, and Sexy asks.

"No. I live alone, and my boyfriend wasn't in town. What is this about?"

"Yasmine Menick," she says, a twinkle in her eye.

"Oh, yes. I heard about her. I house sat for her once a long time ago. It's so sad," I say, offering the truth to a point. Honesty will make me look good in the eyes of the law, right? I just have to turn them to someone else. If they leave, I can set something up. If they just leave...

Still, I have so many questions: How did they find me? Do they have a warrant? If they do, what does it give them access to? Is this all a bluff? Have they spoken to Michael? *Is he why they're here?*

Detective Park cocks one hip. "And when is considered a long time ago?"

"I haven't seen her in years." I keep it brief because my heartbeat pounds in my throat.

This is my paranoia made real. I tried to convince myself that I could get good at this—no, I had convinced myself. But I was foolish.

Detective Park glances at her partner and nods. "An anonymous tip puts you at the scene of the crime. Now, do you think we can talk here, or should we have you come to the station?"

"What? Who? Like I said, I haven't seen her in years. I'm not even sure we would have recognized each other if we'd passed on the street. I'm sorry, but someone has you barking up the wrong tree," I say, trying to mimic the many films I've seen about this. *Stay calm, don't get arrested.*

The detectives are clearly unhappy at my lack of answering the question. "May we come in?" Detective Park pushes.

I imagine her shoving me aside, coming in uninvited. I've gotten rid of almost everything at this point, but I'm sure I've missed something. Are these cops that would beat the truth out of me? Leave me a bloodied mess and tell their boss I *fell*?

"No, I'm not really up for company. I need to go lie down. Work is supposed to be crazy tomorrow. I think you better go... Unless there's something else?" I know that makes me look guilty, but I a*m* guilty.

"Well, we'd like to take a sample of your DNA."

They stand awkwardly on the doorstep, and I think back to that night, how I moved around the perimeter of Yasmine's house, came through her garden, dragged her behind the tree. I wore a full mask, my hair tucked in tight, and I didn't take it off. She's also been in the elements for months before they found her. DNA will not convict me for Yasmine. That's not the worrisome part. It's Holly. Any mistake I made at Holly's could get me caught if I give them a DNA sample now and put it in the system. *In the system…* like I'm a common criminal.

And what of the others? They may be narrowing in on a suspect, but my DNA pops up, and bam!

"No, I don't think I want to give that out—not without a warrant and a lawyer present. I've seen too many movies about people getting convicted because of cross-contamination," I say. That's what people say—people who aren't guilty. *Right?*

I can't remember how DNA collection works *exactly*, but they can't just make me give it to them. I'm almost sure. If my students were here, they would probably tell me. Many of them have had to study the law to protect themselves.

A chill blows by the detectives and sweeps into my warm house. I want to close my door.

Detective Park brushes a flyaway from her ear. "Ms. Dauphine, giving us your DNA could—"

"Call me a conspiracy theorist, but I'm really not comfortable doing that," I say. "If that's all? The cold is starting to hurt my joints." One of the few things I say that isn't a lie.

I go to close the door, but Detective Park's silent partner catches it with his foot. His gaze is intense as it meets mine, and I want to see his teeth, his tongue. I could see his face between my thighs. Not many men get that response from me.

He disappoints me by saying, "We look forward to seeing you soon." *We.* For a police matter.

It's for the best. I'm trying to avoid fucking detectives.

When they leave, I'm left stressed, mortified, and confused.

Before I have a chance to scream or cry into a pillow or video call Adela, I get a text from an unknown number.

"I'm glad you didn't get arrested," it says. Someone is watching me. A second text comes in right after. "I'm so sorry. I didn't want to do it, but I had to tell. I just couldn't live with it if I didn't." It's the third text that sends my vision swimming. "I still love you."

Oh, fuck you, Michael.

He got a burner phone just to tell me he still loves me after ruining my life. That's a new kind of low.

60

surprise.

Phillip Greaves is loudly reporting the same piece of news he's been reporting on and off for days. I've been checking the news on my phone every 30 minutes since the detectives left.

I assume I'll hear that they've identified me on the news before they arrive at the doorstep of my latest house sitting job. Justin O'Pines—a fake name, I'm sure—paid me in cash to watch his new puppies because he had to leave quickly. His house is verging on disgusting, and I'm almost afraid to look around.

Unlike Mrs. Youngstein's home—where I had so many potential photographs it was hard to choose—Justin's house is *too gross* to want to wander. I'm afraid I'll find a stack of money beside used needles and loaded guns.

Justin and I spoke over the phone, and I took the job sight unseen. It's known I'm willing to do that if the need arises. I should squash that, spread the word like herpes: Elizabeth Dauphine must walk through your house before she says *yes*. Bills be damned. I think of the possibilities that come with intimate knowledge of homes I never connect myself with. If I ever figure out a better way to kill someone, and after I set up some asshole for Yasmine's murder, I can think on it.

It's just another job I shouldn't have taken. But in case everything magically blows over, I still have to eat.

The puppies are cute, if not more rambunctious than I want to deal with. Their incessant need to play is another reason I should have turned the job down. I do not enjoy taking care of animals that need much attention.

Adela texts me as I'm contemplating putting all of their food out and leaving them alone until Justin comes back.

"How are you doing?" Adela texts me hourly, it seems. Despite seeing me be *fine*, she's still worried. She thinks I'm repressing feelings or something. "Want me to keep you company?"

I text her back quickly. "Actually, yes. I have an idea and it involves you. I think you're going to like it."

Dots form by her name, then stop. Again and again, until she finally says, "Send me the address."

Knock, knock, knock. It's almost an hour later, and my heart thrums as yesterday flits through my head. The detectives have found me.

"It's me," Adela says. "The doorbell doesn't work."

Of course. I told her to come over, and she said she would. The sound stole my thoughts, though. I try not to show how unsettled I am, how easily I'm shaken today.

Waving her in to avoid the crisp November afternoon, I say, "We are going on a trip."

"This place is gross," she says at the same time. "Wait... a trip?" Adela's eyes light up as she closes the door behind her. "Yes! It's been too long!"

In the living room, we perch on the edge of a clean, ugly plaid couch that is on its way to being used for a film crack house.

"Excellent! Where have you been dying to go?" I ask.

It doesn't matter what she says; I'll be suggesting Nepal. She obviously doesn't know about the detectives, Michael's accusations, the killings. It's her ignorance that makes this such an easy conversation.

"Honestly, everywhere?" she laughs, too excited to notice her surroundings—for the moment. Tapping her finger against her chin, I can tell she's narrowing places down.

Before she spirals I suggest Nepal.

"That's surprisingly exotic for you. I expected Alaska or Canada."

"Exotic? Really?"

She flushes. "Not the best word choice, perhaps, but it's the first word that came to mind. Whatever. I'm just surprised. I'm so down. You've got enough saved?" Adela asks, trying to keep the condescending shock from her voice. I've not mentioned this before, so she's right to be surprised. She's known about the months where having an egg in my ramen was a delicacy.

"This has been something I've been saving for just this moment—to surprise you!" I hate lying to her, but my life is on the line.

She runs her stubby fingers through heat-frizzing hair. "Okay. Nepal. Are we really doing this? When? For real?" *Hook, line, and sinker.*

"How about we leave today?"

"You're so cute! Today!" Adela blanches. After a moment of me not moving, she says, "Oh, hon. Shit… I get it! I can't believe I didn't see it. Of course! Let's get to planning. Obviously, I'll take off as soon as I can. Michael's put you through the wringer."

Of course she makes this about Michael again. In the end, it doesn't matter; she's agreed, and we're leaving. I wish we could leave today—tomorrow at the latest. But she would have questions I don't want to answer. All I can do is push for as-soon-as-fucking-possible.

I lean in to Adela's assumptions. "Thank you. I just... I thought I was okay, but I realized I wasn't when I went home. This is a two-night job, and not sleeping in my bed for a little while longer sounds really nice."

Adela pulls out her phone. "You know what? Heather owes me big. Plus, when was the last time I asked for time off? I have PTO and Sick Leave that are just begging to be taken, and I can do my online stuff anywhere." She's all electricity as she types. "Let me see what I can do."

61

rights.

Passports tucked close at hand, Adela and I are bouncing on our heels in my kitchen. Having to stop at the house before we leave isn't optimal, but I didn't have everything I needed at Justin's. T-minus eleven minutes. *Eleven minutes*, then I'm home free. I just have to lie low for a few months, then come back to a new city with a new name. It's drastic, but they still have no new leads—if Phillip Greaves can be trusted. According to Janes, he can.

Adela only knows about our initial trip, not my sneaking away from her and never coming home. That's okay. Being the best friend that she is, she's dropped life to travel with me—for me. In truth, I think she'd do this if she met the right person too. Travel is big for her. I'm grateful.

I've had the worst two nights' sleep of my life. I've not eaten much, and I took pain pills I swore I wouldn't. Leaving work yesterday, I drove all over the city because I thought I was being tailed. And just this morning, they found Holly. They are trying to link her to Yasmine, according to Phillip Greaves. He does sensationalize sometimes, so it could be that. There are very little similarities between the two women.

Having Adela fly away with me, keep me safe like this… She'll never know how important she is to me. When I leave her at the airport, I hope she puts the pieces together.

Nine minutes.

"Okay, I think we've got everything we could possibly need that Nepal wouldn't have." Adela laughs. "I mean, should we lose our soap or run out, they'll have something for us. *God*, I'm so excited! Honestly. This is probably the most excited I've been in ages."

"Me too!" I say, with enthusiasm she thinks she understands.

"Let's go wait outside for our driver. Says she's around the corner, so maybe less than seven minutes now," Adela says, holding up two sets of crossed fingers—one still wrapped around her phone.

I do a quick check through the house, turn off the lights, make sure the windows are closed and locked, then come back into the kitchen and squeeze her hand. "Let's do this!"

Grabbing my keys is freedom incarnate.

BANG. BANG. BANG. "Elizabeth Dauphine, this is the police."

Adela's eyes go wide. "What the fuck?" I can see her wheels turning as she tries to figure out what they could want from me. "Don't open it," she mouths. Trust runs deep with her, and it makes me love her more. I hate that I'll be hurting her when I step outside, when they arrest me, when she finds out what I've done.

"It's okay," I say.

If they're here, they'll follow me anywhere. They know.

"We've got you surrounded. Come out with your hands up!" *Surrounded? How dramatic.* The voice is familiar—Detective Park. Her faint accent is stronger as she gets louder. It's pleasant, but I'm disappointed that it's her who's here.

"What's going on?" Adela whispers.

I drop my voice. "I love you."

Unlocking the door, I hear guns cock. *For fuck's sake.* I killed some women, I didn't open fire at a concert. I raise my hands and kick the door open with my foot. "I'm unarmed, but I need my cane," I say.

"On the ground," Detective Park shouts. Even though it's sunny outside, they've got lights facing the house. There are also cameras and shouting strangers—or are they my neighbors? I wonder where Phillip Greaves is right now. He's somewhere out there, reporting on me and my crimes, just like he has every other dark event that's happened in Janes.

I slowly get on my knees. With my hands behind my head, I lay face down on the floor of the front entrance. From the floor, I try to project, "My friend Adela is in the house. She's also unarmed and has no idea what's going on."

"I'm on the ground too!" Her voice wavers with unshed tears. The sound is identical to when she and her ex split at a theme park and she couldn't cry. Adela refuses to cry in public.

I have so many questions. But the *how* is all that matters. I gave no DNA. What would give them the right, the *cause* to come arrest me? Surround my home with guns? What if they'd shot Adela? I would have gotten killed rushing them wildly. And yet, I would do it even now.

The next few minutes rush by in a haze of shouts and pounding feet. Spots fill my vision—from fear, devastated acceptance, and excruciating pain.

Finally, rough hands are yanking me up. I cry out, and the officer eases their handling of me, just a little.

"I've got a connective tissue disorder!" I shout. "My joints dislocate easily, and I have nerve damage."

That does Adela in. She starts to cry. "Leave her alone!" she shouts. "Whatever you think she's done, she hasn't! Don't hurt her! No, stop! You're going to break her! FUCK YOU! She's got bad shoulders!"

The officer who is holding me nearly lets go of me, he's started to be so gentle. Whether Adela's scaring him or he doesn't want to be sued is anyone's guess.

Officer Rough Palms begins to recite my rights to me, of which I already know.

"I love you," I shout to Adela. Then, I super glue my lips shut.

The police car door is open and waiting—a monster's mouth ready to consume. Walking to it is a death march. People are shouting my name, asking me why I did it and if I was sorry.

When we get to the car, the officer's hand presses lightly on the top of my skull. He tells me to watch my head and maneuvers me into the car. I wonder if my photo will be as famous as Kore Hockins'.

Life is about to get very messy. This is all my ex-boyfriend's fault, his lies and manipulation. I dumped him; did they know that? I can't tell them that until a lawyer is by my side. But I imagine what happens when I do.

Will they throw out my case?

If not, I can just be another Elizabeth in a long line of murdering Elizabeths.

I will plead insanity if this goes to court. I'm supposed to leave a mark—that's what my mother raised me to believe. Everything I've done is her fault.

She named me, after all.

62

courtroom.

Maria Briggs' closing arguments are impassioned, something out of a film. My sharply dressed attorney demands the jury find me not guilty of the murder of Yasmine Menick. Her soft curls bounce as she addresses the court. It's clear that a disabled woman couldn't do this heinous act, she says in three different ways, each more intense than the next. Women can kill, of course. But, she points out, I need a mobility aid. I need to call in sick for days on end. I need to take pain medication. My joints don't stay in place.

Her words bring some people of the jury to tears. They are horrified we're here. *Same. Same.* There are a few members who are unmoved, have condemned me for being a woman, for having the thinnest connection to her—house sitting. Some believe that having pink cellophane wrapped honey butters at the time of the murder is the clincher. Others are willing to agree that a few blurry cameras that show a white woman with curls driving a compact car are enough to hang one's hat on murder. But if I'm counting correctly, those are in the minority.

"The prosecutor's claim that she was able to bludgeon a woman without being heard, then drag her body behind a tree, doesn't add up in logistics alone. And what of her motive? Who was Yasmine to her? An employer from years ago? This case is a house of cards. It relies on hearsay and circumstantial evidence. How we got this far, I'll never know. While we are debating the conviction of my *disabled* client, Elizabeth Dauphine, the real murderer of Yasmine Menick, is out there. Who knows if they are doing this to someone else?" she says, pounding her fist into her palm.

I tug at my brown pencil skirt like I'm Jamie. The tweed fabric is scratchy, and I'm trying to keep it from touching me as much as possible. The action makes me look fidgety. From subluxations to dislocations, the hard chair and itchy fabric, I've been uncomfortable during the entire trial. Maria has used that as another talking point of my condition being *too bad* to do anything like this.

She ends with, "So, do the right thing. Let this woman go home, get the help she needs, see the doctors and take the medication she needs. Don't keep her locked up for someone else's crimes."

The prosecutor's final argument feels weak after. He's grasping at straws, a kid reaching for something on a high shelf.

I watch the jury's faces more intently as he speaks, not getting caught up or caring. He's a lackluster speaker.

Juror 1 and 2 are unreadable. Both sit straight up, occasionally leaning forward, as if listening requires extra inches of closeness. Juror 3 has exceptional teeth. Though many of them look sharp, they are straight, bleached to a stark white. I try not to look at him much, therefore, I have no idea how he'll vote.

Juror 4, 7, and 9 are on my side without a doubt. 5 is on the fence. 6 hasn't uncrossed his arms since the trial started a month ago. I'd sit like that if I could, to be fair. They've dragged out a nothing case for a month.

Juror 8 isn't on my side, but she seems sympathetic. The footage of me driving at night was enough to seal my fate. Juror 10 doesn't listen when the prosecutor speaks. They took one look at me and voted my way. Juror 11 seems to be leaning the way of my guilt, but she has resting bitch face, so it could go either way. Juror 12 believes in me. He watched me walk to the stand, and that did it. Maybe he was picturing someone he knew.

With 5 swing votes, 2 against, and 5 probably for me, I have no clue where I'll be sleeping tonight

Maria told me not to look behind me, but I know Adela is there with crossed fingers and gritted teeth. She's probably wearing her sensible navy dress with a buckle at the waist—her go-to in professional situations. When she came to visit me last week, her nails were bitten to the quick, so she may have her fingers in her mouth.

There is no one else here in support of me.

The jury takes four hours to decide my fate. Maria doesn't say it, but she doesn't think that bodes well.

Waves crash in my ear as the judge has everyone rise and asks the foreperson to read their verdict.

They find the defendant... They find *me* Not Guil—

My legs give out from under me, and I fall hard into the seat. I gasp with pain that shoots up my spine.

Far away, the judge is calling for order, demanding I stay standing for the rest of the verdict. *All charges.* I'm found Not Guilty of *all charges.*

Of course, I can't stab someone to death or stuff their body in a closet. I'm too disabled to strangle a squirming person. Bludgeoning someone and dragging bodies are actions only strong people can perform. Even a gallon of orange juice is more than I can lift.

The moment the gavel hits the wood, Adela's arms are wrapped around me. I'm still in shock, so I don't turn around and hug back. The physical touch is actually pretty jarring.

"Thank God! No, actually, thank *you*, Maria! This was a ridiculous case, a fucking shit show witch hunt from a jilted lover, and you kept my best friend from going to prison! I cannot thank you enough!" Adela smooches my cheek and pulls Maria into a big hug.

I have no doubt that Maria thinks I did it. *Knows* it even. She sees through the bullshit.

"Headed on your trip, then?" Maria asks.

"As soon as possible, right Elibet?" Adela says, completely unaware of my daze.

I nod. This is such a bizarre conversation to me. Yesterday, I was talking about washing laundry with an arsonist who has a steady supply of cigarettes and matches.

"Just as soon as I tell Jamie the good news and rebook our flight," I say through a dry and gummy mouth. *I'm free.* The thought isn't sinking in yet. It will.

Adela nods furiously, turning towards Maria. Dropping her voice low, she says, "Elizabeth is strong, but I think she needs some time away."

"Prison is no picnic," I say.

My mind wanders to my first night. A big woman named Jules was my cellmate. She thought having a shiv and being pushy would work. One blitz elbow to the spleen, and the sharpened toothbrush was mine. With it pressing into her neck, I told her if she left me alone, I wouldn't use it nor would I join any group that would use much worse. It occurred to me that Sweeney Todd's way of killing could work for me.

I sat alone, read alone, *was* alone after that—for the most part. Big C and Little K jumped me two weeks in, but I guess not crying or begging for mercy made me no fun. It never happened again. I still haven't recovered.

Jules never found out that I was terrified, that I peed myself a little, or that my shoulder had subluxed. All she had to do was push back for one second. Then, she could have done whatever she wanted to me. Her ignorance has been, to date, one of the biggest *little victories* I've ever had.

"But the nightmare is over now," Adela coos.

"Not quite," Maria says. "There's still the press. I think we should go out the back." She gathers her papers and taps them on the desk. "Don't want some crazy attacking you." Laughing, she slides the papers into her attaché case.

The idea *is* laughable. "They'll care tomorrow too."

Adela and I step out of the courtroom and into a zoo, complete with screaming children and animals. She laces her fingers with mine, and together we walk by the demands for an interview and requests for a quote. My cane's usual noise is lost to the reporters' cacophony. I still hurt badly enough that I'm leaning on it a lot. I'm walking slower than usual too.

Out in the fresh *free* air, they follow me. They tear our hands apart, and Adela is lost in the sea of reporters. I hear her saying, "No comment."

Suddenly, a hand is grabbing my elbow. Pain jolts up into my shoulder. In my ear, the most recognizable male voice says, "I still love you, you know." The shock is enough to stop my heart. "I'm so sorry."

I jerk my arm away. "Don't ever touch me again unless you want to end up on the news. Local cop gets sued for harassing disabled woman acquitted of murder." I'll drag myself through more mud for a while if I can take Michael down.

Not a moment later, Adela's voice rises. "What the fuck do you—"

I put my hand on hers. "Let's not be those people. Let's just go, live our lives." I cannot handle another scene, any more questions or scrutiny. Not unless it truly can't be helped.

She and I move forward. Michael starts shouting. "Okay, okay, that's enough." His voice is stern, authoritative. "If she wants to talk to you, she will. But not today."

I turn back to see him. He's in his uniform. Most of the crowd of vultures begins to disperse.

He catches my eye and waves. Those eyes... His smile is sad. Those teeth...

I shake him and his love and betrayal off. It's too much to take in right now. My chest is still tight, waiting for another blow for Little K's fist or Big C's knee. I have little bandwidth, and I know where I'll be putting that energy.

Adela links arms with me. "Where to?"

I turn around and stare at my future in the form of a busy street with taxis and rideshare cars and buses. They can take me to a new city with new houses and new faces with new teeth.

I got away with murder. My mother would be so proud. Now, I can try out the many ideas that I had in prison.

"I could really go for some pomegranate seeds."

THANK YOU!

Thank you so much for reading *Another Elizabeth*!

With millions of other books in the world, the fact that you spent time on mine is humbling. I honestly appreciate your support.

If you enjoyed Elizabeth Dauphine's story, perhaps you could tell your friends, maybe leave a review somewhere fancy people like yourself frequent, and head over to my website to sign up for my newsletter. You'll get a free short horror story about a restaurant that serves something a little more exotic than your average burger and short fiction stories multiple times a year!

Keep reading for a note about my personal experience with Hypermobile Ehlers-Danlos Syndrome, my acknowledgments, and a blurb about me.

AUTHOR'S NOTE

A lot of me is in this book.

No, I'm not a serial killer—yet. I'm still young, so I won't count it out. But I do have Hypermobile Ehlers-Danlos Syndrome. I know how horrible, complicated, depressing, funny, awkward, and life-altering it can be to have dislocating joints and chronic pain.

It's not the *only* thing I have, but I'll save my other diagnoses for other books. Fodder, my dear readers, it's all fodder.

When Elizabeth shouted at me that she must be written, must take priority, must be my entire focus for an entire year, I had to do a little searching. How funny did I want this to be? How dark, how brutal? But beyond that, what was I willing to give? How much of myself, my *true* disability, was I willing to show? I use a cane, have an electric scooter for longer days, and cannot get out of bed at all sometimes. I wasn't sure, at first, how much of that should be shared. I wanted to entertain, but the more I wrote, the more I realized I also wanted to see chronic illness in a way that isn't inspirational or romanticized, that isn't pitiful, and the able-bodied people around them aren't given awards for *putting up* with their existence.

Now, I don't know how you felt about the book. If I did my job, you have more than one emotion right now. But I can tell you that you just read snippets of days from my last decade.

I did visit a geneticist at Duke University. I've had to run into countless walls to put my shoulder back in. *This is not doctor recommended. It's also not Elle recommended.*

I have had spontaneous subluxations and ribs shift because of car stereos and someone banging on the dinner table. But most important to this moment, I have spent countless hours trying to find the best way to describe what's happening inside of me. Some of it can sound downright unbelievable, so making it relatable, visual, and yes, brutal, has helped me and others around me understand this illness.

Whether you loved or hated Elizabeth, loved or hated the book, have already forgotten it and are wondering why you're reading an author's ramblings, I know for sure that you got a glimpse into the life of one of the thousands of chronic illnesses.

I do hope you loved the book, though.

As I always note: this is not necessarily how hypermobility or other co-morbidities show up for everyone with hEDS, and it's certainly not the experiences of someone with the *many* other types of EDS. If you want to know how someone is feeling or what's going on with them, ask them. Trust me when I say, if we don't want to talk about it, we won't. So don't be afraid. It's worse to be those people that stare and make assumptions.

ACKNOWLEDGMENTS

I always have a ton of people to thank because sanity is important, and I'm lucky to have many people help me keep that intact.

I must thank my dear friend, brilliant author, and manuscript whisperer, Valerie Geary. For the first time, I send a first draft to someone and asked them to eviscerate it. I wanted Elizabeth to be the best she could. And Valerie got to work. She rolled up her sleeves, shifted the blinds, opened the windows, and pointed out the good, the bad, the messy, the ugly, the hidden, the unknown, the lacking, the overworked, and the great. Because of her insight and honesty, this book is what it is today. She pushed me, and I'm so grateful for it. So, Valerie, thank you from the bottom of my heart.

Next, I have to thank Alex for beta-reading and finding those little things that, after working on a novel for a year, I honestly just overlooked. A secondary thank you to Kris, her hubby, for helping her with out-of-context passages about construction and curls. All-stars, these two.

My writing group kept me pushing forward, so I'd like to thank the Space Mermaids for showing up week after week.

To my many friends who helped me when I judged myself, encouraged me to take a sabbatical, understood when I didn't text them for weeks, thank you. Your love and support mean so much to me.

My family will always deserve a thank you for existing, for supporting me, and also for making me in the first place. But I would be remiss if I didn't appreciate them for helping me through my chronic illness journey and numerous surgeries. I'm stronger, more open, braver, and more resilient because I've always had you in my corner. I love you so much!

And my husband, the man who literally just brought me a fresh tea and dropped a quick kiss on my cheek, saying, "Don't let me interrupt you." There are not enough words, or maybe I've said them all? What matters is, I couldn't have done this without you. You stepped up in our everyday life more than you already do, so I could put all I needed into this—even when I gave *myself* deadlines. I love you all the more for it.

———

And, as always, if I missed you, I'm sorry.

If you and I have ever come in contact with one another, if I have ever seen a photo you've taken or street art you painted, if you have ever walked past me or held the door for me, you are probably owed a thank you.

So, thank you, strangers, acquaintances, friends, exes. I'd have fewer stories without you.

ABOUT THE AUTHOR

Elle Mitchell is a multidisciplinary artist and author of raw, character-driven dark fiction. She spends her downtime ignoring new story ideas, fighting for disability rights, researching, and eating more than her share of homemade baked goods (when her body allows). Being a woman with several invisible illnesses, she enjoys living a semi-horizontal life with her husband and spoiled furbutts in the PNW.

ANO
THER
ELIZA
BETH

ANO THER ELIZA BETH

CONTENT WARNING

This is a dark book.

Characters are murdered. There are intense descriptions of body manipulation. More characters are murdered.

There is no sexual assault or rape. No animals are tortured or die.

Despite not being written for shock value, you can skip the graphic scenes. You will lose out on Elizabeth's physical and mental state during those moments, but you can still enjoy the story.

Do what's best for your mental health knowing that this is Elizabeth's journey, and we're just along for the ride.

ANO THER ELIZA BETH

little key press

Also by ELLE MITCHELL

ANOTHER ELIZABETH

Published in the United States by Little Key Press.

This is a work of fiction. Names, characters, businesses, places, and events are either the product of the author's imagination or are used fictitiously. Any resemblance to actual persons, living or dead, businesses, companies, or events is entirely coincidental.

First Edition

Cover by Elle Mitchell
Cover font: Gotham Light, Medium
Cover photograph: Elle Mitchell — expensesreceipt.com/store.html

To Mr.'s obsession with Mommy Mouth

Printed in Great Britain
by Amazon

25329895R00179